Sophocles: Oedipus Tyrannus

Sophocles' *Oedipus Tyrannus* (or *Oedipus Rex*) has exerted more influence than any other drama, ancient or modern, on the history of theatre, and this influence has extended far beyond the boundaries of the Western theatrical tradition to include African and Oriental theatre histories as well. This volume traces Sophocles' paradigmatic ancient tragedy from its first appearance on the stage in the fifth century BC to present-day productions. The afterlife of *Oedipus* has played a key role in the history of ideas, and this volume examines its centrality to the history of stage censorship and political and cultural upheaval across the centuries. More recently, the protagonist has come under close scrutiny in his association with the Oedipus of psychoanalytical theory. Macintosh demonstrates how, by following the fortunes of Sophocles' *Oedipus* on the world stage, one witnesses its intersection with and impact upon the history of theatre and the history of ideas.

FIONA MACINTOSH is Reader in Greek and Roman Drama at the Archive of Performances of Greek and Roman Drama, University of Oxford.

Frontispiece – design for British première of Stravinsky's *Oedipus Rex* (1961), Sadler's Wells, London, by Abd'Elkader Farrah

PLAYS IN PRODUCTION

Series editor: Michael Robinson

PUBLISHED VOLUMES

Ibsen: *A Doll's House* by Egli Törnqvist
Miller: *Death of a Salesman* by Brenda Murphy
Molière: *Don Juan* by David Whitton
Wilde: *Salomé* by William Tydeman and Steven Price
Brecht: *Mother Courage and Her Children* by Peter Thomson
Williams: *A Streetcar Named Desire* by Philip C. Kolin
Albee: *Who's Afraid of Virginia Woolf?* by Brenda Murphy
Beckett: *Waiting for Godot* by David Bradby
Pirandello: *Six Characters in Search of an Author* by
Jennifer Lorch
Chekhov: *The Cherry Orchard* by James N. Loehlin
Sophocles: *Oedipus Tyrannus* by Fiona Macintosh

SOPHOCLES
Oedipus Tyrannus

*

FIONA MACINTOSH
University of Oxford

CAMBRIDGE UNIVERSITY PRESS
Cambridge, New York, Melbourne, Madrid, Cape Town, Singapore, São Paulo, Delhi

Cambridge University Press
The Edinburgh Building, Cambridge CB2 8RU, UK

Published in the United States of America by Cambridge University Press, New York

www.cambridge.org
Information on this title: www.cambridge.org/9780521497824

First published 2009

Printed in the United Kingdom at the University Press, Cambridge

A catalogue record for this publication is available from the British Library

Library of Congress Cataloguing in Publication data
Macintosh, Fiona, 1959–
Sophocles : Oedipus tyrannus / Fiona Macintosh.
    p. cm.
Includes bibliographical references and index.
ISBN 978-0-521-49711-4
1. Sophocles. Oedipus Rex.   2. Oedipus (Greek mythology) in literature.
3. Heroes in literature.   I. Title.
PA4413.O7M23   2009
882′.01–dc22

                                                              2009005859

ISBN 978-0-521-49711-4 hardback
ISBN 978-0-521-49782-4 paperback

CONTENTS

ILLUSTRATIONS

ACKNOWLEDGEMENTS

This book has been embarrassingly long in gestation and for this reason I have accumulated debts in very wide circles. From my time at Goldsmiths' College, University of London, I have to thank Chris Baldick, Helen Carr, David Margolies, Bill McCormack and Jerry Sokol for various kinds of encouragement. I remain indebted to many others who have patiently waited for this book and who have provided material and helpful criticism on numerous sub-chapters which have appeared elsewhere: Sarah Annes Brown, Felix Budelmann, Zachary Dunbar, Cécile Dudouyt, Pat Easterling, Barbara Goff, Simon Goldhill, Helene Foley, Isobel Hurst, Lorna Hardwick, Karelisa Hartigan, Eleftheria Ioannidou, Miriam Leonard, Michael Lurje, Marianne McDonald, Martha Oakes, Michelle Paul, Kathleen Riley, Catherine Silverstone, Michael Silk, Michael Simpson, Chris Stray, Michael Walton, David Wiles and Peter Wilson. My students in London and Oxford have contributed in countless challenging and exacting ways – I remain profoundly grateful to them. Martin Revermann very kindly read through the text at the eleventh hour. At Cambridge University Press, I have to thank Vicki Cooper and Becky Jones for their forbearance, and Tom O'Reilly and John Gaunt for their efficiency.

My greatest debt, though, is to my colleagues at the Archive of Performances of Greek and Roman Drama at the University of Oxford: to Amanda Wrigley for the research and technical support she has provided, way beyond the call of duty; to Chris Weaver, Helen Damon and Stephe Harrop for help with pictures; to Peter Brown for indispensable guidance and discussion on opera; and especially to Pantelis Michelakis and Oliver Taplin, for their much-valued intellectual and moral support over a number of years. Edith Hall, who as co-author of another book and close friend of long standing, has heard rather too much of this material over a number of years. My deepest gratitude and debt must go to her for much good humour, incalculable insights and acumen. Finally, I have to thank my family – my husband, Jonathan Marcus and our two sons, Josh and Sam, all of whom have heard far too much about Oedipus.

NOTE ON EDITIONS AND TRANSLATIONS

Sophocles' tragedy is referred to throughout the text as *Oedipus Tyrannus*, as opposed to the rather nineteenth-century, honorific title, *Oedipus the King*. Indeed, many of the twentieth- and twenty-first-century versions under discussion in this volume drop the epithet '*King*'/'*Rex*' altogether as they fashion a post-Freudian/Arthur Miller-esque, Everyman/Ordinary Man, Oedipus. The ancient Greek term *tyrannos* – meaning the non-hereditary ruler who has come to the throne by force and not by birthright – carries with it on occasions the modern connotations of the word 'tyrant'. The ambiguity in the Sophoclean title is also an important factor in various adaptations; and for this reason, it has been maintained here, even if the other titles – *Oedipus the King* or *Oedipus Rex* – are more familiar to many readers.

All translations are my own unless otherwise stated, and all abbreviations of ancient sources are taken from the *Oxford Classical Dictionary* (3rd edition, Oxford 1996).

PRODUCTIONS

The productions listed here are those discussed in this volume, and with their première dates only (revivals have not been listed). For a comprehensive listing, go to the online database of the Archive of Performances of Greek and Roman Drama, University of Oxford (www.apgrd.ox.ac.uk, edited and maintained by Amanda Wrigley).

467 BC	Aeschylus, *Oedipus* (wins first prize with *Laius, Seven against Thebes, Sphinx* [satyr play]) at the Festival of Dionysus in Athens
430–425?	Sophocles, *Oedipus Tyrannus* at the Festival of Dionysus in Athens
409–407	Euripides, *Phonoecian Women* at the Festival of Dionysus in Athens
408–401	Euripides, *Oedipus* at the Festival of Dionysus in Athens
401	Sophocles, *Oedipus at Colonus* posthumously produced by Sophocles' grandson, also called Sophocles, at the Festival of Dionysus in Athens
c. AD 41–9	Seneca's *Oedipus*
64–8	Emperor Nero regularly performs the role of Oedipus
1559–60	Seneca's *Oedipus*, in a translation by Alexander Neville, performed at Trinity College, Cambridge
1585	*Edipo Tiranno*, directed by Angelo Ingegneri in a translation by Orsatto Giustiniani, with music by Andrea Gabrieli, performed at Teatro Olimpico, Vicenza

1659	Pierre Corneille's *Oedipe*, Hôtel de Bourgogne, Paris
1678	Dryden and Lee's *Oedipus*, performed by the Duke's Company at the Dorset Garden Theatre, London
1718	Voltaire's *Oedipe*, Comédie Française, Paris
1858	Jules Lacroix's *Oedipe-Roi*, Comédie Française, Paris, with Edmond Geffroy in title role
1881	Jean Mounet-Sully takes the part of Oedipe in Lacroix's *Oedipe-Roi* at the Comédie Française, Paris
1887	*Oedipus Tyrannus* in ancient Greek, with music composed by Charles Villers Stanford, at St Andrew's Hall, Cambridge, performed by students of the University of Cambridge
1910	*Oedipus Rex*, in a version by Hugo von Hofmannsthal, directed by Max Reinhardt at the Musikfesthalle, Munich, and then at Zirkus Schumann, Berlin, with Alexander Moissi as Oedipus
1912	*Oedipus Rex*, in Gilbert Murray's translation of Hofmannsthal's version, directed by Max Reinhardt at Covent Garden, London, with John Martin-Harvey as Oedipus and Lillah McCarthy as Jocasta
1919	*Oedipe, roi de Thèbes* by Saint-Georges de Bouhélier, dir. Firmin Gémier at Cirque d'Hiver, Paris
1926	W. B. Yeats's *Oedipus the King*, Abbey Theatre, Dublin
1927	*Oedipus Rex* by Igor Stravinsky/Jean Cocteau, Ballets Russes, Théâtre Sarah-Bernhardt, Paris
1932	*Oedipe* by André Gide, dir. Georges Pitoëff, Théâtre des Arts, Paris
1934	*La Machine infernale* by Jean Cocteau, dir. Louis Jouvet, Comédie des Champs-Élysées, Paris
1937	*Oedipe-Roi* by Jean Cocteau, dir. Jean Cocteau, Théâtre Antoine, Paris, with Jean Marais as Oedipus

1945   *Oedipus Rex*, directed Michel Saint-Denis, with
            Laurence Olivier as Oedipus, Old Vic Company at
            The New Theatre, London
1947   Martha Graham's *Night Journey*, dance version, with
            music by William Schuman, Harvard Music
            Department, Cambridge, MA
1947   *Oedipe-Roi*, dir. Pierre Blanchar, Théâtre des
            Champs-Élysées, Paris, designs by Pablo Picasso
1954   *Oedipus Rex*, dir. Tyrone Guthrie, Stratford,
            Ontario, with James Mason as Oedipus
1956   Film of *Oedipus Rex*, dir. Tyrone Guthrie, Stratford,
            Ontario, with Douglas Campbell as Oedipus
1967   Pier Paolo Pasolini's film *Edipo Re*
1968   Ola Rotimi's *The Gods Are Not to Blame*, directed by
            Ola Rotimi (who also played Narrator), Ori Olokun
            Players, University of Ife, Nigeria, with Femi
            Robinson as Odewale (Oedipus)
1978   André Boucourechliev's opera, *Le Nom d'Oedipe*,
            with a libretto by Hélène Cixous, in the Cour
            du Palais des Papes, at the Festival d'Avignon,
            under the direction of Claude Régy, conductor
            Claude Prin
1980   Steven Berkoff's *Greek*, Half Moon Theatre, London
1983   Lee Breuer's *Gospel at Colonus*, music composed by
            Bob Telson, Carey Playhouse, Brooklyn, and
            Brooklyn Academy of Music, New York
1986   *Oedipus Rex*, directed by Yukio Ninagawa, adapted
            by Mutsuo Takahashi, Honganji Temple in Tsukiiji,
            Tokyo (an earlier version dates from 1976 and a later
            version was staged in 2002)
1992   *The Thebans*, translated by Timberlake
            Wertenbaker, dir. Adrian Noble, Royal Shakespeare
            Company, Stratford-upon-Avon

1996   Rita Dove's *Darker Face of the Earth*, dir. Ricardo
               Kahm at Angus Bowmer Theatre, Ashland,
               Oregon
1997   *The Oedipus Plays* (*Oedipus the King* and *Oedipus at
               Colonus*), in a translation by Ranjit Bolt, directed by
               Peter Hall, Royal National Theatre, London
2000   Giuseppe Manfridi's *Cuckoos* (in a version by Colin
               Teevan), Gate Theatre, dir. Peter Hall
2000   *Oedipus Rex*, dir. Tadashi Suzuki, Japan
2001   *Oedipus*, in a version by Blake Morrison, dir. Barrie
               Rutter, Northern Broadsides, The Viaduct Theatre,
               Dean Clough, Halifax
2006   *Oedipus Loves You*, by Simon Doyle and Gavin
               Quinn, Smock Alley Theatre, Dublin
2008   *Oedipus*, in a version by Frank McGuinness, dir.
               Jonathan Kent, Royal National Theatre, London

CHAPTER I

OEDIPUS IN ATHENS

> [T]ragedy is a blessed art in every way, since its plots are well
> known to the audience before anyone begins to speak. A poet
> need only remind. I have just to say 'Oedipus', and they know all
> the rest: father, Laius; mother, Jocasta; their sons and daughters;
> what he will suffer; what he has done.[1]

For the comic playwright Antiphanes, commenting some hundred
years after the composition of Sophocles' *Oedipus Tyrannus*, the task
of the tragedian is simply the art of fine-tuning. Sophocles and his
fellow tragic playwrights, avers the envious Antiphanes, effortlessly tap
into the common source of myth, extract what they need, and then,
with some minor prompting, let the tragic characters speak for themselves. Meanwhile Antiphanes and his colleagues, we infer, are forced
to embark upon a laborious search for the raw material itself, dredging
it up from their own imaginations before they hack and hew it into
some kind of dramatic shape.

Notwithstanding the obvious comic exaggeration underlining
Antiphanes' words, we can, I think, glean more from this slender
fragment of the fourth century BC than just an insight into perceived
differences between the ancient comic and tragic playwrights' art.
First, we can see evidence from the fourth century BC of Oedipus'
increasing emergence as archetypal tragic figure. Indeed, when we
look at the *Poetics*, written in the 330s, we find a similarly privileged
status accorded to the figure of Oedipus. Aristotle recommends that
the would-be tragedian turn to the Oedipus myth in general, and to
Sophocles' reshaping of it in *Oedipus Tyrannus* in particular, to learn
and test the tools of his trade.[2] For Aristotle (Chapter 13), Oedipus is

an exemplary tragic figure whose fall is consequent on an intellectual error (*hamartia*) rather than any morally dubious action.

As we can see from the Antiphanean fragment, Aristotle was not alone in his privileging of the character of Oedipus in the fourth century. But the lionising of Sophocles' play in the *Poetics* was undoubtedly a significant factor in determining Oedipus' subsequent renown. As the solver of the riddle of the Sphinx, Oedipus can be hailed – just as he is by the Thebans in Sophocles' play – as a model for all human intellectual endeavour, and he can serve as living confirmation that brainpower can overcome brute force. Although the Sphinx's riddle is never clearly stated in Sophocles' play, we know from other sources that it asked what goes on four legs, two legs and then three.[3] Oedipus alone can provide the solution (a person: first as baby, second as an adult and finally in old age with a stick), both on account of his intellect and because he turns out to be its hidden subject. As Oedipus enters the stage at the end of Sophocles' play with the staff of a blind man in hand, he is the unwitting embodiment of the final phase of the Sphinx's riddle, and, as such, a stark reminder of the limits of the human mind. Everything about Oedipus turns out to have prefigured his fate: his name alludes to his 'swollen foot' (*oideo* means 'swell' and *pous* 'foot'), his prescience and his blindness (*oida* means 'I know'; but literally translated it means 'I have seen').[4] Even the sharpest human mind had been unable to discern that meanings are multiform rather than uniform, that coincidence and irony are in reality the divine imprint on a seemingly secular world.

Oedipus, then, has readily been construed as the symbol of human intelligence, confident of everything but in reality ignorant of all. But he is also a saviour who is really the pollutant, the stranger who is in reality too closely related to the palace of Thebes. The over-confident Athenians may well have been receiving an object lesson from Sophocles. The fifth-century Greek philosopher Protagoras had confidently argued that 'man is the measure of all things'; Oedipus' example reveals how erroneous the Protagorean dictum really is. For the absent, mysterious gods in the Sophoclean cosmology are shown in the end to have the measure of all. Over the centuries the terms of reference may have been drastically altered, but it is rare for any subsequent generation not to have shared fifth-century Athenian anxieties about their own over-confident predictions concerning themselves and their fortunes. Playwrights through the ages have therefore readily grasped that to reflect upon the fate of Oedipus can teach something of value to each generation.

If Antiphanes' fragment draws our attention to the paradigmatic status of Oedipus by the fourth century, it also raises the important consideration of whether the act of creating from 'amorphous' life is in any sense more demanding than re-creating or adapting what has already been given some kind of life and shape by another, collective source. Many of those who have looked to the Oedipus myth as a starting point for their own compositions may well have cherished hopes that the Antiphanean claim were true. But some have undoubtedly found to their cost that inherited, or appropriated, property turns out very often to be the most intractable material of all, since audiences' expectations and preconceptions can provide a curb to, not a cue for, further creative endeavour. For as Antiphanes also reminds us, audiences receive refashioned material in ways that differ greatly from their responses to the new.

Yet for any playwright, the reworking of a myth yields considerable advantages beyond those of the economy of effort that Antiphanes comically outlines. The very existence of other versions of the story can work to the dramatist's own advantage, providing ample opportunity for expectations and preconceptions to be manipulated accordingly, and for meanings to be generated by omission and elision. Any modern stage adaptation of the Oedipus myth is being played primarily if not exclusively *against* its Sophoclean progenitor, with the interplay between the 'new' and the 'inherited' material providing both resonance and dissonance in the audience's minds.

Indeed, when we think of Sophocles' *Oedipus Tyrannus* we would be mistaken to think of it as some kind of 'original', for in reality Sophocles was no different from any other (ancient or modern) adapter of the Oedipus myth, working on the common material with other versions in mind. In the fifth century BC alone there were at least six plays entitled *Oedipus*, including lost plays by Aeschylus and Euripides.[5] So when Antiphanes says, 'I have just to say "Oedipus", and they know all the rest', he is guilty, perhaps, of more than a little comic licence. But he is commenting some hundred years after the first production of Sophocles' tragedy; and from 386 BC onwards, revivals of classic plays from the fifth century became part of the City Dionysia, the main Athenian drama festival. By Antiphanes' time, a repertoire of Greek tragedies was well established, and a mention of Oedipus may well have meant primarily (as it does to us) Sophocles' version of that myth. However, for the earlier fifth-century audience, sitting down to watch Sophocles' *Oedipus Tyrannus* sometime in the early 420s, the question 'What will happen to *Sophocles'* Oedipus?' must have been uppermost in their minds.

THE POLITICS OF *OEDIPUS TYRANNUS*

The intertextuality that is taken for granted in relation to modern adaptations of Greek myths, therefore, should also be borne in mind when considering tragedies of the fifth century BC, and with Sophocles' tragedy no less than with others. It has often been the practice in the past to attribute the obvious interconnections between, say, Aeschylus' *Libation Bearers*, Sophocles' *Electra* and Euripides' *Electra*, to an alleged, steady decline of tragedy towards the end of the century. But it is important to remember that were our sample of extant tragedies larger, these allusive elements in the plays based on the Orestes myth would in all likelihood turn out to be a common feature of many tragedies. For this reason, the *Libation Bearers*, and the *Electra* tragedies of Sophocles and Euripides, must be understood to be paradigmatic of Greek tragedy in general; and when we think of the Oedipus myth in relation to the fifth century BC, we must think of Sophocles' *Oedipus Tyrannus* as simply one version 'supplementing, challenging, displacing, but never simply replacing all the rest'.[6]

Very few members of the audience who sat down to watch Sophocles'
Oedipus Tyrannus in the 420s would have seen the original production
of Aeschylus' *Oedipus*, which won first prize at the City Dionysia in 467
BC, when it was performed as part of a connected tetralogy with *Laius*,
Seven against Thebes and the satyr play *Sphinx*. But many within the
audience may well have seen a revival of Aeschylus' version, where
Oedipus' fate is but one stage in a family history of sexual transgression
and internecine strife.[7] The only surviving play of the tetralogy is *Seven
against Thebes*, but a Byzantine hypothesis to the play suggests that the
first tragedy, *Laius*, included Laius' homosexual rape of Pelops' son,
Chrysippus, for which he incurred the curse of Pelops, and Sophocles'
decision to omit reference to this version of the myth is no doubt
significant.

In other accounts of the myth, the Delphic oracle demands sexual
abstinence of Laius, which he is unable to maintain.[8] In Sophocles'
Oedipus Tyrannus, by contrast, Apollo appears to have given an
unconditional prediction of Laius' death at the hands of his son
(line 784), and his only 'crime' is to have fathered that fated son,
and to have subsequently attempted to destroy him. As with the
relationship between Oedipus and Jocasta, which Sophocles makes
highly formal to avoid implying any erotic attachment between
mother and son, Sophocles' version makes sexual transgression an
important, but by no means the predominant, motif in his handling
of the myth. The scene in which Oedipus realises that he himself is
Laius' murderer is unusual in its inclusion of the potent and chilling
reminder of the actuality (as opposed to the consequences) of incest.
When Oedipus explains to Jocasta his horrific realisation that it is his
hands, polluted with the blood from Laius' murder, that have been
unwittingly defiling the living body of the dead king's wife, the
audience recoils in horrified sympathy as they view both those
hands and that body in front of them, in the light of the (now
unacknowledged) crime of incest (908 ff.).

The most significant consequence, however, of making the
prophecy to Laius unconditional is to make the Sophoclean world

that much harsher than the Aeschylean counterpart. In *Oedipus Tyrannus* Sophocles presents us with a far more inscrutable world, in which oracles offer seemingly cautionary advice, but in reality predict unavoidable disaster.

Some members of the first audience who watched *Oedipus Tyrannus* would also have seen Sophocles' earlier tragedy *Antigone* (442 BC), where the dead Oedipus' curse extends beyond the death of his sons to include Antigone, Haemon and Eurydice amongst its victims. Antigone's commitment to her brother and the gods of the underworld, which leads her to bury her brother in defiance of Creon's edict, is initially construed by the Chorus as blind intransigence similar, in kind and degree, to that of her father: 'Like father like daughter, passionate, wild … / she hasn't learned to bend before adversity' (lines 525–7). The mould from which Antigone is cast, and the one from which Oedipus too will emerge in the 420s and in the much later *Oedipus at Colonus* (posthumously produced 402–401 BC), is really that of the typical Sophoclean hero(ine), with Antigone's intransigence being the hallmark of what Bernard Knox has aptly termed the 'heroic temper'. Antigone's defiant refusal to compromise even to the point of her own destruction will be a pattern that the Sophoclean Oedipus will repeat in both *Oedipus Tyrannus* and *Oedipus at Colonus*.[9]

As the first audience sat down to watch *Oedipus Tyrannus*, then, they may well have had certain preconceptions about the personality of the protagonist derived from their knowledge of other Sophoclean heroes in general, and from the Sophoclean portrait of his daughter, Antigone, in particular. But any expectations they may have had stemming from the Aeschylean shaping of the material – especially regarding the prominence of sexual transgressions in the myth of the Labdacid dynasty – would have been clearly dashed. By abandoning the Aeschylean connected trilogy, Sophocles has reorientated the focus of his play and established a new centrality for the character of Oedipus, and guaranteed the interrogatory nature of his drama. The Sophoclean Oedipus is like a detective, pursuing his investigation in successive episodes with Tiresias, Creon, Jocasta, the Corinthian

Messenger and finally the Theban Shepherd. Oedipus is no longer the victim of an inherited curse, but a tireless searcher after truth; and the audience – albeit armed with the 'truth' that Oedipus is so urgently pursuing – join him on the quest for his identity, as they piece together the snippets of information from Jocasta about Apollo's oracle to Laius and the details of the baby's exposure (lines 784 ff.), and match them *against* the knowledge they already have from other sources. In other words, already knowing, in Antiphanes' terms, what Oedipus 'will suffer; what he has done' only enhances the complicated nature of the audience's response; it can never simplify.

The new centrality of Oedipus in the Sophoclean version would undoubtedly have prompted responses shaped by recent political events as well. We do not know the precise date of the play's first production, although attempts have been made to date it to 425, after the city of Athens had endured a series of plagues following the outbreak of the Peloponnesian War in 431.[10] Another attempt to highlight its influence on Euripides' *Hippolytus* (428 BC) would indicate a slightly earlier date, around 429.[11] Although any precise dating is clearly impossible, the play undoubtedly reflects upon (even if it does not itself directly reflect) ideas and events that dominated Athenian life at the beginning of the 420s.

Athens was an imperial power which had wielded considerable, and, some might say, overbearing influence over the Greek world throughout the middle years of the fifth century BC. The Athenians had only very recently entered into the war against Sparta and her allies, which was to last nearly thirty years and would eventually lead to the collapse of the Athenian empire. The early years of the war were overshadowed by plagues in Athens, when one quarter of the population was wiped out by the epidemic, including the great Athenian statesman Pericles, who had led the city state through the heyday of its expansionism. The misery and desperation of the Thebans in the opening scene of the play are paralleled in contemporary accounts of the plague at Athens,[12] and the criticism of seers and oracles that runs throughout the text was also symptomatic of the prevailing sense of despair.

The domestic crises at the start of the Peloponnesian War, then, may well have been reflected in *Oedipus Tyrannus*. Moreover, many of the issues under debate in Sophocles' play would have had a decidedly contemporary ring. Oedipus' and Jocasta's responses to Tiresias and the Delphic oracle respectively mirror current debates about the position of religious institutions in the democratic state. The choice of a Theban myth at this time, when, as Sparta's chief ally, Thebes had only relatively recently become the official enemy of Athens, may well also have been significant. Although Sophocles was by no means the only tragedian to represent Thebes as the site and source of disorder during this period, the requisite distancing and the consequent resonance attendant on such a choice of vehicle must have facilitated the playwright's exploration of urgent domestic concerns.[13]

Although the dating of the play with reference to the plagues in Athens has been widely contested, the evident similarities between the Sophoclean Oedipus and Pericles make it hard to imagine that an audience made no connection between their city and the dramatised city of Thebes. As Thucydides explains in his history, the nominally democratic Athens before the outbreak of the war was really under the control of its first citizen, Pericles. It could be argued, for example, that the first part of *Oedipus Tyrannus* is really an exploration of the role of the leader in a democracy: both in the opening scene when Oedipus emerges from the palace to answer the importunings of his grief-stricken people, and especially in the scene of confrontation between Creon and Oedipus.

Furthermore, Pericles' citizenship law of 451 BC, which limited citizenship to the offspring of two Athenian parents, is central to any consideration of the play's preoccupation with biological, as opposed to 'given' or assumed, identity. Indeed, it has been suggested that it was the Periclean legislation above all that determined Sophocles' emphasis on blood relationships (as opposed to incest or parricide) in his handling of the mythical material.[14] The fact that the later play, *Oedipus at Colonus*, deals with Oedipus' past in terms of guilt and pollution, rather than biological identity, would seem to give further credence to the claim that *Oedipus Tyrannus* was reflecting current anxieties over familial relations attendant on the citizenship law.[15] The multiple deaths in families on account of the plague undoubtedly made the effects of the legislation all the more keenly felt. In 429 Pericles was forced to endure the death of his last surviving legitimate son, and the Athenians were apparently so moved by his forbearance at the funeral that they allowed him to waive the legislation and his son by his non-Athenian mistress, Aspasia, became an Athenian citizen. Pericles' citizenship legislation, like Oedipus' curse at the start of the play on whomsoever caused the plague in Thebes, turns out to have a similarly disastrous effect; and yet as Oedipus and Pericles are both hoist by their own petard, so to speak, they display their finest qualities.[16]

That Oedipus himself turns out to be the source of the pollution in Thebes may have called to the first audience's mind the Spartan attempt to intervene in Athenian politics in 432, when they demanded Pericles' expulsion from the city on the grounds of an alleged inherited family curse stemming from a sacriligious murder committed by one of his ancestors.[17] But even if the evident similarities between Oedipus and Pericles are rejected, the connections between the dramatised Thebes and the city of Athens in the last third of the fifth century are plentiful. As Bernard Knox has convincingly argued, Oedipus and his fortunes reflect 'Athens itself, in all its greatness, its power, its intelligence, and also its serious defects. The audience which watched Oedipus in the theatre of Dionysus was watching itself'.[18]

OEDIPUS TYRANNUS IN PERFORMANCE

Sophocles was already over sixty years of age when he wrote *Oedipus Tyrannus*, having led an active public life as well as having thirty years' playwrighting experience behind him. He entered *Oedipus Tyrannus*, together with two other (lost) tragedies and a (lost) satyr play, in the dramatic contest at the City Dionysia in competition with two other tragedians. The festival held in honour of Dionysus, the Greek god of wine, vegetation and drama, was a major religious as well as political event, which all Athenian citizens were able to attend (on account of financial assistance made available by the state), and to which important foreign visitors were invited. Since women did not qualify for citizenship, it is unlikely that Athenian women formed any part of the crowd of between six thousand and seven thousand who watched the plays, but non-Athenian women may well have attended.[19]

The majority of audience members would have participated in some way in the festival's events, making the distinction between audience and participants hard to sustain. Prior to the twelve plays that were to be performed over the three-day period, the audience would have watched, and in many cases participated in, the procession which brought the statue of the patron god, Dionysus, into the theatre to occupy the place of honour in the front row. They would also have seen the sacrifices, and the display of the tribute money paid to the imperial power by the subject states of Athens; and they would have watched the parade of the sons of the war-dead taking a public oath to fight and die for their city. They may also have joined in the dithyrambic contests, which provided narrative through choral song and dance. The eleven (and later fifteen) members of the Chorus were ordinary citizens and so known to many of the audience. The City Dionysia was about putting Athens on display; and by being the centrepiece in this major civic event in the Athenian calendar, Greek tragedy could be said to have played an important part in Athenian democratic life.[20]

It has been suggested that tragedy was born at the time when the mythical mode of thought was giving way to a philosophical mode of analysis; and that it emerged at the same time as political democracy was by no means merely fortuitous.[21] The fifth-century BC theatre itself, with its raked seating and vast circular *orchestra* as focus of the performance area, uniquely empowers the (majority) audience over the (individual) actor.[22] Both Greek tragedy's form and content – its debating characters and its preoccupation with the relationship between the individual and society, the actors and the Chorus – may be said to encapsulate the workings of Athenian democracy. The parallels between the lawcourt, the Assembly and the drama of the period are widely attested in what has been termed the 'performance culture' of fifth-century Athens.[23] It is therefore correct to expect the plays to address the problems and concerns that its audience experienced outside the theatre. But it is clearly inappropriate to reduce Greek tragedy to a historical document. It is important to emphasise the fact that just as its characters and legends were taken from an imaginary heroic past, so too the language (of the Chorus in particular) was heightened and deliberately distanced from that of everyday Athenian speech.

Stage space speaks; and although it is impossible to reconstruct the original production, it is possible and indeed revealing to imagine the play under the performance conditions of the fifth century BC.[24] The very human-centred nature of *Oedipus Tyrannus*, where the remoteness of the gods is a central theme, means that the upper performance level (the roof of the stage building) is left deliberately unoccupied: Oedipus is, at least in the opening scene, the surrogate god in the play in spite of (or perhaps because of) the priest's statement that the people supplicate him not as equal to the gods, but as the first of men (lines 31–3). Oedipus' concern with public (rather than personal) matters in the first part of the play, in combination with his dominance of the stage space in front of the stage building throughout most of the play, merely reinforce this point.[25]

A consideration of the characters' entries and exits is equally revealing. One of the side entrances (*eisodoi*) in this play clearly leads to the city of Thebes, the other abroad, to Corinth and Delphi; and the central doorway of the stage building leads into the palace. When Oedipus stands (presumably) in the *orchestra* following his interrogation of the Theban Shepherd and makes his final discovery of the truth about himself (line 1306), he is again at a place where three roads meet. His re-entry into the palace thus becomes in visual terms a

re-enactment of his arrival at Thebes. The Messenger speech rein-
forces the point with its graphic account of Oedipus' unpinning of
Jocasta's brooches (an action synonymous with disrobing), suggesting
a re-enactment of the nuptial union (lines 1402–14).[26] And Oedipus'
final enforced entry into the palace at the very end of the play – when
both Oedipus and the audience yearn for some cathartic exit from the
city that other versions of the story often allow him – is a powerful
visual statement of the Sophoclean Oedipus' inability to escape the
stigma of his past (line 1678).

Oedipus' dawning realisation of the truth about himself may well
have been accompanied by a movement away from the stage area
(which he dominates in the first part of the play) towards the *orchestra*,
where he must be by the time of the interrogation of the Theban
Shepherd, when proximity between the actors is signalled in the text
(lines 1228 ff.). With such a shift in focus, Oedipus, the surrogate god
of the first part of the play, can be understood to enact his increasing
realisation of human limitations by his movement from the palace
into the communal stage space (strongly associated with the Chorus)
of the *orchestra*.

It is important to remember that the rules of the dramatic contest
restricted the tragedian to only three actors with speaking parts. This
limitation in part explains the use of masks: the actor who played
Creon in the first part would have returned as the Corinthian
Messenger in part two, and Jocasta would have returned with a
different costume and mask to take the part of the Theban
Shepherd. But this apparent limitation is really a strength: it determines the centrality of Oedipus – since the lead actor played this part
throughout – and the interrogatory nature of the successive episodes
between Oedipus and his interlocutors – Tiresias, Creon, Jocasta, the
Corinthian Messenger and finally the Theban Shepherd. The nature
of the investigation changes in the pivotal scene with Jocasta (lines
778 ff.), when the pursuit of the killer of Laius becomes intermeshed
with the search for self-identity: the theme of regicide is from now on
eclipsed by the question of parricide.

The changes in register in Greek tragedy may not always be obvious to an audience watching the play in translation, but they are crucial to an understanding of the mood and tempo of the Sophoclean tragedy. In addition to the obvious divisions between the (predominantly) spoken parts of the episodes and the sung parts of the choral odes, it is important to remember that the actors also use song at moments of high emotional tension, making Greek tragedy much closer to the twentieth-century Western musical than to other modern drama. Such a transition occurs after Jocasta's first entry to intervene in the altercation between her husband and her brother, when the Chorus, in sung lyrics, echo her entreaty to Oedipus to show clemency to Creon. There is then a lyric dialogue between the Chorus and Oedipus which underlines the highly emotionally charged nature of the exchange (lines 725–41). With Oedipus' concession (line 742) comes both a return to reason and a significant return to the spoken iambic metre. But the Chorus and Jocasta continue to sing, supplying both an emotional and aesthetic diminuendo to the interlude that ends with the Chorus's appeal to Oedipus to be their helmsman. This lyric exchange is an interesting variant on the traditional choral ode which it supplants at this point, separating as it does the episode between Oedipus and Creon from the pivotal one between Oedipus and Jocasta that follows.

The final scene, following the Messenger's account of Jocasta's suicide and Oedipus' self-blinding, involves a similar interplay between lyric and spoken utterance. The horror of witnessing the entry of the blinded Oedipus and the extremity of his suffering are conveyed in the highly wrought lyrical dialogue that begins the final scene (lines 1432–96). The contortions of syntax and rhythm mirror the confusion and chaos that Oedipus' actions have unwittingly brought upon himself and his family. When Oedipus returns to the spoken word (lines 1496 ff.), his sentiments remain unaltered; it is merely the key that has changed, allowing for the human frailties of the chastened Oedipus to come into full play in the thoroughly political exchange that occurs between himself and the proto-tyrant, Creon, in the final moments of the play.

OEDIPUS AND THE 'DISCOVERY' OF THE HERO

The story of Oedipus in some senses reverses the normal pattern of heroic myth, which charts the path of the outsider's dawning realisation of his true birth and his eventual accommodation within society. Although Oedipus in this sense is a kind of antihero, he has clearly been responsible for shaping modern definitions of heroism.

In Chapter 13 of the *Poetics* (1453a ll, 1453a 20), Aristotle seems to imply that the 'tragic hero', as we know it – the central figure in a tragedy – was invented by Sophocles in *Oedipus Tyrannus.* It may well have been that Sophocles wrote his play with a particularly outstanding actor in mind (possibly the one who took the leading part in Euripides' *Medea* a few years earlier in 431 BC). However rare the single, central figure is in Greek tragedy in general – apart from *Oedipus Tyrannus* and the *Medea*, we only find this central figure in Sophocles' *Electra* and *Oedipus at Colonus* and in Euripides' *Hecuba* and *Trojan Women* – all Sophoclean characters do share with Oedipus certain distinctive 'heroic' features. Oedipus, like his other tragic counterparts, is unyielding even in extremis.

In fifth-century Athens, the term 'hero' referred specifically to notable, dead persons, who were worshipped in religious cults. Oedipus himself was worshipped as such a hero in Athens during the fifth century; and Sophocles' later play, *Oedipus at Colonus*, may well provide for Sophocles' audience an explanation for the existence of a shrine to Oedipus in Attica.[27] During the course of *Oedipus at Colonus*, we watch Oedipus as an old man beginning his ascent into 'hero-cult' status as he is poised on the threshold of death.

Although the phrase 'tragic hero(ine)' is better omitted from discussions of Greek tragedy altogether in order to avoid confusion with these heroes of cult, it is hard to resist in relation to the Sophoclean characters. The hallmark of the typical Sophoclean character is social and psychological isolation attendant on their refusal to abandon an original choice; and fixity of purpose becomes a source of both personal strength and weakness, as incredulous onlookers find it increasingly hard to communicate with them. The tragic characters, for their part, very often turn to the landscape or to the dead for solace and guidance as the world of the living appears to recede from their vision. It is as if accession to heroic status entails the beginning of the process of the tragic character's own death.

Aristotle, in the *Politics* (1253a), describes the person who is incapable of working in common with others as either god or beast; and like gods and beasts, the tragic characters in Sophocles occupy a liminal position in society in terms of their source of power for both good and evil. Oedipus appears, through enormous energy and personal integrity, to extend the boundaries of the humanly possible; and his supra-human achievement turns out to be coincident with the discovery that the very boundaries he has, in reality, crossed are those humanity would least wish to exceed.

Oedipus displays extraordinary determination and vigour in his efforts to unravel the truth about Laius' murder and his own identity. His fixity of purpose is evident from the outset when he pronounces his decision to find Laius' murderer on receiving news from the Delphic oracle (lines 149 ff.). Even though there is a shift in focus as Oedipus becomes increasingly concerned with the question of his own paternity, he remains doggedly determined to rid the city of its pollution, despite all efforts to deter him (by Tiresias, 359 ff.); by Jocasta, 1158 ff.); and finally by the Theban Shepherd, especially 1280 ff.).

But determination and integrity in the 'tragic hero' very easily give way to overbearingness and narrow intransigence; and we watch an increasingly isolated Oedipus as he pursues his goal to the exclusion of all other considerations. Tiresias' evasiveness and subsequent denunciation of Oedipus as the murderer provoke a tirade of abuse and invective in response, and signs of gross insecurity in Oedipus that verge on paranoia (lines 402 ff.). As the *tyrannos* – the ruler from outside who has not inherited his position – he immediately infers that Creon (who has been deprived of inherited successsion) must be Tiresias' conspirator. And during his subsequent encounter with

Creon, we learn that the only evidence for Oedipus' suspicion is the fact that it was Creon who urged him to seek Tiresias' advice in the first place (line 622). Oedipus, who alone of the Sphinx's interlocutors had the intellectual capacity to solve the riddle, turns out to have too much faith in his own interpretative powers. Instead of heeding Creon and the Chorus's advice when they urge patience, Oedipus mistakes his own impetuosity for sure-footedness:

> When my enemy moves against me quickly,
> plots in secret, I move quickly too, I must,
> I plot and pay him back. Relax my guard a moment,
> waiting his next move – he wins his objective,
> I lose mine. (lines 693–6)

Oedipus fails now, just as he did during the fatal encounter with Laius at the crossroads, to notice the true nature of his adversary; he is blind to the truth, and it is only through his literal blindness that he will, paradoxically, be able to see the truth of his own situation.

As with other tragic heroes, Oedipus' world view becomes increasingly one enjoyed only by himself: Jocasta's attempts to prevent him finding out the truth are construed as wilful obstruction (lines 1169 ff.) and royal pique (lines 1186 ff.). The apparent outsider of the opening of the play now embraces the prospect of being a foundling nurtured by Mount Cithaeron, only to discover very shortly that he belongs all too much to the Theban city. When he finally comes face to face with the Theban Shepherd, the only man who can dispel his delusions, he pursues his goal with a terrifying (but paradoxically admirable) ferocity that is typical of the tragic hero. The requisite Aristotelian tragic emotions of pity and fear combine here in a state of turmoil throughout this breathtaking scene, as the audience is both drawn in sympathy towards Oedipus the man, and yet recoils in horror at the fierceness of his interrogation and the dawning of his fate.

It is only after the Messenger speech, and during the final scene of the play, that these tragic emotions can be held in some kind of check: now that the tragic hero has been 'tamed' through his discovery of the truth and his action of self-blinding, pity can be given unreservedly, and fear of the inscrutable divine machinery can be felt absolutely. The final few minutes of the play, which some commentators and adapters have found too emotive for comfort,[28] show Oedipus in the company of his daughters (lines 1613 ff.); and it is here that the biological confusions in the family are poignantly enacted before our eyes. The blinded Oedipus now painstakingly gropes for his daughters'/sisters' hands; and by rejecting the traditional father–son farewells as he pronounces his sons' ability to cope by themselves (lines 1599 ff.) – a theme that is to run throughout *Oedipus at Colonus* – we watch Oedipus assume instead the traditional role of mother as he laments the anomalies that lie in store for his abandoned daughters.[29] Antigone may be said in her eponymous play to embody the typical features of the tragic heroine in her encroachment upon the traditional masculine preserve of the *polis*. Here in Sophocles' *Oedipus Tyrannus*, we witness her father's final confirmation of his heroism in his ability to occupy traditionally feminine territory as he bids farewell to his daughters. Even though Sophocles has evidently chosen to downgrade the sexually transgressive features inherent in the mythical material, it is important to emphasise that his treatment refigures rather than represses those elements in the last few moments of the play.

THE THEBAN BROTHERS

Sophocles, then, like other later adapters of his play, was reworking traditional material both in the light of his current circumstances, and in contradistinction to the work of predecessors and contemporaries. In addition to the earlier *Seven against Thebes* of Aeschylus, there are three other extant plays – Euripides' *Phoenician Women*, his (fragmentary) *Oedipus*, and Sophocles' *Oedipus at Colonus* – that were inevitably written and undoubtedly watched with the Sophoclean *Oedipus Tyrannus* in mind.

The kind of intertextual references that Sophocles' audience may well have appreciated on watching *Oedipus Tyrannus* can be glimpsed, perhaps, by looking at the interrelationships between Aeschylus' *Seven against Thebes* (the only extant play from the tetralogy of 467 BC) and Euripides' *Phoenician Women* produced sometime between 409 and 407, both of which deal with the internecine strife between Oedipus' sons.

Euripides' version is clearly written with the Aeschylean tragedy in mind. Midway through Euripides' play, Eteocles (the son who has denied the throne to his brother Polynices) announces to Creon his intention to go and appoint seven captains to defend each gate of the city against the invading forces (lines 855 ff.). In an earlier scene we have watched Eteocles and Polynices fail to reach agreement over their respective claims to the Theban throne, despite Jocasta's importunings. Now towards the end of the episode with Creon, Eteocles states that to name each captain would be a waste of precious time when the enemy is camped outside the city's walls (lines 858–60). Eteocles' lines here are often taken to be a barbed reference to a lengthy scene in Aeschylus' *Seven against Thebes*, where some 220 lines (some fifteen minutes' playing time) are given over to fourteen highly stylised set speeches in which a soldier gives seven separate accounts of the enemy leader at each gate, to which Eteocles responds in turn with an account of his chosen Theban adversary (lines 456–846). The seventh gate turns out to be beseiged by Polynices: Eteocles will now be forced to confront his own kin in mortal combat, as Oedipus' curse on his ungrateful sons had predicted.

The contents of this lengthy and (in modern terms) 'stilted' scene have been reworked in Euripides' play in a number of ways. First, the details of the leaders of the invading force have already been given to the audience in the second part of the prologue when Antigone, standing on the roof of the stage building/the city wall with her Tutor, learns the identities of the invaders (lines 84–234). And later in the play, we are to learn details of those who fought at each of the gates in the first Messenger speech that follows the battle (lines 1233–1338). Any argument that attempts to account for Eteocles' earlier remarks in terms of a self-conscious attempt at so-called dramaturgical 'sophistication' seems limited. Instead of seeing the Euripidean comments as simply a joke at the expense of the conventions of early tragedy, it is perhaps more fruitful to see Polynices' remarks as Euripides' playing *against* the earlier version in rather more subtle ways.[30]

Aeschylus' Eteocles is presented as a decisive leader of state in public from the prologue onwards, and is only unsettled in private by presentiment that his father's curse may well be about to be enacted (lines 97–107).[31] His Euripidean namesake, by contrast, has shown himself to be a cynical oath-breaker from the outset, for whom power alone is the absolute reality. Now in this scene with Creon, he turns out to be indecisive as well, and completely dependent on the military skills of his uncle. Eteocles' comments therefore on the shortage of time (lines 858–60) would seem to be less concerned with probing the limits of Aeschylean dramaturgy than with revealing the ways in which an acquaintance with the Aeschylean version can deepen our understanding of the episode. In Aeschylus' scene it is the moral turpitude of the invaders that is being stressed through the elaborate accounts of the emblems on the shields; and Eteocles is caught in a battle which is essentially an impersonal clash of shields, until the moment comes when he realises that it is his own brother whom he is to meet in armed combat (lines 815 ff.).

Euripides, by contrast, has made the war all too obviously a personal issue from the start, in a play in which all the characters (except Tiresias, but including the Chorus) are blood relations. It is the Euripidean Eteocles' shortcomings that are being compounded by our awareness of his Aeschylean counterpart. The pretext of time-saving seems implausible from an Eteocles who has already been forced to delay the counter-attack on account of his need for Creon's lengthy lesson in military tactics (lines 815 ff.). His refusal to place captains at the gate serves, above all, to show him to be no leader at all, with no intrinsic interest in the broader context of the battle; he is only interested in destroying his brother in combat. In marked contrast to the Aeschylean *dramatis personae*, there is no sense in which Euripides' characters can be seen as reluctant victims of their father's curse. In an earlier scene Tiresias has already explained to Creon that there is a much older curse on Cadmus, which the sacrifice of Menoeceus will end, making the role here of Oedipus in his sons' destruction recede even further from the audience's minds (lines 1071 ff.). Both Eteocles and Polynices are shown actively pursuing 'destructive and self-destructive ends'.[32] Indeed, both the subsequent choral ode prefiguring their encounter and the Messenger speech that follows and reports it serve to emphasise the atavistic nature of the brothers' encounter (lines 1432–4;1513 ff.).

Writing his play with the events of 411 BC in very recent memory, Euripides has made the war in Thebes an intensely personal affair from the outset. The oligarchic coup of 411 and its aftermath had left Athens on the brink of civil war, and in the *Phoenician Women* Euripides is showing that it is family misalliances and personal inadequacies that make war, rather than, as in the Aeschylean version, the operations of fate over which the characters themselves come to realise they have no power. Like the (near-)contemporaneous *Orestes* by Euripides (408 BC), the tragic characters enact their undignified, self-seeking and self-regarding roles in a world that bears little or no resemblance to the alarming, but divinely ordered, cosmos over which Zeus prevails in the Aeschylean tragedies. The *Phoenician Women* demonstrates, in this respect, the considerable advantage the tragic playwright does have in being able to play his scene *against* an analogous scene by another tragedian.

THE EURIPIDEAN OEDIPUS

Both *Seven against Thebes* and the *Phoenician Women* have endings that appear to anticipate the events of Sophocles' *Antigone*,[33] suggesting that the *Antigone* had become part of the standard repertoire by at least between 409 and 407 BC, when the *Phoenician Women* received its first performance. In the *Phoenician Women*, we can also see evident links with Euripides' later fragmentary *Oedipus*, which contrast strongly with Sophocles' treatment of the character of Oedipus in both *Oedipus Tyrannus* and the later *Oedipus at Colonus*.

The *Phoenician Women* opens with Jocasta's prologue, where her account of the events leading up to the play is broadly in line with Sophocles' *Oedipus Tyrannus*, except with regard to her own fate. The blinded Oedipus, we learn, has been incarcerated alive in the palace behind her by his sons in an effort to erase the family's shameful past. But as with the anomalous imprisonment of Oedipus' daughter in Sophocles' *Antigone*, the actions of the incarcerators must be punished; and here in the *Phoenician Women* Oedipus has cursed his sons with the fate of dividing their inheritance with 'sharpened steel' (lines 61 ff.). Jocasta explains that their subsequent pact to rule independently, and in turn, was soon broken by Eteocles' failure to honour the terms of the agreement; and Polynices, she explains, has now returned with the Argive force to secure his claim to power.

In the *Phoenician Women*, Oedipus' brooding presence inside the stage building is felt throughout the play, through the allusions of others. Jocasta sings of his deep despair and suicidal longings (lines 366 ff.) as she enters after the choral entry-song to act as broker for the debate between her doomed sons. Even though Jocasta enjoys a prominent role in the stage action of the play, she nonetheless shares with Oedipus a kind of spectral existence, having gone into premature mourning with Polynices' exile (lines 343 ff.). The house itself towards the end of the play takes on a life of its own (lines 1639 ff.), with Antigone calling significantly upon the House of Oedipus (not, as elsewhere in the play, the House of Cadmus/Laius); and she invokes the head of the household as if she were Electra raising the dead Agamemnon from his tomb in Aeschylus' *Libation Bearers*. When Oedipus finally emerges from the palace, it is exactly as if he had been raised from the dead:

> Girl, why do you goad me into the light
> with your terrible tears, a bedridden creature

> from dark chambers, this stick support for my
> blind foot? A shadow of thin air,
> a corpse from the clay,
> a winged dream? (lines 1700–45)

At the end of the tragedy, the audience gain a brief glimpse of the defiant Oedipus in the Sophoclean mould ('Well, I'll not be abject and twine my arms around your knees. I won't betray my nobility / of birth, even if it goes the worse for me': lines 1790–2); but Euripides' Oedipus is essentially a spent man who proclaims the solver of riddles as dead (line 1689).

It is generally understood on metrical evidence that Euripides' *Oedipus* came after the *Phoenician Women* (*c.* between 409 and 407 BC), and before Sophocles' *Oedipus at Colonus*, which was posthumously produced by his grandson, also called Sophocles, in 401 or 402.[34] There is no consensus regarding the ordering of all the fragments of the Euripides *Oedipus*, but the main differences between Euripides' and Sophocles' versions appear to hinge on the means of the discovery of the truth about Oedipus. One fragment of the Euripides version announces:

> Pressing Polybus' son firmly to the ground we blind him and
> destroy the pupils of his eyes (fragment 541, p. 117).

It is usually inferred that these words come from a Messenger speech, and report the account by Laius' servants of their savage blinding of Oedipus under Creon's orders.[35] What is striking here, of course, is absence of the traditional theatrical motif of self-blinding (it is there in Aeschylus and Sophocles, although absent from the one detailed Homeric account of the myth in Book 11 of the *Odyssey*, lines 271–80). But perhaps the most significant difference (implicit in the appellation 'son of Polybus') lies with Euripides' separation of the discovery of regicide from the act of parricide.

Numerous fragments suggest that the lost play presented a sharp contrast between an intellectual, but essentially passive, Oedipus and a ruthlessly opportunistic Creon, who is the jealous would-be usurper of the throne (as Oedipus mistakenly accuses him of being in Sophocles' play).[36] The lines of (possibly) Jocasta bemoan the fact that 'Envy which ruins the wits of many men destroyed him, and destroyed me with him' (fragment 551, p. 121). Creon in Euripides' version appears to have hired the Theban servant who survived the incident at the crossroads to find out evidence against Oedipus. When Queen Periboia (Sophocles' Merope) arrives from Corinth with the news of Polybus' death, the Theban servant seems to have recognised her chariot as that used by the killer of Laius.[37] Euripides' play of subterfuge and savagery is clearly a very far cry from Sophocles' tragic trajectory, which is driven by the investigatory powers of its protagonist. Chance, not direction, brings about the discovery of the truth in Euripides' version; and as with the (possibly) earlier *Phoenician Women*, Oedipus appears to have little likelihood of survival against the shamelessly manipulative characters who surround him. If the dating based on metrical evidence is correct, and we are speaking of a date between 408 and 402/1 BC, the *Oedipus*, like Euripides' other plays at this time, is reflecting the domestic turmoil and political skulduggery in Athens of the latter years of the Peloponnesian War.

As with the *Phoenician Women*, Jocasta is given the space to emerge as a powerful tragic character in the Euripidean *Oedipus*. In a potentially much more emotive scene of recognition following the blinding, the discovery of Oedipus' true paternity is made in a thoroughly domestic context that has been stripped of all Sophoclean political ramifications. As Jocasta and Oedipus listen to Periboia speak of the baby she found in a chest that had been put to sea, Jocasta is forced to deduce, and to endure, the fulness of her own role in Oedipus' life. By 'loosening the structure'[38] of the Sophoclean play, by separating the regicide from the parricide, Euripides has done something that many subsequent adapters have also done. He may well have made his scene that much more poignant by narrowing its focus and by removing the question of regicide from view, but by doing so he has denied himself the very universalising qualities that attracted subsequent audiences and adapters to the Sophoclean play.

OEDIPUS AT COLONUS

It is only in Sophocles' last tragedy, *Oedipus at Colonus*, that Oedipus returns in the recognisable mould of the Sophoclean hero. Indeed it is in this play that we uniquely witness the accession of a character into hero-cult status during the course of a tragedy. Elsewhere that ascendancy is usually implicit in the ending, as in Sophocles' *Ajax*, rather than enacted during the course of the play. The structure of this last play is much looser than that of the *Oedipus Tyrannus* and much more like the episodic plot of the *Phoenician Women*, with the preparations for the second and last momentous event in Oedipus' life taking place at the grove of the Eumenides in Colonus. These preparations are interwoven with discussion about Oedipus' own personal fate and responsibility, as well as the more topical consideration of the relationship between Thebes and Athens.

After the defeat of Athens in 404 BC, Thebes became estranged from Sparta, and offered sanctuary to Athenian exiles hostile to the Thirty Tyrants put in place by the Spartan victors. It was from Thebes that the Athenian democrats launched their successful counter-attack that led to the gradual restoration of the democracy from 403 onwards. Sophocles, it should be recalled, had died before the end of the war in 406 or 405; and when his play was produced in 402 or 401 by his grandson, also called Sophocles, it may well have been reworked in the light of recent events. Produced as it was during the construction period, *Oedipus at Colonus* must have been viewed as an exercise in Athenian confidence-boosting, as well as an exploration of past hostilities between Athens and Thebes, and as an attempt to provide an explanation for a permanent and mutually beneficial alliance between the states in the future.

When Theseus arrives to meet the old man who has encroached upon the sacred grove of the Eumenides and asked for audience with the King of Athens, he immediately recognises the stranger as Oedipus (lines 549 ff.). Theseus goes on to re-enact in reverse the sanctuary afforded to Athenians in Thebes in 404 by promising to provide sanctuary for Oedipus in Athens. When Oedipus points out the magnitude of such an undertaking, warning of the imminent Theban invasion to retrieve him, Theseus wonders what on earth could cause conflict between Athens and Thebes. In response, Oedipus delivers a long speech on the transience of all living things and especially all human alliances, speaking with the start of a prophetic voice that will resound in the last part of the play:

> and a day will come when the treaties of an hour,
> the pacts firmed with a handclasp will snap –
> at the slightest world a spear will hurl them to the winds –
> some far-off day when my dead body, slumbering, buried
> cold in death, will drain their hot blood down,
> if Zeus is still Zeus and Apollo the son of god
> speaks clear and true. (701 ff.)

Sophocles may well have been writing the kind of play that Aristophanes was looking for in the *Frogs* in 405, when Dionysus goes to Hades in search of a tragedian to save the city. But when *Oedipus at Colonus* was produced, at least, not only must it have reminded the Athenians of the beauty of their countryside at a time when the ravaged plains must have been all too apparent (lines 18 ff.; 668 ff.), but it also provided them with a reason to trust in their new relations with Thebes at a critical moment during the construction period.

It has been pointed out that 'the road is the single most dominant spatial metaphor in the play'.[39] In some senses we are invited to witness the parallels between the first and final momentous event in Oedipus' life through the use of the stage space in this play. Unlike the practice in other tragedies, the stage building does not function as a point of exit/entry during the course of the play:[40] as the sacred grove of the Eumenides, it is only used once at the very end when it provides the path for Oedipus and Theseus as Oedipus approaches his death.

Acting as a potential rather than an actual exit, the stage building becomes all the more significant as the point at which the two *eisodoi* meet with the entrance to the grove. In this sense, it could be argued that *Oedipus at Colonus*, and the final exit of Oedipus especially (lines 1695 ff.), is being deliberately played *against* analogous exits in Sophocles' *Oedipus Tyrannus.*

Whilst the events of *Oedipus Tyrannus* enact the traditional hero-myth in reverse, the *Oedipus at Colonus* goes some way towards putting the hero-myth back on its traditional course. As the opening of *Oedipus Tyrannus* serves to highlight the fortitude and pre-eminence of Oedipus in Thebes, the events of the first part of *Oedipus at Colonus* are designed to emphasise the physical vulnerability of the blind, aged Oedipus in exile. In the opening scene, Oedipus' beggarly garb and scarred body, together with his dependence on Antigone, are highlighted as is his new chastened acceptance of his sufferings (5 ff.). Oedipus declares himself to be 'this harried ghost of a man, / this Oedipus … Oedipus is no more / the flesh and blood of old' (lines 132 ff).

If Oedipus in Sophocles' earlier tragedy provides the dynamic to his own play, here in the later play his vulnerable shell is beseiged at every turn. First, the chorus of old men of Colonus fear his entry into the sacred grove, and guide his slow perilous path from the grove to the threshold where they can safely question him, before recoiling in horror as they learn his identity (lines 192–219). Frail and fragile though Oedipus is, there are moments during this choral interchange when Oedipus' inner strength is summoned and we gain a glimpse of the power that is prophesied in Apollo's oracle. To the Chorus, he proclaims: 'I come as someone sacred, someone filled / with piety and power, bearing a great gift / for all your people' (lines 312 ff.); and his powers do not go unnoticed: 'You fill me with awe, you must, old man – / you express your arguments with such force' (lines 316 ff).

Even if Oedipus' inner strength is never far from sight, his physical limitations are never forgotten. The bitter exchange with Creon may again adumbrate the spiritual power of Oedipus (lines 897 ff.), but it is the impotence of Oedipus the man that is emphasised as he hears of

Creon's capture of Ismene, and is forced to act as helpless bystander during the violent assault on Antigone. The lyric exchange at lines 953 ff. enacts an escalation in emotional and physical intensity, which is almost unparalleled in Greek drama, and which reaches its climax with Creon's sacrilegious attempt to grab Oedipus, the suppliant. As with the parallel confrontational scene between Creon and Oedipus in *Oedipus Tyrannus*, a third party is desperately sought to defuse the conflict. Here it is Theseus, the legendary pre-eminent Athenian king, who arrives in the nick of time to save Oedipus from violent assault and to pledge the return of his daughters. The touching scene of reunion that follows serves to underline the frailty of Oedipus the man, as he is forced to realise that he is unable, as pollutant, to embrace Theseus, his benefactor (line 1282). Hailed as the saviour of Thebes in *Oedipus Tyrannus*, Oedipus turns out, in reality, to be its pollutant; in *Oedipus at Colonus*, by contrast, he is the true saviour of Athens, and yet ironically remains all too aware of his own pollution. The lengthy first part of the later play, when time the destroyer is shown at its most merciless, reaches its culmination with the third choral ode in which the Chorus conclude that 'not to be born is best' (lines 1211 ff.).

From now on the physical shortcomings of Oedipus no longer matter; indeed they seem to vanish altogether. First we watch Oedipus curse his sons before our eyes – a Sophoclean touch that enables the audience to witness the growing power of Oedipus and makes the quarrel between the ignoble sons independent of their father's curse. Here, in this powerful scene, Oedipus is not simply able to reassert his strength through his verbal and spiritual defeat of his son, Polynices, he is also able to find his own oracular voice, even having been himself destroyed by prophecy (1554 ff.).

The significance of this oracular pronouncement is underlined by Oedipus' withdrawal from ordinary human exchange henceforth (lines 1585–1655): Oedipus' accession to heroic status is now nearly complete as he is no longer fully of this world. It is only with the thunder clap that Oedipus returns to the present, and only then to usher into the stage space the divine portents that only he can interpret. Although

Oedipus is most anxious for Theseus to come so that he can divulge to him his secret, he ultimately has no need of his benefactor because, in marked contrast to the earlier scenes, he can now provide his own dénouement; it is Theseus, by contrast, who needs him.

At this point in the play, we are reminded of parallel scenes in *Oedipus Tyrannus*: both Oedipus' entry into the palace on learning the truth about himself, which re-enacts his arrival in Thebes and resembles in all respects an exit for death; and his final and involuntary entry into the palace at the close of the play, blinded and newly disempowered in sharp denial of the rewards of traditional heroism. In this penultimate scene in *Oedipus at Colonus*, Oedipus is again at the crossroads, but the exit for death is now real and he is poised to enact his final *rite de passage* that is to proclaim him hero. Moreover, in marked contrast to the final scene of the earlier tragedy, now Oedipus' physical disability vanishes and the blind man is empowered to lead the sighted through the sacred grove that has remained untouched since Oedipus' first premature incursion in the opening scene.

Whereas the Oedipus of *Oedipus Tyrannus* was forced to confront his human limitations at the end of the play, Oedipus in *Oedipus at Colonus* does indeed extend the boundaries of the humanly possible in the last scene. The manner of his dying is recounted in enigmatic terms in a lengthy Messenger speech; but with Theseus alone as witness, the Messenger can only imagine 'the lightless depths of Earth bursting open in kindness / to receive him'. Oedipus has thus received the 'promised rest' that Apollo predicted (line 107), but he has not been divinely recompensed. His ending, like the hero he himself has now become, is both mysterious and chilling, both of and not of this world.

FROM OEDIPUS TO EVERYMAN

When Dionysus searches amongst the dead tragic poets in Hades for a saviour for Athens in Aristophanes' *Frogs* (405 BC), the comic playwright seems to be looking back to the good old days of tragedy.

But Greek tragedy did not run out of steam at the end of the fifth century BC, as has sometimes been suggested. The inclusion of revivals of fifth-century plays into the dramatic festival in 386 tells us more about the formation of a repertoire than about any alleged decadence in tragic dramaturgy. Already in the fifth century Attic tragedy was being exported around the Greek world; and by the end of the fourth century it was being performed in the local theatre of every city in the Greek world, and its popularity is reflected in its representations in the visual arts.[41]

In Sophocles' day there were probably only a very few papyrus copies of his plays in circulation in the city, but by the late fourth century there were clearly so many copies that legislation had to be passed in Athens preventing wholesale alteration of the plays by actors (Plutarch's *Life of Lycurgus*, 841 f.). Thenceforth, official copies were held in the Athenian archive and these probably became the basis for the Alexandrian texts from Ptolemaic Egypt dating from the third century BC. to which our texts can ultimately be traced.

Even though *Oedipus Tyrannus* did not win first prize when it was initially performed in the fifth century,[42] it seems to have enjoyed a privileged status very soon after. Regular performances of the play in the fourth century would seem to be attested by the Antiphanean fragment that serves as epigraph to this chapter. That famous actors appeared in the part of Oedipus is certain: at the Dionysia between 341 and 339 BC, the actor Neoptolemus is said to have played Oedipus (presumably the *Tyrannus*); and in the next generation, Polus, one of the most celebrated actors in antiquity and performing in the late fourth century and early third century BC, is closely associated with Sophocles' plays in general, and his Oedipus plays in particular.[43]

Although Aristotle in the *Poetics* (Chapter 14) shows little appreciation for performances in general, and seems to imply that *Oedipus Tyrannus* can be equally, or possibly more intensely, appreciated by being read rather than watched onstage, it is nonetheless his assessment of Sophocles' tragedy, above all, that enhanced the growing status of the play and guaranteed that it would influence all subsequent tragic theory and practice. According to him, Sophocles' tragedy is the finest example of the genre, with its perfect plot and central tragic figure designed to arouse both pity and fear in the audience, and thereby to purge the audience of an excess of those emotions. As we have already seen, it is from Oedipus as Aristotle's ideal central tragic figure that the modern tragic hero(ine)'s ancestry is ultimately traceable.

However unrepresentative this Aristotelian paradigm is of Greek tragedy in general, it does offer some valuable insights into Sophocles' *Oedipus Tyrannus*. In Chapter 11, Aristotle cites the arrival of the Corinthian messenger with the supposedly good news of Oedipus' foundling status – the scene which leads to Jocasta's realisation of the truth and eventually Oedipus' own – as one of his examples of reversal (*peripeteia*). Fragments of a Sicilian vase dated to the time of the *Poetics* seem to represent the same scene from Sophocles' play. The vase depicts four figures on a platform – the Corinthian Messenger, Oedipus, and two little girls – and a young woman, Jocasta, half-covering her face to one side. Although one may ask why Antigone and Ismene have been included in this scene – notwithstanding the question 'who is the mysterious figure who lurks behind Jocasta?' – this vase is generally considered to be the only example of a depiction of a particular moment of a tragedy in performance on a Greek vase.[44] Its subject, moreover, attests at the very least to the popularity of Sophocles' play in the Greek world in the latter part of the fourth century, and to the popularity of the scene that Aristotle singles out for commendation in his treatise.

Moreover, Aristotle (Chapter 11) is surely correct to identify the structural principle of the play as one of reversal, with its ironic twists and turns in the plot, and also the overall reversals in Oedipus' fortune (the hunter who becomes the quarry; the doctor who is the disease and so on). Furthermore, his praise of the coincidence of reversal and discovery (*anagnorisis*) in the play goes far in explaining the reason why Oedipus' fate moves the audience so intensely. We may well bear

Aristotle's observation in mind when we turn to other modern adaptations of the myth. For just as Euripides' *Oedipus* may well have lost much of the tautness of the Sophoclean plot when he chose to separate the discovery of the regicide from the parricide, so other modern playwrights who separate the two strands of the story clearly dilute the tragic formula that Aristotle identified as an essential ingredient for success.

In his account of Greek tragedy, Aristotle makes no mention of the gods, of the democratic city, and, as we have seen, bizarrely he makes little mention of the performances of the plays themselves. By taking Greek tragedy out of its Athenian context, he has clearly misled many of his readers over the centuries about the nature of his avowed subject. But by presenting such a partial picture of Athenian tragedy, he also ironically guaranteed that both tragedy and his theory would make an easy transformation into an international art form.[45] Furthermore, by removing Athens and Pericles from Sophocles' play, Aristotle may be said to have paved the way for its survival and transmutation in the future: without Aristotle, one might say, Oedipus would never have become Everyman.

NOTES

1. Antiphanes, in R. Kassel and C. Austin, *Poetae Comici Graeci* (Berlin 1983–), 189.

2. Aristotle, *Poetics*, Chapters.11, 13, 14, 15, 16, 26. But see Stephen Halliwell, *The Poetics of Aristotle: Translation and Commentary* (London 1987), 9–10, who argues against seeing *Oedipus Tyrannus* as the paradigm for Aristotle's theory.

3. On the myth in general see Jan Bremmer, 'Oedipus and the Greek Oedipus complex', in Jan Bremmer (ed.), *Interpretations of Greek Mythology* (London and Sydney 1987), 41–59; and Lowell Edmunds, *Oedipus* (London and New York 2006).

4. This widely shared view is not, however, endorsed by R.D. Dawe in his commentary *Sophocles, Oedipus Rex* (rev. edn, Cambridge 2006).

5. R. Kannicht (ed.), *Tragicorum Graecorum Fragmenta*, vol. 5.1, *Euripides* (Göttingen 2004), 569–70, for commentary.

6. Peter Burian, 'Myth into Muthos: the shaping of tragic plot', in P. E. Easterling (ed.), *The Cambridge Companion to Greek Tragedy* (Cambridge 1997), 178–210, 180.

7. Aeschylus was accorded the rare/unique privilege of having his plays revived in the fifth century (see Aristophanes' *Acharnians*, line 10). But there is a strong possibility that the plays were also performed at other smaller festivals in Athens (see further, e.g., P. E. Easterling, 'A show for Dionysus', in Easterling (ed.) (1997), 40; Eric Csapo, 'Social and economic conditions behind the rise of the acting profession in the fifth and fourth centuries BC', in C. Hugoniot, F. Hurlet and S. Milanezi (eds.), *Le Statut de l'acteur dans l'antiquité grecque et romaine* (Tours 2004), 53–76. NB the evidence for the dating of Sophocles' *Oedipus Tyrannus* is circumstantial and highly controversial. See further note 10 below.

8. E.g. Euripides' *Phoenician Women*, lines 19 ff., 998–1001. Translations in this chapter are from the Penguin Classics editions, unless otherwise stated.

9. Bernard Knox, *The Heroic Temper* (Berkeley and Los Angeles, CA and London 1964). See further below, 14–17.

10. Bernard Knox, *Word and Action: Essays on the Ancient Theater* (Baltimore and London 1979), 112–24. Sophocles was defeated that year by Aeschylus' nephew, Philocles, who is known to have won first prize the year Sophocles competed with *Oedipus Tyrannus*.

11. R. M. Newton, 'Hippolytus and the dating of *Oedipus Tyrannus*', *Greek, Roman and Byzantine Studies* 21 (1980), 5–22, is endorsed by Richard Janko, 'Oedipus, Pericles and the plague', *Dionysus* 11 (1999), 15–19.

12. Cf. Thucydides, *The Peloponnesian War* (hereafter Thuc.) 2. 47 ff.

13. See Froma Zeitlin, 'Thebes: the theater of self and society in Athenian drama', in J. P. Euben (ed.), *Greek Tragedy and Political Theory* (Los Angeles and London 1986), 101–41.

14. See David Konstan, 'Oedipus and his parents: the biological family from Sophocles to Dryden', *Scholia* 3 (1994), 3–23.

15. Ibid., 10.

16. Plutarch, *The Life of Pericles*. See Janko (1999), 15–19.

17. Herodotus, *The Histories*, 70; Thuc. 1. 127–8.

18. Knox (1964), p. 77.

19. On the evidence see Simon Goldhill, 'The audience of Athenian tragedy', in Easterling (ed.) (1997), 54–68, 62–6. On the size of the audience see J.R. Green, *Theater in Ancient Greek Society* (London and New York 1994), 9–10; and H.R. Goette, 'Choregic Monuments and the Athenian democracy', in P. Wilson (ed.), *The Greek Theatre and Festivals Documentary Studies*, (Oxford 2007), 122–49.

20. See Simon Goldhill, 'The Great Dionysia and civic ideology', in J.J. Winkler and F. Zeitlin (eds.), *Nothing to do with Dionysos? Athenian Drama in Its Social Context* (Princeton 1990), 97–129. For a qualification of this position see Chris Pelling, 'Tragedy, rhetoric, and performance culture', in Justina Gregory (ed.), *A Companion to Greek Tragedy* (Oxford 2005), 83–102.

21. J.-P. Vernant, 'The historical moment of tragedy in Greece: some of the social and psychological conditions', in J.-P. Vernant and P. Vidal-Naquet, *Myth and Tragedy in Ancient Greece*, 2 vols. (Cambridge, MA 1988), vol. I, 23–8.

22. See David Wiles, *Tragedy in Athens: Performance Space and Theatrical Meaning* (Cambridge 1997), 35–6.

23. Edith Hall, *The Theatrical Cast of Athens: Interactions between Ancient Greek Drama and Society* (Oxford 2006), 353–92.

24. Oliver Taplin's *The Stagecraft of Aeschylus* (Oxford 1977) and *Greek Tragedy in Action* (London 1978), and Rush Rehm's *Greek Tragic Theatre* (London and New York 1992), are the best examples of performance criticism. For the considerable debate surrounding the legitimacy of this approach, see David Wiles, 'Reading Greek performance', *Greece & Rome* 34 (1987), 136–51 136 ff.; and Simon Goldhill, 'Reading performance criticism', repr. in Ian McAuslan and Peter Walcot (eds.), *Greek Tragedy* (Oxford 1993), 1–11. See too Martin Revermann, *Comic Business: Theatricality, Dramatic Technique, Performance Contexts of Aristophanic Comedy* (Oxford 2006), Chapter 2.

25. See Felix Budelmann, *The Language of Sophocles: Communality, Communication and Involvement* (Cambridge 2000), 214–19, for an excellent account of the public nature of Oedipus' language in the first part of the play. My comments about the use of space here, it should be

pointed out, run counter to the recent emphasis on the *orchestra* as the main performance space for actors as well as the Chorus. See Rehm (1992); Wiles (1997).

26. Cf. Charles Segal, *Oedipus Tyrannus: Tragic Heroism and the Limits of Knowledge* (2nd edn, Oxford 2001), 110.

27. Edmunds (2006), 26–30, 50–4. On Greek hero cult in general see B. Currie, *Pindar and the Cult of Heroes* (Oxford 2005).

28. Dawe (2006), 192–203, argues that the ending (lines 1424–1530) is spurious and was interpolated to align the plot with the *Oedipus at Colonus* and perhaps the *Antigone*.

29. Cf. the farewells in Euripides' *Medea, Hecuba* and *Trojan Women*; and see further Fiona Macintosh, *Dying Acts: Death in Ancient Greek and Modern Irish Tragic Drama* (Cork 1994), 91–107.

30. Cf. Peter Burian, 'Introduction' to Euripides *The Phoenician Women*, trans. P. Burian and B. Swann (Oxford 1981), 7–8. All translations are from this edition.

31. Most editors/translators assume that the Scout exits at this point, leaving Eteocles alone to deliver one of the rare soliloquies (albeit in a prologue where different rules prevail) in Greek tragedy.

32. Burian (1981), p. 7.

33. On the ending of Aeschylus' *Seven against Thebes* as interpolation, see Gregory Hutchinson (ed.), *Aeschylus, Septem contra Thebas* (Oxford, 1985).

34. For the dating of Euripides' *Oedipus*, see T.B.L. Webster, *The Tragedies of Euripides* (London 1967), 245–6; Martin Hose, 'Überlegungen zum "Oedipus" des Euripides', *Zeitschrift für Papyrologie und Epigraphik* 81 (1990), 9–15; and Christopher Collard, 'Oedipus', in C. Collard, M.J. Cropp and J. Gibert (eds.), *Euripides: Selected Fragmentary Plays*, 2 vols. (Oxford 2004), vol. II, who proffers *c.* between 415 and 410 BC. Translations are Collard's; fragment numbers are from Kannicht (2004).

35. The Scholiast to Euripides' *Phoenician Women*, at line 1760, comments that the servants blinded Oedipus (see Collard (2004), 109 n. 1).

36. Fragment 542 (Kannicht, 575; Collard 117): 'I tell you pale silver and gold are not the only currency, but virtue too is an established currency for all mankind, which they should use.' Fragment 547 (Kannicht, 579; Collard, 121): 'Although love is a single thing, its pleasure is not

single: some love what is bad, some love what is good.' Fragment 552 (Kannicht, 581; Collard, 121): 'Is it indeed more useful to be intelligent without courage, than both headstrong and crass? The one of these is foolish but defends itself, the other, which is peaceable, is lazy; and there is weakness in both.'

37. Hose (1990), 12.

38. Webster (1967), 245.

39. Charles Segal, *Greek Tragedy: Myth, Poetry, Text* (Ithaca 1986), 368 ff.

40. Of course, early tragedies did not have a *skene* building.

41. See P. E. Easterling, 'From repertoire to canon', in Easterling (ed. 1987), 211–27; Green (1994).

42. According to the hypothesis of some medieval manuscript (but not attested elsewhere), the prize went to Philocles for whom there are no extant plays.

43. For Neoptolemus, see *Inscriptiones Graecae*, ed. F. H. de Gaertringen et al. (2nd edn, Berlin 1924–), no. 2320; for Polus, see Epictetus, *Dissertationes*, ed. H. Schenkl (Leipzig 1894), fragment 11, 464: 'Don't you see how Polus did not play Oedipus the Tyrannos with a better voice or more sweetly than Oedipus at Colonus, the wandering beggar?' I am indebted to Edith Hall for these references.

44. For discussion, see Green (1994), 61; O. Taplin, 'The pictorial record', in Easterling (ed.) (1997), 69–92, 87–8; and O. Taplin, *Pots and Plays: Interactions between Tragedy and Greek Vase-Painting of the Fourth Century BC* (Los Angeles 2006), 90–2.

45. E. Hall, 'Is there a Polis in Aristotle's *Poetics*?', in M. S. Silk (ed.), *Tragedy and the Tragic: Greek Theatre and Beyond* (Oxford 1996), 295–309, 305–6. For discussion of Aristotle and the 'viewing' of tragedy see M. Revermann, 'The competence of theatre audiences in fifth- and fourth-century Athens', *Journal of Hellenic Studies* 126 (2006), 99–124.

CHAPTER 2

THE ROMAN OEDIPUS AND
HIS SUCCESSORS

'Yet would anyone in his senses put the whole series of Ion's
works on the same footing as the single play of *Oedipus*?'[1]

Sophocles' tragedy appears to have continued to enjoy pre-eminent
status throughout the Roman period, both in its own right and also,
more particularly, as a source of emulation for Roman playwrights.
The whole of Roman literature was predicated upon the notion that
it should imitate the Greek example. Horace's dictum in *Ars Poetica*
(*c.* 28–21 BC) to 'give your days and nights to the study of Greek
models' (lines 268–9) had already been heeded by the young Julius
Caesar in the previous generation, who is said to have composed a
version of *Oedipus*, which was later suppressed by his adopted son,
Augustus.[2]

Whilst Julius Caesar's version was a tragedy, the other deeply
serious, but highly popular theatrical genre of the period, the pantomime, included at least one *Oedipus*. The Roman pantomime was
essentially a masked ballet based on a serious Greek mythological
theme, performed by one highly skilled dancer, one actor and a choral
accompaniment. The celebrated dancer of the Augustan era, Hylas,
was said by Pylades, his tutor and subsequent rival, to have recklessly
danced the part of Oedipus. Pylades reprimanded him with the
reminder: '*You* can see'.[3]

By the time of Nero, Roman writers appear to be alert not only to
the political potential of the Oedipus myth, but to its psychological
depths as well. In *The Satyricon*, for example, Petronius casts his
narrator, Encolpius, as a parodic Oedipus, who discovers that his

killing of a troublesome goose (a symbol of potency) can create as much furore as the crime of parricide itself. And when Encolpius finds himself jilted in love, he threatens his impotent member with castration, adding: 'Don't some tragic heroes chastise their eyes ...?'[4] Petronius' implied association here between Oedipus' blinding and Encolpius' intended act of castration is a startling piece of literary jesting, which anticipates connections not made again until the advent of psychoanalytical theory towards the end of the nineteenth century (see further Chapter 6 below).

The emperor Nero himself, who was renowned as actor both on and off the stage, is said to have taken the part of Oedipus on numerous occasions. His frequent theatrical public performances from AD 64 to 68 seem to have consisted of solo renderings of Greek tragic characters in an operatic style, but his close association with Oedipus in particular appears to have had less to do with the powers of his onstage performance than with the real-life rumours that found him guilty of Oedipus' unwitting crime of incest.

The Roman historian Suetonius gives an account of Nero's attempted incest with his mother, Agrippina, whom he subsequently killed in striking imitation of Orestes, another of his favourite tragic roles.[5] And if Nero's life brought to the historian's mind the character of Oedipus, we find a similar association being made by Dio Cassius in an account of Nero's suicide in AD 68:

> And he now repented of his past deeds of outrage, as if he could undo any of them. Such was the tragic part that Nero now played, and this verse constantly ran through his mind: 'Both spouse and father bid me cruelly die.'[6]

The 'tragic part' and 'this [clearly notorious] verse' are an obvious allusion to Nero's recent stage performance as Oedipus, which concluded (according to Suetonius) with the verse: 'Wife, father, mother drive me to my death'.[7]

Neronian Rome was a dangerous and luxuriant place, with extravagant displays of wealth being publicly paraded alongside scenes of flagrant and excessive violence and cruelty. According to the historian

Tacitus, the theatrical mode was an inevitable, and indeed the paradigmatic, stance under an absolutist regime.[8] The audiences in the theatre watching Nero's performances were as much under the imperial gaze as the actor was under theirs: negative or reluctant reception of Nero's performance met with fatal consequences. Moreover, as the site of gladiatorial combats and real-life sex shows, the theatre during the imperial period was less an imitation of life than an extension of it.

The playwright Lucius Annaeus Seneca was tutor to Nero from AD 49, and he remained at the centre of power in Nero's court until AD 65, when he was ordered to kill himself, a task which he performed in the true Roman high style, in calm acceptance of his fate.[9] In his letters, Seneca reveals his deep-seated reservations about the mass entertainment of the time, and his plays are clearly 'a reaction against typical Roman drama'[10] rather than representative of the period as is sometimes assumed. His ten extant tragedies (two of which are generally considered to be by later dramatists) are not without the excesses of violence, cruelty and strident display that are characteristic of the period in general, and which form the content of the popular theatrical entertainment of the time. But excess in his tragedies is strictly marshalled within a highly wrought rhetorical frame, which affords a strong measure of aesthetic distance denied to the popular performances. Rhetorical training in Rome had become an activity in itself at this point; and the rhetorical speeches in Seneca's plays must be understood within the political context of Neronian Rome, where conspiracy and subterfuge led to an inevitable divorce between word and deed.

When T.S. Eliot compared Seneca's plays with their Greek forebears, he commented:

> Behind the dialogue of Greek drama we are always conscious of a concrete visual actuality, and behind that of a specific emotional actuality. In the plays of Seneca, the drama is all in the word, and the word has no further reality behind it.[11]

For Eliot, the absence of a 'concrete visual actuality' in Seneca's plays was due primarily to a presumed oratorical (rather than enacted) mode of delivery. And whilst it is true that there is evidence that some plays in the imperial age were written for declamation alone, there is equally ample evidence of performances of comedy and high tragedy in theatres and private houses at the time. Moreover, Seneca's plays contain implicit stage directions, extras and multiple spoken and mute roles, all of which would tell against recitation. One authority on Seneca's tragedies maintains: 'there is little possibility that either recitation or (even less) private reading was their intended primary mode of realisation', and 'Senecan tragedy belongs, if anything does, to the category of Roman performance theatre'.[12]

The imperial period of Rome saw the construction of permanent stone theatres, which replaced the temporary wooden structures of the republic. That these permanent structures were designed as an expression of the immovable power invested in the new rulers is certain.[13] The seating of these theatres also reflected the power structures of the age, with strictly socially stratefied seating replacing the Greek theatre's allocation of seat according to area of residence.

The semicircular *orchestra* was now occupied by senators instead of a singing and dancing chorus participating in the action. From as early as the fifth century BC, the participatory role of the chorus in tragedy was being challenged, with the Greek playwright Agathon substituting transferable 'interludes' for the traditional choral ode. Republican Roman tragedy included choral odes, but the chorus could now readily absent themselves from the stage in the middle of the action.[14] In Seneca's tragedies the role of the chorus is marginalised in the new monarchical context, being reduced to a very occasional interjection in the dialogue in the acts, and to the singing of odes that often have very little immediate bearing on the action proper.

With the disappearance of the *orchestra*, the odes were now delivered from a raised stage, which was enclosed both from above (by a roof) and behind (by a towering facade). The Roman audience was thus denied both the privileged viewpoint and the vista beyond that the Greek theatre afforded its spectators. With the introduction of a stage curtain, the audience's new role as spectator rather than participant was enhanced. Here in Rome, audiences witnessed an interior space that mirrored the claustrophobic, repressive atmosphere of the world beyond the theatre.

However, the characters within that interiorised stage space were at an even greater remove from the everyday world of the audience than the legendary heroes of the Greek tragedies had been from their own. The masked Roman tragic actor's distance, moreover, was emphasised by raised boots, which gave him the necessary stature to be viewed in ample relief against the towering stone backdrop. The acting style was consequently highly expressive, and consisted of virtuoso performances of voice and gesture. In sum, Roman theatre of the time of Seneca was concerned with both distance and display, just as real life in imperial Rome consisted of spectacles designed to dwarf the individual and to magnify the centres of power.

SENECA'S OEDIPUS

Seneca's treatment of the story of Oedipus is not confined to a single play. In addition to his *Oedipus*, there are also two substantial fragments which are generally understood to form a part of his *Phoenician Women*.[15] The fragments are interesting not least because, like the *Oedipus* itself, their treatment of the Theban myth of necessity reflects specifically Roman concerns and anxieties.

In the first fragment, which resembles Sophocles' *Oedipus at Colonus* rather than Euripides' *Phoenician Women*, we are presented with an exiled and thoroughly broken Oedipus who is on the brink of suicide. Antigone performs the role of the loyal and devoted daughter, whose advocacy of stoic detachment seems unable to deter Oedipus from his suicidal longings. What is of especial note here is that Oedipus' despair derives from his horror at the crime of incest, not (as he maintains) at the lesser crime of parricide (lines 264 ff.). Under Roman law, the purity of the male bloodline was sacrosanct and it was essential to maintain its dignity, and the penalty for incest was (variously) deportation or violent death.[16]

The second fragment recalls the scene in Euripides' *Phoenician Women*, when Jocasta vainly attempts to intervene in the conflict between her two sons to prevent the destruction of Thebes. Just as the scene in Euripides' play explores the conflict in the light of the recent events of the civil war in Athens, so the Senecan fragment explores the fratricidal mania of Polynices and Eteocles as a paradigm for the fratricidal realities of the Roman world from the first century BC.[17] More specifically, the Neronian horrors are conveyed in Eteocles' flagrant denial of any possibility of rule by popular consent.

When we turn to Seneca's *Oedipus*, we find a similar prominence granted to the crime of incest. Jocasta in Seneca's play is afforded the same degree of space that Euripides grants her both in his *Phoenician Women* and in his *Oedipus* (see Chapter 1). Seneca's (albeit truncated) Sophoclean-inspired scene of recognition with the Corinthian Messenger and the Theban Shepherd (lines 764–909), does not lead (as in Sophocles) to Jocasta's silent departure for her death. Instead, Seneca's heroine fades from the action altogether before the arrival of the Corinthian Messenger, only to return at the very end of the play. But with her return, she goes on to play a major role in the dénouement, during most of which she manages to upstage the blinded Oedipus (lines 1004 ff.).

The most notable consequence of granting Jocasta an enhanced role at the end of the play is to underline the incestuous nature of their marriage. In Sophocles' version, it will be recalled, there is only one brief moment in the tragedy when the actuality (as opposed to the unacknowledged reality) of incest is enacted, at the point when Oedipus recoils in horror at his regicidal hands that have touched the body of the wife of the dead king (lines 908 ff.). In Euripides' play the scene of recognition between Periboia (Merope), Jocasta and Oedipus must have been both deeply affective and highly effective in emphasising the transgressive nature of Oedipus' life (see Chapter 1). Here in the final scene of the *Oedipus* we find the preoccupation with the purity of the male line of descent in Roman law being reflected in the increasing emphasis on the crime of incest, with the (ethically lesser) act of parricide all but receding from the dialogue.

When Jocasta enters she addresses the blinded Oedipus as her son, and he in turn is forced to acknowledge their newly defined relations formally by addressing her as mother. As Oedipus realises, their actions have tainted the very naming process itself (*per omne nostri nominis fas ac nefas*; line 1023). Having decided on death, Jocasta first invites the parricide to add matricide to his crimes in order to relieve her of her shame and guilt. But Jocasta swiftly rejects any passive end, grabbing instead Oedipus' own parricidal sword, and proclaiming:

> Strike here, my hand, strike at this teeming womb
> Which gave me sons and husband! ... (lines 1038–9)[18]

In a gesture that parallels both other Senecan suicides and the suicide of Nero's mother, Agrippina,[19] Jocasta symbolically re-enacts onstage the incestuous union in her very attempt to erase every trace of that physical relationship. As with the Oedipal echoes in Petronius' *Satyricon*, Seneca's *Oedipus* is further testimony to the Roman anticipation of psychoanalytical readings of the myth. The Sophoclean tragedy of the painful quest for self-knowledge has become Seneca's Roman tragedy of familial chaos. If Sophocles' Oedipus does not himself suffer from the complex that Freud was to associate with his name, Seneca's character comes perilously close to doing so in the final moments of this play.

Seneca's handling of the Oedipus myth, then, is very much at variance with Sophocles' *Oedipus Tyrannus*, but it does bear some striking similarities to the fragmentary *Oedipus* by Euripides (see Chapter 1). Like Euripides' eponymous hero, Seneca's protagonist is the victim of circumstances rather than the author of them. From the outset he is paralysed by forebodings of his doomed fate, living in dread of parricide and incest, and believing himself to be the cause and source of the plague in Thebes merely on account of escaping Apollo's prophecy rather than its fulfilment (lines 35–6).

The cowering, doom-dominated Oedipus at the start of Seneca's play is the antithesis of the Stoic man for whom patient endurance is all. The world he occupies offers a perverted view of the traditional

Stoic universe, where the natural world is understood to coexist harmoniously with its inhabitants. Here the scenes of destruction in Thebes described by Oedipus turn out to mirror his own unwitting crimes. As Oedipus reports the horrors of parents being forced to cremate their children (lines 59 ff.), we recall the confusions over generational rites and responsibilites that are hidden within the royal house, and Oedipus' account of intrafamilial strife attendant on the shortage of funeral pyres (lines 65 ff.) sharply prefigures the civil war that Oedipus' curse of his sons will ultimately unleash, and to which the Chorus allude later in the play (lines 747–50). Finally Thebes is now polluted, as will be the case in the next generation, because the dead remain unburied (lines 66–8). Seneca's Oedipus, like his Euripidean forebear, is forced into the role of witness; and here, as in the remaining sections of the play, he can never be more than the semi-conscious author of his immediate circumstances.

Seneca's Oedipus is in this sense the antithesis of the Aristotelian tragic hero: for him there is no coincidence of *anagnorisis* (recognition) and *peripeteia* (change of circumstances). Indeed there is no true *peripeteia* in the play, and no one scene of *anagnorisis*. The anxieties and presentiments of Oedipus in his opening soliloquy (or monologue, depending on when Jocasta enters) are given their objective correlatives in subsequent scenes. First Manto performs what turns out to be a perverted sacrifice of a bullock and heifer under the direction of her father, Tiresias. This scene, often invoked as evidence for recitation rather than performance, could easily have been performed in a highly stylised, perhaps even balletic, mode (as in ancient pantomime, as has recently been suggested). The bullock resists the death blows and fights back, and Manto discovers a mangled and displaced foetus in the young heifer's womb. Just as the transgressions of the royal house run contrary to nature's laws, so too the actions of the sacrificial victims defy the dictates of nature.

Although the perverted sacrifice is not difficult for the audience to decode, Tiresias urges consultation with the dead king himself in order to find out the identity of the regicide. Creon returns in the next scene to give a lengthy account of his (offstage) evocation of Laius' ghost on the periphery of the city, during which the dead king named his son as his killer. The disbelieving Oedipus can only deduce (and with more reason than in Sophocles) that a conspiracy is afoot, and in the world of Neronian realpolitik, appropriately retorts: 'The king must guard against the possible / As against certain danger' (line 699). But he re-emerges in the subsequent scene with misgivings and memories of a fatal encounter that can only deepen his initial self-doubts.

The unrelenting nature of the Senecan world, dominated as it is by the fixity of Fate that even the gods are powerless to alter (lines 988–90), is a far cry from the bleakness of the Sophoclean cosmos where ignorance alone is seen to obscure providential order. Here in Seneca, uncertainty and dread are the only appropriate responses in a world from which the gods have seemed to retreat. Like the empire itself, where the emperor masqueraded as a merciless and unpredictable god, Oedipus is prey to forces that can inspire only fear and foreboding. Whilst the Sophoclean progenitor is carried along by the dynamic of discovery prosecuted with the peerless mind of its protagonist, Seneca's play reveals an Oedipus whose encounter with the Sphinx involved brawn rather than brain (lines 92 ff.), and whose onstage response to events is to enact in minor and then major key the presentiments of guilt he felt from the outset. Seneca's play is – no more, no less – a play about an incestuous parricide.

If Seneca's *Oedipus* follows Euripides both in the prominence it affords to Jocasta (and consequently mother–son incest) and in its portrait of a passive protagonist, it may also be said to follow Euripides in its broad contextualisation of the myth. The Senecan tragedies are far more densely mythically allusive than their Greek counterparts, and here in the *Oedipus* the odes range broadly over Theban myth in ways that recall the Euripidean wide focus on the Labdacid dynasty in the *Phoenician Women*. Whilst the Chorus in Seneca's *Oedipus* is most probably absent altogether from the private first act between Oedipus and Jocasta, it is likely that this Senecan chorus remained onstage (somewhat atypically) during the rest of the action.[20] This is not to imply that their involvement in the scenes proper is substantial – on the contrary, with the exception of one line when they introduce Creon, they do not involve themselves directly until some four hundred lines into the play, when they respond (again very unlike a Greek chorus) to Tiresias' order to sing a hymn to Bacchus. In this sense, as with Senecan tragedy in general, the Chorus in the *Oedipus* makes its contribution to the play almost entirely through the odes.

Whilst the entry song of the Chorus (as in Sophocles) may be informed by their experiences of the horrors wreaked by the plague within the city (lines 110 ff.), they continue in the next two odes to act less *in propria persona* than in the capacity of chroniclers of Theban history. The hymn to Bacchus, although deftly fitted into context with Tiresias' exhortation to cover the passage of time needed for the offstage invocation of Laius' ghost, bears the hallmark of the choral 'interlude' that could be easily slotted into any play. The second ode, however, has a much more direct bearing on the action, broadening the perspective on Oedipus' fate both back in time and far into the future. Like Euripides in the *Phoenician Women*, Seneca allows the chorus to locate the cause of Theban misery at its Cadmean inception, and to allude obliquely to the fratricidal battle that is to follow (lines 709–63).

The Chorus's perspective may turn out to be a limited one in many ways – Oedipus is not, as they maintain in the third ode, without responsibility – but its prophetic insights into Theban history remain pertinent to the end of the play. When the blinded Oedipus gropes his way slowly and hesitantly, careful not to stumble on his mother's corpse, he promises his departure will bring an end to the sufferings of his city. Oedipus in the Senecan mould has now emerged as the Theban scapegoat, permitted, as he is not at the end of Sophocles' *Oedipus Tyrannus*, to begin the life of exile that forms the subject of *Oedipus at Colonus*.[21] But as with the Euripidean example, the wide mythical lens reminds the audience that Oedipus' departure at the end of the play will not succeed in relieving the city of all its misery. As the

Senecan Oedipus departs in the final moments of the play, he is as isolated in his suffering as he felt himself to be in the opening scene of the play: in the Neronian world of public display, intrigue and deception, the lonely individual is left to negotiate his own fate.

OEDIPUS IN EARLY MODERN ENGLAND

Whilst Aristotle's references in the *Poetics* led to the privileging of Sophocles' *Oedipus Tyrannus* in the modern world, the earliest attempts to re-create tragedy in the Greek mould and to recapture the power of Sophocles' *Oedipus Tyrannus*, in particular, were in fact more indebted to the Roman *Oedipus* of Seneca than they were to the Sophoclean version. The *Oedipus* reworkings in the early modern period are variously Senecan, with their tormented, passive heroes and onstage horrors and especially in the prominence they grant to the crime of incest and in their tendency to marginalise or dispense with the Greek chorus.

In England, in particular, the predominance of Seneca in the Renaissance was due to the Roman tragedian's ready accessibility, following the appearance of a number of vernacular translations of individual plays from 1559 onwards (which formed part of a collection of translations of the ten plays in 1581), and a complete Latin edition of the tragedies in 1589.[22] In 1566 during the Christmas revels, the audience of Gascoigne and Kinwelmershe's *Jocasta* at Gray's Inn, London, witnessed a scene deeply indebted to Seneca's *Oedipus*, as the Priest performed a ritual sacrifice and read the auguries before a chorus of twenty Bacchanales. *Jocasta* was the first English vernacular tragedy to be inspired (albeit indirectly) by an ancient play, being heavily based on Ludovico Dolce's *Giocasta* (1549), which was in turn indebted to Euripides' *Phoenician Women*. That the English playwrights should have happily followed Dolce in incorporating this scene from Seneca's *Oedipus* was hardly surprising, since Seneca's tragedy would have been broadly familiar to many members of their audience. Gascoigne's friend and fellow member of Gray's Inn,

Alexander Neville, had completed his English translation of Seneca's *Oedipus* by 1560, when he was an undergraduate at Trinity College, Cambridge. And indeed, it may well have been Neville's text that was used for a production of *Oedipus*, performed together with the *Hecuba* at Trinity College in 1559–60, about which nothing is known except that it made considerable demands upon college funds.[23]

Neville intended his translation for performance, just as he believed had been the case with Seneca's play. In the Epistle to Doctor Wotton appended to the play, Neville pronounces that his translation would similarly

> by the tragical and pompous show upon stage, [serve] to admonish all men of their fickle Estates, to declare the unconstant head of wavering Fortune, her sudden interchanged and soon altered Face; and lively to express the just revenge, and fearfull punishments of horrible crimes, wherewith the wretched worlde in these our miserable days piteously swarmeth.[24]

Neville's few additions make the Senecan tragedy into a medieval mystery play, with Oedipus' 'horrible crimes' being fully atoned for by a chastened Oedipus at the end, who openly acknowledges:

> ... (Alas) the fault is all in me,
> O Oedipus accursed wretch, lament thine own calamity (p. 94)

The choral entry ode sounds more like a psalm than a marching song; and Neville omits the hymn to Bacchus altogether, at a time when the chorus was clearly felt to be little more than a group of choristers.

The increased marginalisation of the chorus in Neville's translation was, as we have seen, by no means against the Senecan grain. And given the confined performance space of a college dining hall – which hardly lent itself to a singing and dancing chorus – the Senecan tendency was inevitably continued. Indeed, when Elizabeth I and her entourage turned up at the chapel of King's College, Cambridge to watch a performance of Plautus' *Aulularia* in 1564, she provided the focus of the production by being seated upon her throne onstage.[25] The audience in this essentially medieval theatrical context provided their own 'choral' perspective on account of their proximity to the actors within the confined space of the dining hall. Moreover, this selective audience was probably not so markedly different from the audience for whom Seneca himself was writing; and clearly the English Renaissance audience shared the essentially monarchical outlook of Neronian Rome, for whom a participating chorus would have been an alien (and, of course, a potentially subversive) intrusion.

Neville's translation of Seneca was not the only vernacular translation of *Oedipus* around at this time,[26] nor indeed was Cambridge alone in taking an interest in the character of Oedipus. William Gager, a don of Christ Church, Oxford, wrote a Latin playlet entitled *Oedipus* around 1578. Gager was the leading neo-Latin dramatist of the day and Christ Church was one of the Oxford colleges most prominent in the promotion of drama in English and Latin. It is not clear whether Gager's 195-line playlet was intended for performance as it stands, or whether it is only a first attempt at a larger play.[27] Despite the brevity of the text, the main details of Oedipus' life are placed within a broad context that includes the dispute between Polynices and Eteocles (sc III) (made recently popular by its rendering in Gascoigne and Kinwelmershe's *Jocasta*). As with the medieval morality play, it seems that the exemplarity of these tragic characters is only completely grasped through the full sweep of their lives.[28]

Also in keeping with the medieval morality tradition is the inclusion of the ordinary citizen's perspective on the momentous events. In a bold extension of the Euripidean programmatic prologue (lines 1–39), a Theban Citizen bewails the plague and all the earlier disasters that have stricken Thebes since Cadmus' day. He then goes on to inject a highly poignant personal note into his generalising lament: the plague has already taken his wife, five of his sons, his three daughters, his slaves and his cattle; but now that his father and one surviving son have met their deaths as well, he cannot find wood enough for their funeral pyre. The particularity of the citizen's complaint here renders the traditional lament suddenly direct and new.

The desire to see Oedipus' life diachronically appears to be one that lasts down to the early part of the seventeenth century as well, with a version by Thomas Evans published in 1615. Evans's *Oedipus* was subtitled *Three Cantoes wherein is contained: 1) His unfortunate Infancy 2) His execrable Actions 3) His Lamentable End.*[29] Whether the play was performed or not, it was perhaps by no means merely fortuituous that Evans should have turned to the same classical subject that had been chosen by two French playwrights the previous year. Not only was Evans writing at a time when the 1603 and 1608 London outbreaks of the plague were in relatively recent memory and remained a constant, potential threat; but like the two French playwrights, he was also writing at a time when the institution of the monarchy was coming under sharp scrutiny and appearing increasingly insecure.

THE FRENCH NEOCLASSICAL OEDIPUS

Whilst the 1614 *Edipe* of Jean Prévost is less Senecan than Greek in terms of its form – unusually at this time, it has a participating chorus[30] – it is Senecan in its presentation of an Oedipus (abandoned by the gods) who ends up killing himself with his son's sword in the final moments of the play. In Tallemant des Réaux's *Edipe* of the same year we find Senecan fate meeting up with Huguenot fatality and leaving Edipe unable to escape the mark of original sin. In both these early French versions the peerless monarch is posited as an ideal rather than a reality, and both Prévost and Tallemant des Réaux in many ways set the pattern for French dramatic treatments of the Oedipus myth over the next two centuries, when it became impossible to conceive of Oedipus without some kind of political reference.[31]

From 1624, when France came under the overweening direction of Richelieu, aesthetics and politics became intermeshed: the so-called neoclassical 'rules' advocated in French poetics with the dubious authority of Aristotle were held to impose 'order' on the otherwise formless drama, and aesthetic rules were regularly invoked to justify strictures within the political domain. The row attendant upon Corneille's tragicomic *Le Cid* in 1636 was as much about the political implications of generic breakdown as it was about aesthetics pure and simple.

According to at least one younger contemporary, Corneille 'paints men as they should be' and was thus readily assimilable (in accordance with the Aristotelian formula) to Sophocles, while his younger rival Racine, who 'paints them as they are', became a latterday Euripides.[32] Commenting on Aristotle's *hamartia*, then generally misunderstood as 'moral flaw', Corneille expresses incomprehension about Oedipus' alleged guilt;[33] and he deliberately sets himself apart from his contemporaries in focusing upon Oedipus as an individual whose extreme suffering commands our compassion. But writing his own version of the myth in the wake of the internecine struggles during *La Fronde*, it was inevitable that Corneille's Oedipus should appear as a distinctly fallible, and essentially Senecan (as opposed to Sophoclean), tragic hero. Senecan too is the prominence granted to the apparition of the admonitory Laius, who appears imaginatively in Corneille's version (through the power of the Messenger's words) to the whole populace (see Figure 1).

Corneille grew up in Rouen, where he received a Jesuit education that instilled in him a passion for theatre and especially for Seneca, who remains his principal ancient source in *Oedipe*. But now in accordance with the neoclassical spirit of the age, Corneille does not simply set out to usher Oedipus into the modern world; he sets out to improve upon earlier attempts to dramatise his painful discovery of the tragic events of his life. In deference to contemporary taste the marginal Senecan chorus is now omitted altogether, with Corneille substituting a subplot of love and intrigue in its stead. But it was not only the limited stage space at the Hôtel de Bourgogne in 1659 that would have precluded a Greek participating chorus. It was also that Corneille's theatre already had its own Greek 'chorus' of sorts, in the significant number of distinguished onstage spectators, who (even more acutely than was the case with the audience at English Renaissance performances in

1. Chaveau, engraving, frontispiece to Corneille's *Oedipe*

great halls) were unwittingly mimicking some of the ancient choric functions. Moreover, Corneille's play also provided its own equivalent of the Senecan choral interludes, with five *entr'actes* composed and choreographed by Jean-Baptiste Lully, when it was revived in Fontainebleau on 21 July 1664.[34]

Sophocles' tragedy of self-discovery is confined in Corneille's version to the last act of his play, whilst the first four acts consist of a series
of episodes that reflect on the conflicting demands of private and
public duties. Oedipus remains resolute in the first part of the play in
his conviction that his oath to Hémon must be upheld. He has already
promised Hémon the hand of his stepdaughter, Dircé, on political
grounds, even though arguments from the heart first from Thésée
(who is in love with Dircé) and then his wife, Jocaste, attempt to make
him waver. In the eyes of Dircé, Oedipe is the overweening *tyrannos*,
who has usurped her rightful position on the throne, and who now
seeks to deny her any chance of establishing a power base by marrying
her off to some second-rate royal.

But the reality seems otherwise: Oedipus here in Corneille's version
is, in fact, not resolute enough and he breaks his oath despite fears of
the gods' disapproval and presentiments of his own ruin. Furthermore, Corneille's Oedipus ironically suspects that the endogamous
nature of the Dircé/Thésée match may well be the cause of the plague
in Thebes. This is Oedipus cast in the Senecan rather than the
Sophoclean political mould; and it was this 'inferior', equivocating
Oedipus that subsequent dramatists sought to redress.

After Oedipus has discovered his true identity in the final act of
Corneille's play, it is not shame but anger that marks his response. The
blinded Oedipus in deference to contemporary taste never appears
onstage in the Cornélien version. It is from Dymas's report alone that
we learn the significance of Oedipus' self-mutilation: he blinds himself here not (as he does in Sophocles) to avoid the shame of seeing his
parents in Hades, but rather as an act of defiance against the unjust
gods, and as a constant reminder to others of the tyranny of the sky. As
Corneille's Oedipus tears out his eyes with his hands in true Senecan
style, Dymas informs us that as his blood spilled on the ground, all
discord in Thebes came to an end. This neoclassical Oedipus may be
an aberrant, vacillating king, but as Christ-like saviour of his people at
the end of the play he becomes a true king; and as the man who
defiantly confronts his destiny, he finally becomes tragic hero.

Whilst Oedipus fails in the political arena in Corneille's tragedy, there is no doubt that his alter ego, Thésée, represents a symbol of hope for the institution of the monarchy, when he is left to steer the newly restored Thebes to safety in the last moments of the play. That Corneille was employing the Oedipus myth for deeply political reasons is without question: the tragedy was written after seven years' silence at the time when Mazarin, Richelieu's successor, was enjoying enormous power during the last few years of the regency before the accession of the young Louis XIV. If the figure of Mazarin lurks behind Oedipus the *tyrannos* (the outsider who rules by popular consent rather than hereditary entitlement), there is little doubt that the character of Theseus is the long-awaited future monarch waiting in the wings. And when the young king turned up at the Hôtel de Bourgogne on 8 February 1659 to see the play shortly after it opened on 25 January,[35] it must have been hard to avoid the obvious inference that Corneille was calling upon the ancient Oedipus to instruct those in authority no less than those in waiting.

OEDIPUS IN THE ENGLISH RESTORATION PERIOD

Corneille's *Oedipe* was written at the time of the Interregnum in England, when Royalists had sought refuge in either France or Holland. When they returned to England with the restoration of the monarchy in 1660, they brought with them the dramatic developments and tastes that they had witnessed and acquired on the Continent. Dryden and Lee's *Oedipus* of 1678 was written very much in response to Corneille's tragedy, and consequently presumed in its audience a broad familiarity with the French version. But there were two other indirect engagements with Sophocles' tragedy around this time, which would have also had some bearing on Dryden and Lee's choice of subject in 1678.

William Joyner's *The Roman Empress* was performed by the King's Company at Lincoln's Inn Fields in 1670. In the preface to his play, Joyner explains his choice of *Oedipus Tyrannus* as his primary source:

> Having consider'd, that of all tragedy the old Oedipus, in the just estimation of the Antients and moderns carry'd the Crown: a Story as yet untoucht by any English Pen, I thought, though defective in my art, I could not be but very fortunate in this my subject.[36]

Yet Joyner's play is no faithful rendering of Sophocles' tragedy, and he goes on to outline the reasons behind his numerous liberties with Sophocles' text: his protagonist can now be a great Roman emperor rather than a 'petty' Greek prince; and unlike Oedipus, his protagonist really existed (albeit with a different name). But Valentius is nonetheless like Oedipus because he

> incurs those very misfortunes, which with all imaginable care he shun'd; condemning his son without knowing him; and after death knowing him with all benefit: which makes him the best, and greatest of all Tragical subjects.[37]

Joyner's tragedy is Sophoclean, then, in its focus on the metaphorical blindness of his protagonist and in its concern with the theme of parricide (threatened, presumed or actual); and in the final moments of the play when Valentius realises that he has not simply lost a trusted general, but his own son too, that allusion is made explicit in Valentius' complaint before killing himself in true Roman fashion: 'Are these my eyes thought worthy of the light?' (p. 66).

Joyner's play is clearly a warning to those anti-Papists who were seeking to deny England the continuity and stability promised by the Restoration: the unerring emphasis on the breakdown in intrafamilial relations that have come about because of the civil war in Rome presages conflict ahead closer to home. And it is, of course, this concern with unwitting intergenerational chaos that provides his point of reference with Sophocles' bleak ending in *Oedipus Tyrannus*. Milton's tragedy *Samson Agonistes* was published in 1671 (the same year as the text of Joyner's play) and it also chooses to focus on the politics of the Restoration period with reference to the Oedipus myth.[38] In marked contrast to Joyner, however, Milton engages with the second part of Oedipus' life, and with Sophocles' *Oedipus at*

Colonus in particular. And although this might make Milton's closet drama appear to fall beyond the scope of this study, the equal engagement with the politics of the Restoration theatre and the Sophoclean tragic figure make *Samson Agonistes* central to the discussion. In the 'Epistle' to the play, for example, Milton similarly invites comparison with the Greek tragedians, but here (unlike Joyner) the parallels he makes refer primarily to formal rather than thematic concerns. Indeed, Milton's use of a permanently onstage and participating chorus makes his debt to the Greek example obvious. But his statement of debt is not simply about aesthetic preference; his deployment of a Greek-inspired interrogatory chorus in *Samson Agonistes* is in many ways a reflection of his unfailing republican sentiments and his rejection of Royalist neoclassical strictures.

Formal and thematic parallels can be made with Aeschylus' *Prometheus Bound*, but the comparison with *Oedipus at Colonus* is the most sustained. Samson's embittered blindness and devastating revenge on the Philistines not only recall Milton's own personal response to his straitened circumstances, but also allude to the blinded Oedipus, whose fatal curse on his sons will ultimately wreak havoc on all the Thebans, who had formerly rejected him and now cynically require his body. In this respect, the physically mutilated and enchained Samson shares with the elderly, stateless Oedipus the ability to draw for one last time upon the suprahuman energies that propelled him into greatness in the first place. Like Oedipus, he too has presentiments of this resurgence of strength ('I begin to feel / Some rousing motions in me, which dispose to something extraordinary my thoughts'[39]); and we infer that Samson too departs this world in the knowledge that his death will reward those he loves and exact a devastating revenge upon his enemies.

Milton's verse drama was not designed for performance, even though recent stagings have shown just how intensely performable it is.[40] And the power of the play derives in large part from its being deliberately cast in contradistinction to the 'heroic' plays and to the performance conditions of the Restoration theatre. From the

messenger speech at the end of the play, we learn that the site of
Samson's revenge was 'a spacious theatre' (line 1605). In the 'intermission' (line 1629) during the games, when Samson is seemingly
seeking respite after the physical exertion demanded of him by the
crowd, he leans on the pillars that support the roof of the theatre and
proclaims:

> Hitherto, Lords, what your commands imposed
> I have performed, as reason was, obeying;
> Not without wonder or delight beheld;
> Now, of my own acccord, such other trial
> I mean to show you of my strength yet greater
> As with amaze shall strike all who behold. (lines 1640–5)

With these words, the messenger tells us that Samson bowed and
tugged down the pillars, forcing the entire theatre roof to come
crashing down over the heads of 'Lords, ladies, captains, counsellors,
or priests' (line 1653) and of Samson himself. With more than a touch
of republican spirit, perhaps, Milton's messenger adds that only those
'vulgar' (line 1659) members of the audience who could not afford the
privileged seats with a roof over their head managed to escape the
widespread destruction.

In marked contrast to the 'heroic drama' being performed at the
Lincoln's Inn theatre, in which the aristocratic hero typically engages
in chivalric acts in order to win the love of a princess, Milton's
protagonist is deemed too filthy for even the giant Harapha to
challenge to a fight (line 1107). In the same year as the publication
of *Samson Agonistes*, the Duke's Company moved to the Dorset
Garden Theatre, ushering in a new era of spectacular theatre.
Indeed, the theatre of the 1670s as a whole is marked by a significant
increase in the use of sophisticated stage machinery, and the extensive
use of stage spectacle may well be considered the defining feature of
English tragedy by the end of the decade.[41] In returning to Greek
tragic form in *Samson Agonistes*, Milton was deliberately eschewing
current aesthetic tastes; and in setting the revenge of his decidedly

'non-heroic' hero in a theatre, we see how (as was the case in France) aesthetic and political preferences were inextricably linked at the time.

John Dryden and Nathaniel Lee's *Oedipus* was performed at the Dorset Garden Theatre in 1678 and is the epitome of the tragedies of spectacle against which Milton was casting his verse drama. At Dorset Garden – as at the new Drury Lane theatre which opened in 1674 – there were three separate performance spaces. The first and most routinely used was the forestage in front of the proscenium arch, which served as the site of Restoration comedy. With the select members of the audience now seated in the onstage boxes situated to the sides of the forestage, this (intrinsically French-inspired) performance space was in many ways a vestige from the medieval theatre, and reminiscent of the Renaissance performance spaces in college dining-halls, in which the enactment of the play was primarily a rhetorical event.[42] Here in Dryden and Lee's tragedy the scenes of intrigue and deception that fuel the subplot take place upon the forestage.

New in the Restoration theatre were the two additional stage spaces behind the proscenium – the scenic stage and beyond that the vista stage – both of which were used for the scenes of spectacle. In Dryden and Lee's *Oedipus*, the scenic stage was used extensively for the processional entries and the Shakespearean crowd scenes, during which the speaking actors would comment from the downstage position of the forestage on the tableau taking place in the distance on the scenic stage. The vista stage was reserved for the numerous supernatural events in the *Oedipus*, notably the appearance of the apparitional figures of Oedipus and Jocasta that appear in the sky during the portentous storm in Act II, the evocation of Laius and the other ghosts in Act III and the appearance of Laius' ghost again in Act V. Oedipus' final suicidal leap from the western tower may also well have taken place from the distance of the vista stage, in which case Dryden and Lee intended Oedipus' departure from this world to be as much an apotheosis as it is in *Oedipus at Colonus*.[43] Indeed, Oedipus'

final defiant words, refusing to acknowledge any guilt, would imply at
least some kind of supernatural strength:

> May all the gods as well, too, from their Battlements,
> Behold, and wonder at a Mortal's daring;
> And, when I knock the Goal of dreadful death,
> Shout and applaud me with a clap of Thunder.
> Once more, thus wing'd by horrid fate, I come,
> Swift as a falling Meteor; lo, I flye,
> And thus go downwards, to the darker Sky.
>
> *[Thunder. He flings himself from the Window:*
> *The Thebans gather about his Body.]*[44]

In Oedipus' last words, we detect more than a note of Senecan
bombast (as well as a nod towards Milton's Samson);[45] and in a very
real sense Seneca is Dryden and Lee's main source. In the Preface,
however, Dryden also cites Sophocles and Corneille as sources, and
the English Oedipus is clearly designed to counter the Cornélien
vacillating Oedipus, who is upstaged by the 'greater hero', Theseus.
The debt to Sophocles is considerable, with the Sophoclean prologue
being adopted almost verbatim in the second part of Act I; Sophocles'
pivotal scene (when the question of regicide is linked to the fear of
incest and parricide) appearing here in Act II following Oedipus'
dream; and finally in Act IV, the recognition scene with the
Corinthian Messenger and the Shepherd reads much like a close
translation of Sophocles' text.

Indeed, in some circles the play was criticised for being too dependent on its principal Greek source and perilously close to an act of pure
plagiarism.[46] To the modern audience, however, the unacknowledged
debts to Shakespeare are glaring (generally, in the crowd scenes taken
from *Julius Caesar* and *Coriolanus*, and in the use of ghosts, the
sleepwalking motif and the proliferation of bodies at the climax; and
more particularly in the casting of Samuel Sandford, famous for his
Richard III, as Creon). In the Prologue, the unsuspecting spectator is
led to believe that they will receive Sophocles *au naturel*; and Dryden

and Lee's *Oedipus* is best understood as an attempt to follow the Miltonic example by returning to ancient precedent directly, and especially, without French neoclassical mediation. Here, in *Oedipus*, Dryden seeks to reconcile the conflicts between the ancients and moderns debated within his *Essay of Dramatic Poesie* (1668) by reproducing the 'best' aspects of all his sources, both ancient and modern.

The Senecan hallmark, however, remains the strongest on *Oedipus*, with incest and fate being the two central controlling forces in the play. Fate is felt in two ways: externally through the supernatural events – the storms, the prodigies in the sky and (as in Sophocles) the coincidences in the plot (so Jocasta walks in at the time of Oedipus' curse and unwittingly wishes it upon both him- and herself – Act I sc. I). But Fate also works internally through the incest motif, which (as in Seneca) becomes the governing force in the play. Here in Dryden and Lee, we get the sense that Oedipus and Jocasta are driven to incest; that Oedipus, propelled to Thebes to escape the workings of the oracle that prophesy incest with his mother, is nonetheless governed by the oracle's ordinance, which is never far from his consciousness nor indeed from the consciousness of the other characters in the play. At the very beginning, we are reminded of Oedipus' striking resemblance to Laius (p. 123). As in Corneille, this Oedipus fears the match between Creon and Eurydice on grounds that uncle and niece 'are too near … 'tis offence to kind'; and with his excessive response 'Nature would abhor / To be forced back again upon herself / And like a whirlpool, swallow her own streams', he confesses, 'I know not why, it shakes me, / When I but think on incest' (Act I sc. I, p. 140).

In Act II, before retiring to bed, Oedipus alone confesses to an 'unusual chillness' in his sexual encounters with his wife: 'An unknown hand still checked my forward joy, / Dashed me with blushes … / That ev'n the act became a violation' (Act II sc. I, p. 150). Oedipus then sleepwalks, with dagger in one hand and taper in the other, clearly witnessing the events that are soon to be played out in the waking hours; and later he confesses to Jocasta that he dreamt of her as his mother, magnifying for the Restoration audience what are the

intentionally reassuring words of Sophocles' Jocasta. In the penultimate scene of the play (as in Seneca), when the blinded Oedipus meets
up with his mother/wife, the incestuous nature of their relationship
comes most obtrusively to the fore. Oedipus pronounces:

> O, in my heart I feel the pangs of Nature;
> It works with kindness o're: Give me way!
> I feel a melting here, a tenderness,
> Too mighty for the anger of the Gods!
> Direct me to thy knees: yet, oh forebear,
> Lest the dead Embers should revive. (p. 204)

This is an Oedipus for whom nature's compulsions are too strong to
resist. Dryden and Lee's Jocasta, as in Seneca, proclaims their inno-
cence and blames fate, declaring passionately: 'For you are still my
husband' (p. 205). Oedipus wishes to believe her espousal of nature
over conventional taboo, and promises to

> … steal into thy arms,
> Renew endearments, think then no pollutions,
> But chaste as spirits' joys. Gently I'll come,
> Thus weeping blind, like dewy night, upon thee,
> And fold thee softly in my arms to slumber. (p. 205)

But immediately Laius' ghost appears from beneath in the vista stage
to prohibit this ultimate violation of taboo. Seneca's play became a
play about a guilty incestuous parricide; here in Dryden and Lee's
version, the play has become a meditation on the prohibition of incest
altogether.

During the Commonwealth, incest was made a criminal offence for
the first time and punishable by death under the Act of Parliament for
May 1650.[47] Hitherto and following the Restoration (and until 1908,
see further Chapter 4 below), the offence was not punishable by the civil
courts, only the ecclesiastical courts, who rarely exercised their jurisdiction. For this reason alone, Dryden and Lee's play was a bold espousal of
Restoration values, and it provided a strong dose of titillating and risqué
sensationalism for the libertine courtiers within the audience.

But Oedipus is also political in other Senecan respects as well, especially in its removal of the chorus altogether. The marginalised Senecan chorus is here denied a voice altogether, except the baying one of a heckling crowd for whom the occasional interjection is permitted (Acts I and II). For Oedipus, they are simply 'the wild herd' (p. 149). By Act IV the rebellion is well under way, and by Act V Oedipus has to take refuge in the western tower. In this deeply political play, written shortly after the Great Plague of 1665, and not long after the regicide of Charles I, the parallels with contemporary figures are not hard to find. Behind Laius clearly lurks Charles I, and behind Oedipus we have allusions to both Charles II and to Cromwell himself; but the clearest allusion is to the Earl of Shaftesbury behind Creon, the Machiavellian Richard III figure, who will shortly instigate the Monmouth Rebellion (1685) in a bid to remove Charles II and replace him with Charles's illigitimate son, the Earl of Monmouth, in order to preserve Protestant succesion.[48]

In Act I of Dryden and Lee's play, Oedipus is presented as both absent ruler and political 'outsider' in the rhetoric of Creon and his cronies; and in Act IV we watch the opposition to Oedipus being carefully orchestrated by Creon's faction. Following the bloodbath of retribution that is unleashed in the subplot in the final act, and after the tableau presented on the scenic stage (alluding as it does to the stock Restoration rape scene)[49] of *'Jocasta held by her Women, and stabb'd in many places of her bosom, her hair dishevel'd, her Children slain upon the bed'* (p. 211), Oedipus makes his own suicidal leap from the top of the tower. At the end of the play, Haemon is left together with Tiresias, who first reassures, then warns, the Thebans/English audience confronted with Oedipus' corpse:

> The dreadful sight will daunt the drooping Thebans,
> Whom Heav'n decrees to raise with Peace and Glory.
> Yet, by these terrible Examples warn'd,
> The sacred Fury thus Alarms the World.
> Let none, tho' ne're so Vertuous, great and High,
> Be judg'd entirely blest before they Dye. (p. 213)

Left with the clerical authority of Tiresias and the political and
military skills of Haemon (here Captain of the Guard and no member
of the royal family), there is nonetheless no indication to the audience
as to what monarchical 'authority' will fill the vacuum now the king
is dead.

With its sympathetic portrayal of a flawed but defiant leader, Dryden
and Lee's *Oedipus* was perhaps open-ended enough to guarantee the
play's popularity in the ever-changing political circumstances that were
to unfold in the latter part of the seventeenth century and well into the
eighteenth. Indeed, Dryden and Lee's play is arguably the single most
important version of Sophocles' tragedy on the stage for at least one
hundred years following its first performance. In many ways, it continued to exert considerable influence on theatre history long after it
ceased being performed on the stage. For when people thought of
Oedipus well into the nineteenth century in England, it was generally
Dryden and Lee's play rather than Sophocles' that they had in mind.
When Sophocles' own tragedy met with the stringencies of the Lord
Chamberlain's Office towards the end of the nineteenth century, it was
on the grounds of its incestuous content. The ban was in many ways on
that better-known version by Dryden and Lee that loomed long and
large in the British theatrical memory, and which placed a proud and
defiant, and by no means wholly contrite, incestuous parricide centre
stage (see further Chapter 4 below).

Like all great plays, Dryden and Lee's *Oedipus* has a colourful (and
often elaborately contrived) performance history that involves star
performers and 'playlets' within the play proper. Among the star
performers attracted to the leading role were Thomas Betterton, the
most celebrated actor of the Restoration period; the eighteenth-
century actor–manager Thomas Sheridan (father of the playwright
Richard Brinsley Sheridan), who took the part of Oedipus in a revival
of Dryden and Lee's tragedy in 1755 (see Figure 2); and towards the
end of the eighteenth century, John Philip Kemble, who also appeared
on at least one occasion in the part of Oedipus, and the frontispiece to
a 1791 edition of the play commemorates that role. In a memorable

Act III. OEDIPUS. *Scene 6.*

I. Roberts del. *Publish'd for Bell's British Theatre, June 7th 1776.* *Reading sc.*

Mr SHERIDAN in the Character of OEDIPUS.
What mean these exclamations on my Name?

2. Burnet Reading, engraving of Thomas Sheridan in the title role of Dryden and Lee's *Oedipus* (post-10 January 1755, when he first took the role), Act III, sc. VI, 'What mean these exclamations on my name?'

revival in 1692, the requisite Aristotelian tragic balance was somewhat upset when Oedipus (George Powell) almost met his death at the hands of Creon (Sandford), after Sandford had inadvertently been handed a real dagger by the property-man. But this revival is not simply recalled in theatre annals for this reason; the 1692 production is important because it was the first time the play benefited from the addition of incidental music by Henry Purcell for the Senecan incantation scene – music that was to act as the source of the famous song 'Music for a while'.[50]

Although Dryden and Lee's tragedy remained a stock play in the repertoire during the first part of the eighteenth century (Hogarth's engraving *Strolling Actresses Dressing in a Barn* (1738) appears to draw on at least one provincial revival),[51] the English *Oedipus* was not without its detractors. Whilst there were those who levelled charges of plagiarism against the playwrights at the time of its composition, by the end of the seventeenth century there were those who objected that Dryden and Lee's play was not Sophoclean enough.[52] And what these commentators were resisting, above all, was the Senecan and the neoclassical imprints upon the Greek material at a time when literary and dramatic tastes were beginning to look beyond what was seen as the increasingly oppressive influence of French aesthetic prescriptions.

NOTES

1. Ps.-Longinus, *On the Sublime*, Chapter 33 (the end of the first century AD). Ion of Chios was a contemporary of Sophocles, and had been admitted into the canon of great tragedians by later Hellenistic scholars.

2. Suetonius, *Life of Caesar*, 56. See further Leofanc Holford-Strevens, 'Sophocles at Rome', in Jasper Griffin (ed.), *Sophocles Revisited: Essays Presented to Sir Hugh Lloyd-Jones* (Oxford 1999), 219–59.

3. Macrobius, *Saturnalia*, 2.7.14: 'Saltabat Hylas Oedipodem, et Pylades hac voce securitatem saltantis castigavit: sù blépeis.' For Roman

pantomime, see the essays in Edith Hall and Mary-Rose Wyles (eds.), *Ancient Pantomime* (Oxford 2008).

4. See Petronius, *Satyrica*, ed. and trans. R.B. Branham and D. Kinney (London 1996), 137.3, p. 145 n.; 132.4, p. 138 n. I am indebted to Edith Hall for drawing these references to my attention.

5. Suetonius, *Life of Nero*, 28.2; 34.1–4. For comment, see S. Bartsch, *Actors in the Audience: Theatricality and Doublespeak from Nero to Hadrian* (Cambridge MA, 1994), 38–42.

6. Dio Cassius, *Epitome*, 63.28.3–5. The translation is taken from Vol. VIII of the Loeb edition of Dio Cassius, *Roman History*, trans. E. Cary and H.B. Foster (Cambridge, MA 1925).

7. Cf. Suetonius, *Life of Nero*, 46.3. The translation is taken from Vol. I of the Loeb edition of Suetonius, *The Lives of the Twelve Caesars*, trans. J.C. Rolfe (Cambridge, MA. 1914).

8. Bartsch (1994), 22. On the theatricality of the period, see A.J. Boyle, *Tragic Seneca: An Essay in the Theatrical Tradition* (London and New York 1997).

9. Tacitus, *Annals*, XV, 60–4.

10. David Wiles, 'Theatre in Roman and Christian Europe', in J. Russell Brown (ed.), *Oxford Illustrated History of Theatre* (Oxford 1995), 49–92, 61. Wiles gives a very helpful overview of the interaction between theatre architecture and politics in the period.

11. T.S. Eliot, 'Seneca in Elizabethan Translation' (1927), repr. in T.S. Eliot, *Essays on Elizabethan Drama* (New York 1956), 6–7.

12. Boyle (1997), 11, 12. Cf. P. Kragelund, 'Senecan tragedy: back on stage?' in J.G. Fitch (ed.), *Oxford Readings in Seneca* (Oxford 2008), 181–94.

13. Wiles (1995), 58–9. Generally on Roman theatre and theatre audiences see F. Sear, *Roman Theatres: An Architectural Study* (Oxford 2006).

14. P.J. Davis, *Seneca Thyestes* (London 2003), 22–7.

15. They may well be from separate plays. The republican tragedian Accius, whose works have not survived, also wrote a play called *Phoenissae*. See Boyle (1997), 96, n. 21.

16. Ibid., 103. See further S. Hornblower and A. Spawforth (eds.), *The Oxford Classical Dictionary* (3rd edn, Oxford 1996), sv. 'incest'.

17. Boyle (1997), 103.

18. Line references are to the Oxford Classical Text and all translations from the *Oedipus* are taken from E.F. Watling's Penguin Classics edition of *Seneca: Four Tragedies and Octavia* (Harmondsworth 1966).

19. On the parallels with the suicide of Agrippina, see Boyle (1997), 102.

20. Davis (2003), 23.

21. For Sophocles' Oedipus and the scapegoat motif see J.-P. Vernant, 'Ambiguity and reversal: on the enigmatic structure of *Oedipus Rex*', in J.-P. Vernant and P. Vidal-Naquet, *Myth and Tragedy in Ancient Greece*, English translation by Janet Lloyd (New York 1988), 113–40.

22. Alexander Neville's Senecan *Oedipus*, which dates from 1560, was first published in 1563 (see below in this chapter for discussion) and appeared in *The Tenne Tragedies of Seneca*, ed. Thomas Newton (London 1581).

23. See Bruce R. Smith, *Ancient Scripts and Modern Experience on the English Stage 1500–1700* (Princeton 1988), 205–11

24. Alexander Neville, '"The Epistle" to Oedipus the Fifth Tragedy', in *The Tenne Tragedies of Seneca*, ed. T. Watson (repr. New York 1967), Part I, 158.

25. Smith (1988), p. 110.

26. There is another one in the Bodleian, MS Rawlinson poet.76 (Summary cat.iii, 297, No. 14 570). See R.H. Bowers, 'William Gager's *Oedipus*', *Studies in Philology* 46 (1949), 141–53.

27. J.W. Binns (ed.), *Renaissance Latin Drama in England* (Hildesheim and New York 1981), 1–8.

28. The diachronic account of the myth is part of an older tradition, which is mediated via the Italian and French romance traditions. See Lowell Edmunds, *Oedipus* (London and New York 2006), 64–78.

29. H.R. Palmer, *List of English Editions and Translations of Greek and Latin Classics Printed before 1641* (London 1911), 100; and R.A. McCabe, *Incest, Drama and Nature's Law 1550–1700* (Cambridge 1993), 111.

30. Prévost is following Italian, rather than French, theory at this time. See further Chapter 3 below.

31. The standard study is Christian Biet's excellent book *Oedipe en monarchie: Tragédie et théorie juridique à l'âge classique* (Paris 1994).

32. La Bruyère, *Les Caractères de Théophraste, traduits du Grec, avec les caractères ou les mœurs de ce siècle* (2nd edn, Paris 1688), 170–1: Corneille '*peint les hommes comme ils devraient être*' and Racine '*les peint tel qu'ils sont*'.

33. For a discussion of Corneille's theoretical stance, see B. Louvat (ed.), *Corneille Oedipe Tragédie* (1659) (Toulouse 1995), xxii–xxiv, xxvii–xxxii.

34. For details of Lully's revival see Grove 1980 II: 327.

35. Louvat (ed.) (1659), xvi–xvii.

36. William Joyner, *The Roman Empress: A Tragedy* (London 1671), A2.

37. Ibid., A5.

38. See Edith Hall and Fiona Macintosh, *Greek Tragedy and the British Theatre 1660–1914* (Oxford 2005), 11–12. There is some suggestion that Joyner read *Samson Agonistes* in MS. See E. Sauer, 'Milton and Dryden on the Restoration stage', in C. J. Summers and T.-L. Pebworth (eds.), *Fault Lines and Controversies in the Study of Seventeenth-Century Literature* (Columbia, MO and London 2002), 88–110. I am indebted to Margaret Kean for this reference.

39. John Carey (ed.), *John Milton: Complete Shorter Poems* (London and New York 1997), 390, lines 1382–3. Subsequent references appear in parentheses after the citation.

40. E.g. the Northern Broadsides production in autumn 1998.

41. P. D. Cannan, 'New directions in serious drama on the London stage, 1675–1688', *Philological Quarterly* 73 (1994), 219–42.

42. Smith (1988), esp. 51 ff.

43. Ibid., 256–7.

44. *The Works of John Dryden*, ed. M. E. Novak (Berkeley and Los Angeles 1984), 2133. Subsequent references appear in parentheses after the citation.

45. For Dryden's debts to Milton in this play, see Hall and Macintosh (2005), 14–21, esp. 20.

46. Paulina Kewes, *Authorship and Appropriation: Writing for the Stage in England, 1660–1710* (Oxford 1998), 157–8.

47. C. H. Firth and R. S. Rait, *Acts and Ordinances of the Interregnum 1642–1660*, 3 vols. (London 1911), vol. II, 387. See further, McCabe (1993), 262.

48. For a detailed account of the politics of the play, see Hall and Macintosh (2005), 24–9.

49. J. I. Marsden, 'Spectacle, horror and pathos', in D. Payne (ed.), *The Cambridge Companion to English Restoration Theatre* (Cambridge 2000), 181–9.

50. J. Doran, *'Their Majesties' Servants': Annals of the English Stage from Thomas Betterton to Edmund Kean*, rev. R. W. Lowe, 3 vols. (London 1888), Vol. I, 349. See further *Works of John Dryden* (1984), 447, 466; and R. Thompson, *The Glory of the Temple and the Stage: Henry Purcell 1659–1695* (London 1995), 41.

51. For discussion see Hall and Macintosh (2005), 1–2 and notes.

52. Kewes (1998), 157–8.

CHAPTER 3

OEDIPUS AND THE 'PEOPLE'

I will grant it probable that at the suffering of kings several should be concerned; at the same time you must grant it absurd that they should sing and dance at their sufferings ...[1]

The marginalisation, and in many cases the omission, of the Chorus from the seventeenth-century plays dealing with Oedipus is clearly related to the political conditions under which they were produced. The Greek interactive chorus was an alien and unrealistic encumbrance to neoclassical theorists and practictioners residing in the post-feudal monarchical societies of seventeenth-century Europe. Here, as in other respects, aesthetic decisions were informed by political ones; and the reference by the French neoclassical theorist La Mesnardière to the 'vile populace'[2] makes it clear why a modern equivalent of a Greek chorus would have been intolerable at this time.

The omission of the Chorus was regularly explained with reference to the neo-Aristotelian concept of *vraisemblance*: as John Dennis's character Freeman states in the epigraph to this chapter, it was deemed 'absurd' to find an intrusive group, singing and dancing onstage within the confines of the royal palace. However, the role of the chorus had also been supplanted by the audience itself in the early modern period: just as Elizabeth I and her entourage had been on display during performances of ancient plays in the great halls of colleges and country houses in the previous century, so now a prominent 'chorus' of aristocrats took up residence in the pit in the seventeenth-century theatres. Moreover, following the success of Corneille's *Le Cid* in 1636, select members of the audience (male dignitaries at first, women as well from 1710) were able to occupy seats on the stage proper at the Comédie Française, as was to be the case some years later at the Dorset Garden Theatre and the new Drury Lane Theatre in Restoration London. And if the chorus had previously fixed 'place' in the ancient theatre by their (generally) unfailing presence, that function was now being fulfilled by an audience who remained in their seats after the actors had left the stage at the end of the scenes.

This chapter focuses on the ancient chorus proper rather than on its modern surrogates; and it charts the early fortunes of Sophocles' group of Theban elders and their relation to the play's protagonist upon the modern stage. This was never a continuous relationship because it was inevitably contingent upon the changing political and material circumstances in which the tragedy was produced.

OEDIPUS AT VICENZA

Whilst the audience at the sixteenth- and seventeenth-century performances of ancient plays in colleges and public theatres acted as a surrogate chorus, a different, more Greek, choric model existed in the modern world. The French alternatives to the Greek chorus (notably the *confidant* and the regular onstage presence of at least one character during the interval between scenes or *liaison des scènes*) were in many ways a reaction against Italian Renaissance theory, in which the idea of 'community' (especially under the republican state of Venice) had greater currency.[3] Moreover, the Aristotelian privileging of the Sophoclean chorus as 'one of the actors' (*Poetics,* Chapter 18, 56a 25–32) was considered during the Renaissance (as with all things Aristotelian) something to which modern practitioners should aspire. The most notable example of that body of Italian dramatic theory being put into practice occurred in the Venetian town of Vicenza in March 1585, when a performance of Sophocles' *Edipo Tiranno* was given to mark the opening of Palladio's Teatro Olimpico.[4]

The Chorus for this first modern vernacular production of Sophocles' tragedy consisted of fifteen performers, who, following their entry song, remained onstage throughout the play. The composer was Andrea Gabrieli, who at the age of 75 was already one of Italy's most emininent composers; and here at the end of his life he produced an entirely new musical idiom, inspired by his understanding of the ancient world, to accompany Orsatto Giustiniani's words.[5] According to Angelo Ingegneri, the play's director, tragic choruses (in marked contrast to other kinds of choral performance) required a simplicity that reflected their affinity with the style and rhythms of ordinary speech. In Gabrieli's music for the play there is no modern melody or counterpoint; and it is the verse rhythm that prevails. Whilst the odes, according to Ingegneri, were there to provide relaxation to the audience between the acts, it is clear that 'relaxation' was not intended to preclude edification on this occasion. Elsewhere the director explains the absence of any instrumental accompaniment for the choral odes with reference to the primacy of the lyrics; and the variety within the choruses, which range from unaccompanied solo delivery to six-part choral ensemble, also suggests a concern with the intelligibility of the words.[6]

If the chorus in the Teatro Olimpico conveyed a sense of community by their consistent onstage presence, the inclusion of a huge number of extras – twenty-eight for Oedipus' entourage, twenty-five for Jocasta and six for Creon – similarly served to underline the public nature of this late sixteenth-century production. The chorus was not a homogeneous group – its leader alone intervened in the dialogue in the acts, much to the consternation of one critical eyewitness who finds the interrogatory leader worryingly far apart from the Chorus and 'on a level with the king'[7] – and the confinement of singing to entr'acte choral odes reflected the well-established Italian tradition of *intermedi* (the songs and dances which offered respite from feasting and provided frames for spoken drama). But the absence of dance on this occasion and the prominence of the choral voice within the dramatic structure as a whole also looked forward to early opera – and especially to Monteverdi's in the very early seventeenth century – in which choral performance predominates over the aria.

However, the importance of *Edipo Tiranno* in theatre history in general is clearly not confined to its Chorus, its large cast of extras and consequently elaborate stage business; it is its setting, above all, for which it is remembered. The decision to build Continental Europe's first permanent stone theatre in Vicenza was taken as early as 1579 by the members of the Academia Olimpica, which included the eminent artist and architect Andrea Palladio.[8] Palladio died the following year after completing the plans and it was left to Vicenzo Scamozzi to oversee the building works and to add the five three-dimensional sets behind the doorways. The inspiration for Palladio's design was Vitruvius' *De architectura* (particularly in the Barbaro translation of 1567) and the extant example (albeit at that time full of houses) of the ancient theatre at Orange.[9] Even if the upper-class audience who attended *Edipo Tiranno* was far removed from the cross-section of citizens who sat in the Theatre of Dionysus in fifth-century Athens, its relative homogeneity (there were no ducal grandees in the Republic of Venice) meant that the non-socially stratified seating of the ancient theatre could be adopted in the three-thousand-seater (and, at that time, roofed) theatre at Vicenza without difficulty.

However, this was not simply an attempt at an authenticating revival: like early Italian opera which was in its embryonic stages at this time and to which this production (and especially Gabrieli's music) may be said to have significantly contributed, it was as much an attempt to build upon the spirit of the ancient world as it was to revive it. Just as Gabrieli's choral singing was (unlike ancient singing) unaccompanied in order to guarantee the full intelligibility of the word, so other aspects of the production sought to 'improve' upon ancient theatre practice where necessary. The absence of masks at Vicenza was also explained by Ingegneri with reference to the superior powers of the human face in the enhancement of the emotional range of the performance. The Aristotelian nature of the production was also registered through the director's concern with the need to move the spectator; and the decision to perform at night (from 1.30 a.m. to 5 a.m.) in torchlight (despite the dubious success of this) no doubt stemmed from a similar concern to foster conditions most favourable to the effect of Aristotelian catharsis.[10]

The decision to dress Oedipus (played by Nicolò Rossi at the first performance, by Giambattista Verato at the second) as the Sultan in lavish gold vestments, with an entourage of Turkish archers, not only shows a desire to refashion ancient Thebes as an exotic 'other'; it also reflects an understanding on the part of the Academicians of the contemporary political potential of Greek tragedy. Indeed, with the main extant accounts of the play being so widely divergent,[11] it is impossible to overemphasise the political nature of the production overall: the two performances (on 3 and 5 March) and the excessively protracted build-up before the 1.30 a.m. start time, were as much about the importance (or perhaps the self-importance, as the statues that adorn the facade would testify) of Vicenza and its Academicians as they were an exercise in the revival of Sophocles' tragedy.[12] It may well be this politicisation that is responsible for the interrupted performance tradition at Vicenza: it was not until 1618 that the next play was performed, Torquato Tasso's elaboration of Sophocles' play, *Re Torrismondo* (1587); and thereafter the theatre was not used for theatrical performance until the late nineteenth century.

FROM 'KING' TO 'TYRANNOS'

The prominence granted to Sophocles' *Oedipus Tyrannus* in Aristotle's *Poetics* (especially since it alone of Aristotle's main examples was extant), together with the neoclassical preoccupation with formal dramaturgical questions, guaranteed the pre-eminence of Oedipus within the early French dramatic tradition. When André Dacier published his enormously influential translation and commentary of *Oedipus Tyrannus* and *Electra* in 1692, he secured Oedipus' centrality well into the eighteenth century.[13] But Dacier did not merely place Oedipus centre stage; he placed the Sophoclean Oedipus within the French tradition, banishing the Senecan version to the wings until the very end of the eighteenth century. The *Oedipus Tyrannus* was the most frequently translated and adapted of the Greek texts from 1614 to 1818, when about thirty adaptations and six French translations appeared.[14] In France, as indeed in England during this period, to invoke Oedipus meant inevitably to confront and explore in dramatic form the political potential or indeed the political actuality of regicide, tyranny and patriarchy.

Dacier followed Aristotle in commending the coincidence of recognition (*anagnorisis*) and reversal (*peripeteia*) as the hallmark of the Sophoclean success with *Oedipus Tyrannus*; and given the fact that Corneille's unwieldy five-act play – and later Voltaire's *Oedipe* of 1718 – had placed the discovery of regicide in Act IV and the discovery of Oedipus' parentage in Act V, Dacier was able to appreciate the demonstrable effectiveness of the Sophoclean formal structure on account of its very absence from French neoclassical example. Voltaire followed Corneille in this respect, but less for aesthetic than thematic reasons: how, he wondered, could Oedipus implausibly forget about the regicide following his discovery of his true identity?

However, the political climate also meant that regicide could not be relegated to a secondary role. Indeed, just as the Oedipal regicide had been of utmost importance in the Restoration period in Britain, it was to prove central again to the eighteenth-century French readings of Sophocles' play. The links between incest and the *ancien régime* were longstanding; and now in the eighteenth-century versions of Oedipus, we find a new interest in the *tyrannos* of the title as the monarchy itself comes under increasing scrutiny. Whilst the Senecan version had denied Tiresias divine insight and consequently excluded the scene between Oedipus and Tiresias, now it is this scene in the Sophoclean text that gains prominence. Here we witness a new Oedipus in many French and English translations, which follow Dacier as well as the

Jesuitical commentators René Rapin and Pierre Brumoy in their sharp scrutiny of the king's conduct. Oedipus is now the non-hereditary monarch with tyrannical tendencies; and in the French republican versions we also see the return of the chorus, who had been excluded for so long from the modern stage on the grounds that they worked contrary to the dictates of verisimilitude. Now, in a world where monarchical excesses needed to be held in check, the chorus (under the influence of the radical readings of Rapin and Brumoy) increasingly assume an interrogatory function akin to their role in the democratic drama of fifth-century Athens.[15]

For Dacier, the causes of Oedipus' misfortune are his rashness and blindness, not the crimes of parricide and incest. Dacier's guilty Oedipus was in many ways a response to Corneille's ultimately 'redeemed' protagonist, who was regularly appearing on the stage at the Comédie Française (and did so until 1730);[16] and it was in part against Dacier's limited 'moralising' reading of Sophocles' play that the most important French eighteenth-century reworking was cast. When Voltaire began working on his *Oedipe* in 1715, he relied heavily on Dacier's translation;[17] and whilst he followed many of the recommendations in Dacier's commentary, he took particular exception to the claim that Oedipus' inquiring mind was a problem. In Voltaire's damningly literalist reading of Sophocles' tragedy, it was the fifth-century Oedipus' curiosity alone that impressed the eighteenth-century philosopher. For the enlightenment mind, Oedipus' dogged pursuit of the truth in the scene with the Theban Shepherd is the only reasonable action performed by the Sophoclean Oedipus.[18]

Whilst Dacier's translation proved an invaluable guide and an excellent sounding board for Voltaire during his composition of *Oedipe*, the importance to him of Corneille's version of 1659 as well cannot be understated. The evident parallels between the two plays in terms of the love interest in both subplots led to immediate charges of plagiarism, which Voltaire spiritedly refuted. But it is perhaps the parallels between their political circumstances that prompted Voltaire's choice of subject. As had been the case for

Corneille's *Oedipe* in 1659, the regent – this time the Duc
d'Orléans – was beginning to behave as 'sole' absolute monarch,
having disbanded the Council of Regency that was set up in 1715
to rule in the five-year-old Louis XV's stead. Voltaire had already
published scurrillous verse about the regent on two previous occasions; and the allegations of the Duc's incestuous relations with his
daughter must have made Voltaire's *Oedipe* potentially explosive
when it opened at the Comédie Française on 18 November 1718
(see Figure 3).[19]

However, the fact that Voltaire went on to receive a substantial
pension from the Duc on the strength of his version would seem to
imply that any perceived identification between the ancient Oedipus
and the Duc was considered flattering rather than offensive.[20] *Oedipe*
may well be construed as a revolutionary play in its strident attack on
the gods and the clergy – it has been described by at least one
commentator as the first bomb hurled at the *ancien régime*[21] – but
Voltaire is offering no proto-republican reading of the myth. Oedipus
in Voltaire's tragedy is, in fact, a much more impressive leader
than his counterpart in Corneille's earlier play. As a figure of the
Enlightenment, he is both compassionate in his identification with his
people and prescient in his assessment of the facts. Yet Voltaire's
Oedipus remains the outsider – he is not even loved by Jocaste,
whose earlier passion for Philoctète is revived at the start of the play.
Oedipe is no ideal king either, because his reign is based upon false
beliefs. But as with Corneille, the ideal king is Oedipe's alter ego, in
this case Philoctète (rather than Thésée), who is significantly left at the
end of the play as a symbol of hope for the next generation. According
to Philoctète, it is inner qualities rather than inherited status that
count.[22] When accused by Oedipe and the people of being Laius'
killer, he appeals to Oedipe not as king but as a fellow hero, one who
must have faith in the heroism of his peers (Act II, sc. IV, lines
545 ff.). As in the real world, these perfect kings in the French
Oedipus plays are by necessity only embryonic, posited as ideals rather
than actualities.

3. Décor for Voltaire's *Oedipe* (1718), Comédie Française

When Philoctète in Voltaire's play is urged to stay to face the accusations made against him and to await news from the High Priest to absolve him entirely, he disdainfully agrees to stay, not out of any interest but through pity for the people (Act III sc. III, lines 735 ff.). In the subsequent scene, the High Priest arrives, followed by a chorus of two who represent the people. In Corneille's version the chorus was not simply marginalised, it was omitted altogether; and the other eleven versions written between 1718 and 1731 also omit the Greek chorus.[23] And while Voltaire (unlike Dacier) is generally rather dismissive of the Sophoclean chorus on the grounds that it moralised excessively and intruded unnecessarily,[24] what we witness here in his *Oedipe*, albeit in rudimentary form, is the beginning of the French eighteenth-century interest in the Greek chorus as representative of *le peuple*.

The success of Voltaire's play was immediate, with plaudits for star performances from Mlle Charlotte Desmares, known as la Desmares (as Jocaste), Abraham-Alexis Quinault, known as Quinault-Dufresne (as Oedipe), and his brother, Maurice (as Philoctète). As was the case with all successful tragedies in the eighteenth and nineteenth centuries following the return of the Italian Company to Paris after the death of Louis XIV in 1715, Voltaire's tragedy inspired a lively burlesque version entitled *Oedipe travesti* by Pierre François Biancolelli (called Dominique), which opened at the Théâtre Italien on 17 April 1719.[25] In Biancolelli's burlesque, set in a village to the north of Paris, the ready applicability of the Oedipus myth to modern France is under-lined by its updating to include fortune-tellers, the abandonment of children and a fatal drunken brawl which provides the backdrop for the parricide.

However, in some senses it was the notoriety of Voltaire's *Oedipe* that guaranteed its longevity: it spawned numerous critical pamphlets charging its author with impiety and plagiarism. Voltaire went on to write supplementary, and additionally contentious, lines for the printed edition, especially those which heightened the attacks on the gods ('the gods want blood and they alone are listened to' – Act II sc I), the clergy ('A priest, whomsoever he be, whichever god inspires him, ought to pray for his kings, not lie to them' – Act III, sc. IV) and, most contentiously as the century progressed, the monarchy ('What would I have been without him, nothing but the son of a king' – Act II sc. II).[26]

Although Voltaire omits the scene between Creon and Oedipus, this particular Sophoclean scene of confrontation – together with that between Tiresias and Oedipus – gains prominence during the course of the eighteenth century as the role of the monarchy comes under increasing scrutiny. Now Oedipus begins to assume characteristics more often associated with the ancient label *tyrannos*, with its loose association with the modern 'tyrant', than with those qualities more commonly implicit with the generally honorific title 'king'.[27]

Although there were numerous other versions following in the wake of Voltaire's controversial play,[28] the next most significant event for the production history of Sophocles' play was not in fact a performance, but the publication of two translations of *Oedipus Tyrannus* and *Oedipus at Colonus* in *Le Théâtre des Grecs*, by Pierre Brumoy. Brumoy's preface registered a new (non-neoclassical) historical awareness of Greek drama. As early as 1674, René Rapin had noted a marked distinction between the ancient Greek delight in the humiliation of kings and the modern French preference for gallantry and sentiment. But Brumoy now went a step further in implying that Greek tragedy provided the fifth-century audiences with an object lesson in the evils of kingship.[29]

That Brumoy's proto-republican readings were to exert influence during the years leading up to the Revolutionary period was hardly surprising. And the increasing adoption of the Greek model of a participating chorus in the Oedipus plays in the last part of the eighteenth century can be seen as the aesthetic correlative to the growing revolutionary ethos.[30] There are six versions of the Oedipus around the turn of the century (1784 to 1818), all of which have prominent choruses. There is only one exception, in the version by Nicholas G. Léonard (posthumously published in 1798) where the king is the victim of a popular rebellion. That Oedipus was also called upon by those in positions of power is evidenced by the promise of Marie Antoinette that the first work at the Théâtre de la Cour would be the *Oedipe à Colone* of the Italian composer Sacchini.[31]

The most interesting of these republican Oedipuses is *Oedipe Roi* by Marie-Joseph Chénier (written before 1811, published posthumously in 1818), where the Chorus appears in every scene. Although there is no evidence that this play was performed, it was highly influential owing to the status enjoyed by Chénier as a playwright. Like Voltaire, Chénier proclaimed the aim of tragedy to be to promote a love of virtue, laws and liberty and a loathing of fanaticism and tyranny; and with the help of his participating chorus, his Oedipus is first revealed as tyrannical king of the *ancien régime*, who is warned by both Tiresias and Creon on separate occasions in terms that echoed the warnings issued to Louis XVI and his queen against putting private interest over public good. But from being the tyrant who denies his people the right of individual speech at the start of the play, Chénier's Oedipus becomes by the end a man at war with the tyrannical side of himself.[32]

The Romantic period's fascination with transgressive conduct in general meant that Oedipus' crimes could be construed as part of a collective act of social defiance. The neoclassical preoccupation with poetic justice was shown to be thoroughly tainted and compromised; and the neoclassical rules over which the court of Louis XIV had presided under Mazarin were to be rejected. A return to the Greeks now meant a complete break with the aesthetic and moral strictures of the moribund *ancien régime*.

If both the form and content of Sophocles' tragedy in the Revolutionary period were found to express and explore aspirations and ideas that dominated that period, it is important to bear in mind that the growing interest in formal aspects of the original was still only very rudimentary. The age of high neoclassical tragedy, when tragic actors besported themselves in togas and plumes, had only recently disappeared; and it was only in 1759 that the modern surrogate chorus of aristocrats had finally been removed from the stage at the Comédie Française. Voltaire himself went on to become instrumental in promoting increased historical accuracy in sets and costumes at the Comédie Française in the second half of the eighteenth century. French revolutionary ideals led to changes in fashion in the 1770s, which were adopted both on the street and on the stage.[33] The 'free' French citizen wore a chitonesque tunic and Greek-style sandals (slip-ons, with no heel, which were tied at the ankle with a ribbon), and the newly liberated women, for whom public breastfeeding was to be celebrated as a natural Rousseau-esque act rather than a mark of primitivism, wore garments to reveal one breast (in striking imitation of, say, the Roman sculpture in the Louvre, which Napoleon was to bring from Rome to Paris in 1807). The famous Revolutionary tragic actor François Joseph Talma caused a sensation when he brought the classical fashion from the streets into the theatre, appearing as a tribune in Voltaire's *Brutus* in 1789 in a toga that revealed his bare arms and legs.[34] But when Voltaire sites Sophocles at the start of a tradition rather than as a model – in, say, his 'Troisième Lettre' – he is expressing ideas that were no different to those of Corneille and his contemporaries. At the end of the eighteenth century, changes to the chorus notwithstanding, there was little advancement upon Voltaire's programme of appropriation, which advocated adaptation and improvement rather than imitation and revival on the grounds that the spirit and needs of the modern age must be accommodated and respected above all other considerations.

FROM *TYRANNOS* TO EVERYMAN

Voltaire's *Oedipe* remained in the repertoire of the Comédie Française until 1852, totalling a record 336 performances since its première.[35] Its eclipse may well have come about with the arrival at the Odéon of the Potsdam production of Mendelssohn's *Antigone* in 1844, which made Parisian audiences realise that the French neoclassical model was

not the only one available to them. The Romantic poet Gérard de
Nerval pronounced in advance of the opening of the production:
'Greece has risen from the grave'.[36]

The French translation of the German version of Johann Jakob
Christian Donner (1841) was by two ardent Romantic poets, Paul
Meurice and Auguste Vacquerie. The involvement of Meurice and
Vacquerie guaranteed that this Prussian Greek revival was hailed by
many as an illuminating contribution to the vibrant French Romantic
theatre, which was still doing battle with the ossifying neoclassical
tradition. Greek tragedy – like Shakespearean tragedy – was now
enlisted on the side of French Romanticism. In the preface to their
translation (which appeared fifteen days after the performance),
Meurice and Vacquerie eloquently outline the reasons for their appropriation of a Greek tragedy: the greatest mistake, in their estimation, is
to take Greek tragedy as tragedy; with its ability to evoke both laughter
and tears in the audience, and with its inclusion of music, it is best
understood not in relation to neoclassical tragedy, but to Romantic
melodrama instead. This highly contentious claim inevitably led to
opposition towards the translation per se, and we find many traditionalists playing down the content of the play in their reviews and
emphasising instead (as in London in 1845) the impressive set and the
arresting (but not necessarily immediately pleasing) Mendelssohn
score. What these traditionalists found hardest to cope with was that
tragic drama was now being expected to encompass a new, less
restrained emotional range (*'une violence de sentiment'*). At the
Odéon, Antigone's passage to her death was said to have been char-
acterised by deliriously convulsive movements as she clung onto the
Theban elders in the chorus in despair and desperation.[37]

These divided responses apart, the overall impact of the
Mendelssohn *Antigone* was inspirational. It showed French audiences
that Greek drama could be played out in a theatrical space that
incorporated two performance levels – one for the actors and one
for a singing chorus. And it fuelled the already burgeoning interest
in Greek drama that had captured Europe as a whole since the

publication of the widely translated (frequently reprinted and much plagiarised) *Lectures on Drama* by A. W. Schlegel, which began to appear in 1809.[38] It also led to an increase in the number of translations of Sophocles' tragedies in particular, some seeking to erase the 'vulgarity' they detected in Meurice and Vacquerie's *Antigone*, others to emulate it.[39]

One translation that dates from this politically turbulent decade is the *Oedipe-Roi* by the poet and playwright, Jules Lacroix. Although Lacroix's text had to wait until 18 September 1858 to be used in performance, his project had been fired by a desire around 1843 or 1844 to translate '*Oedipus the King* faithfully, religiously, and to translate it for the French stage, with its choruses, verse by verse without changes, without any sacrifice to modern taste – simple and grotesque, in all its tragic horror'.[40] Here in the dedication to his play, Lacroix is placing himself in marked contrast to the Voltairean tradition which sought to improve upon the ancients; a faithful copy in Lacroix's estimation is worth much more than any adaptation. More than one reviewer of Lacroix's play recalled the famously ironic comment of Voltaire after a performance of his *Oedipe*: 'Applaud, Athenians! It's Sophocles!'[41] Now the reviewers could rebut Voltaire with the example of a genuinely French Sophocles.

What is striking about Lacroix's pronouncement is that he appears to be deliberately dissociating himself from two contemporary camps: in his desire to eschew modernity, he is rejecting both the Voltairean neoclassical tradition and the 'vulgarising' tendency detected by some in the avowedly Romantic translation of the *Antigone* by Meurice and Vacquerie. But in his desire to translate Sophocles' play 'faithfully, religiously' and to bring it to the French stage with its chorus and in 'all its tragic horror', Lacroix betrays his own Romantic allegiances. What is significant about his version of *Oedipus Tyrannus*, and what seems to have secured his success, is that he has combined the strengths of both the neoclassical and the Romantic traditions. His adoption of rhymed alexandrines puts him firmly within the neoclassical tradition; and his style and his scholarship were for the most part admired by the academic and literary establishments. But he was equally admired by at least one theatrical critic for bringing to light the source of the boulevard melodramas that pulled in the crowds in the popular theatres of Paris.[42]

Lacroix's first translation for the stage had been *Macbeth* in 1840 – he later went on to translate *King Lear* in 1868 – and the Shakespearean influences are felt in his Roman-inspired plays, *Testament de César* (1849) and *Valéria* (1851), as well as in his general preference for large crowd scenes and fast-moving changes of scene. In his *Oedipe-Roi*, which was performed for the first time at the Comédie Française on 18 September 1858, the Shakespearean influence can be felt equally in the large cast of extras who first appear onstage as the supplicating citizens in the opening scene, but who come and go from the scene in the company of major characters. They are, moreover, distinct from the chorus proper, which Lacroix has reduced (somewhat bizarrely for a 'faithful' rendering) to a group of four consisting of two young girls, a woman and an old man. This change to the chorus's identity did not go unchallenged, with at least one commentator finding it deeply inappropriate that young girls should be allowed to discuss incest.[43] Nor indeed did the choral chanting (as opposed to singing) of the odes to the musical accompaniment go unnoticed, or uncriticised, especially since the language they used was not noticeably different from that of the protagonist.

Why indeed did the 1858 production include a chorus of four, of mixed age and gender? Was it to make the chorus a truly representative group rather than an obvious political grouping as was the case with the Theban elders of Sophocles? If Lacroix wished to depoliticise his chorus and dissociate himself from, for example, Chénier's revolutionary version, his inclusion of a large crowd of extras was a mistake. For by making a large crowd of extras exit with one of the actors, you have, *faute de mieux*, political drama. At the end of the scene of confrontation between Oedipus and Creon, and following Jocasta's intervention, the stage direction reads: '*Creon exits, accompanied by a section of the people. The chorus keep a distance from Oedipus, so as to show disapproval of his violence.*'[44] Oedipus' paranoia in Lacroix's reading may well seem justified, as Creon's 'faction', so to speak, is seen to follow him from the stage. But at the same time it is important to point out that Oedipus' own language up until this point in the Lacroix version has been that of imperial ruler: 'No. Punishment is necessary [for Lauis' murderer]! Today, this country is under my laws, and this hand is their custodian' – where the imperial arm of the state metonymically replaces the human arm. Later, with Creon himself, Oedipus imperiously exclaims: 'Do you want to disobey my sovereign law?'[45] Creon may well be seen to be fomenting trouble unwittingly in Lacroix's text, but there must have been little doubt in the minds of some members of the audience that opposition in Thebes was both inevitable and vital.

Lacroix's *Oedipe-Roi* received sixteen performances in 1858 and was revived again in 1861, going on the next year to win the Prix Extraordinaire from the Académie Française which is normally reserved for original works. At the ceremony, the permanent secretary praised Lacroix's text for not being troubled by 'recent social disturbances'.[46] But at the time of its première in 1858, the honeymoon period of Napoleon III was fading; and despite the economic gains of the 1850s, France was living under one of the most repressive political systems it had experienced. By the time of its first revival in 1861, the political mood in France was decidedly gloomy. To claim that Lacroix's translation succeeded precisely because it was not political seems disingenuous. As we have seen, to stage an apolitical Oedipus in France was an impossible task: questions of kingship, clerical authority and free will had been regularly broached and confronted on the stage of the Comédie Française with the help of Sophocles' tragedy throughout France's theatrical history. Following the coup d'état of 1851, the urgency of these questions returned to the fore, and remained there throughout the Second Empire period to a greater or lesser extent.

That the political climate of the period suited the Lacroix version is certain, but there were other factors that guaranteed both its durability and its eventual leading role in the dramatic repertoire of Europe as a whole. We have heard how neoclassical readings of the *Poetics* exaggerated the role of the single central tragic figure in Aristotle's prescriptions, and how these readings led in turn to the emergence of the modern tragic hero(ine). Indeed it is by no means merely fortuituous that the only other Greek tragedy of this period to gain such prominence in the European repertoire from the 1850s onwards was that other atypical central figure Greek tragedy – Euripides' *Medea*.

The *Medea* of Ernest Legouvé first appeared on the Paris stage in 1856, with the Italian tragedienne Adelaide Ristori in the title role. Both the centrality of the character of Medea and the performance of Ristori in the part contributed to its theatrical success at this time. The modern star system in the theatre that replaced the old established companies was well established in the second half of the nineteenth century. As well as having a deleterious effect on the theatre in general – it resulted, for example, in the long run and the consequent decline in the number of new plays – it may nonetheless be seen to have played a major role in the revival of certain Greek plays. Now with a return to the Greek originals and an avoidance of neoclassical busy subplots, there had been (as we have seen) some attempt to restore the Greek chorus. But as was the case with Lacroix's *Oedipe Roi*, by granting the chorus generally no more than a marginal role (in Legouvé's case omitting it altogether), the single central figure gained even greater prominence. In this sense, the nineteenth-century revivals merely extended the European tradition of the tragic hero(ine) that can be traced from Shakespeare via Racine and then via its more recent German examples, Schiller and Goethe. In 1841 Thomas Carlyle's lecture entitled *On Heroes, Hero-Worship and the Heroic in History* was published; and in an age of hero-worship the stars of the stage were definitely not excluded.

With Lacroix's version the French stage was able to witness the blinded Oedipus for the first time. Both Corneille and Voltaire had omitted the final scene for reasons of decorum; and it is significant that it is this scene in Lacroix's version that seems to have captured the minds of the reviewers. The part of Oedipe was taken from 1858 onwards by Talma's successor at the Comédie Française, Edmond Geffroy, whose performance in the part received unanimous acclaim especially for this final, hitherto unseen, act. A renowned theatre critic of the period, Francisque Sarcey, wrote that he had felt sure before he went that he would have nothing to learn from the 1861 revival. The last act had always struck him on the page as being too long; but onstage with Geffroy in the title role, he learned otherwise:

> I know nothing more beautiful than this crushed Titan ... He cries, and with what an abundance of tears! With what accents of torn tenderness! There were scarcely any women in the auditorium; one could have counted them on one hand. But I saw some wiping tears from their eyes.[47]

Even though Sarcey clearly feels that the crying was confined to the female members of the audience, there is evidence elsewhere that the emotive nature of the final moments of the play did not affect the audience on gender lines. Lacroix, for example, claims that his greatest reward for his translation was granted when he witnessed tears running down the face of the elderly permanent secretary of the Académie at the end of the first performance of his play.[48]

Another reviewer praises Geffroy's performance highly, adding nonethess that he is perhaps a little less 'touchy' (*ombrageux*) and less 'quick-tempered' (*emporté*) than the Greek original. The result of these changes, however, is deemed a success, with the French Oedipus being altogether more touching and more 'pitiable' than the Sophoclean character.[49] Far removed from the eighteenth-century *tyrannos*, this is a new 'human' Oedipus that audiences can under-stand. By 1861 Geffroy had become so closely identified with the role of Oedipus that one reviewer feared that in the event of his imminent retirement, there would be no one to take over the role.[50] Indeed the ancient Oedipus now had to wait until the next generation before the star system could produce another tragedian, Jean Mounet-Sully, who was deemed worthy of donning his heroic mantle.

In his memoirs published in 1914, Mounet-Sully records his visit to Émile Perrin (presumably sometime in the late 1870s), then general

administrator of the Comédie Française, to ask him if a revival of
Lacroix's *Oedipe-Roi* was possible. Perrin eventually agreed to his
request, on the condition that Mounet-Sully consulted the creator
of the role, Geffroy. The meeting of the two stars was apparently
something of a success because Mounet-Sully reports that their ideas
about the role broadly coincided.[51] When Mounet-Sully speaks of his
understanding of the character of Oedipus, it is clear that his own
interpretation is an extension of the tragic hero that emerges through
Dymas' report at the end of Corneille's tragedy. For Mounet-Sully, as
for Corneille, Oedipus in his rebellion against the gods is a kind of
Prometheus, 'and each of his cries is like a shaking of invisible chains'.
Oedipus is representative of 'the revolt of instinct and intelligence
against blind fate and the terminal defeat of man'.[52]

In this sense Mounet-Sully's interpretation of Oedipus, a role he
assumed on 9 August 1881, is very much a part of the French tradition
in its focus on the tragic figure in an unjust cosmos. When he is asked
in an interview in 1888 what he thinks about the role of fate in the
play, he replies: 'I've only seen a man, an unfortunate king. I don't
know the secrets of the gods and I don't believe in oracular predictions
when they don't conform to justice. I'm always on the side of humanity.'[53] This is Oedipus for the modern secular world, with the religious
dimension of the original being subsumed into the performance.
According to Mounet-Sully, as he performs the role he feels that 'a
sacred responsibility weighs upon me'; and he maintains that he
always has 'a religious respect' for the role: 'I arrive on stage each
time like a priest going to the altar.'[54] This deeply religious reverence
that the actor feels for his role is frequently echoed in reviews of the
production. A critic's account of his attendance at a performance of
Oedipe Roi in the open-air theatre at Cauterets in 1910 converts
theatre-going into participation in a religious ceremony. He recalls
Oedipus' clamour echoing round the Pyrenees, the tripods on the
turfed mounds wafting incense into the air, the trees groaning a dirge
in sympathy, the fateful blind man wending his lonely way, far from
the palace, towards the unknown mountaintops beyond.[55]

This Senecan-inspired ending is, of course, a very far cry from Sophocles, and indeed far from Lacroix's own text (which is much closer to Sophocles), where Oedipus, trying to cling to his children, is separated from them, and, supported by a slave, and leaning on a stick, starts on his way (and we presume) back into the palace. The 1881 revival included numerous other changes to the original production: under Perrin's direction the set was altered and was considered by some to be disappointingly modern through its new lick of paint. It should, it was averred, have included the kind of archaeological details that had been on display in the Greek Galleries at the Exposition of 1878.[56] In marked contrast to the 1844 *Antigone*, this was no authenticating revival: although the set appeared 'classical' enough, there was no one central facade against which the actors performed because the palace was situated to the right, the temple of Apollo to the left and the Acropolis in the distance. There is a busy-ness about the set at the Comédie Française, which owes more to nineteenth-century stage pictorialism than it does to any ancient staging (Figure 4). Furthermore, despite the addition of a new score by Edmond Membrée, there appear to have been even more noticeable cuts to the choral odes in the 1880s with the result that the emergent lonely modern hero of Lacroix's text becomes the unerring focus of the new production.

That the audience was being offered a new psychological reading of Oedipus is clear from Mounet-Sully's comments in an interview of 1888. People often noted an increase in Oedipus' humanity since Mounet-Sully took over the role, and he was either aware of Stanislavsky's work in Moscow or at least was working along similar lines. He speaks like a method actor *avant la lettre* in his account of his preparations for his role. He makes the character enter inside him and live under his skin: 'I am with him in complete intimacy. I question him, I discuss with him.'[57] As he rehearsed his lines, Mounet-Sully claims to have pared down the Lacroix text in order to render it fully accessible to his late nineteenth-century ears. The confrontation with Tiresias, for example, he translated into a cabaret brawl; Jocasta in the

COMÉDIE-FRANÇAISE. — *OEDIPE ROI*, tragédie de Sophocle, traduite en vers par M. Jules Lacroix; musique de M. Edmond Membrée.
Voir page 574.

4. *Oedipe-Roi* at Comédie Française with Mounet-Sully in title role, from *L'Univers illustré* 20 August 1881

vernacular of the street becomes for him 'a woman of the people' (*une femme du peuple*). Seen thus in the raw, Mounet-Sully is suddenly struck by the passionate intensity of all the characters, and claims to be able to reveal to himself the Theban tragedy in all its sublime horror.[58]

By stripping off the layers of self and text, Mounet-Sully is of course anticipating the parallel that Sigmund Freud so eloquently expressed between the experience of watching *Oedipus Tyrannus* and the practice of psychoanalysis. If Freud found the source of his psychoanalytic theory in Sophocles' treatment of the Oedipus myth, it is hardly surprising that Mounet-Sully's interpretation of the role made such an impact on him.[59] When Mounet-Sully included Hamlet in his repertoire in 1886, one is tempted to infer that this prompted or possibly confirmed Freud's linking of the Sophoclean and Shakespearean tragedies in relation to his theory of the Oedipus complex.

OEDIPUS AND THE SCULPTURAL IDEAL

Reviewers from around the world speak of the plasticity of Mounet-Sully's movements, of the power of gesture in his performance. These gestures could be intensely, actively physical – he apparently threw the Shepherd to the ground in the interrogation scene in an effort to get the truth from him (much to the consternation of one conservative Athenian critic).[60] But, more famously, they were fluidly sculptural. He claimed that each of his postures, each of his gestures and even the fold of his chiton came from his careful observation of statues in the Louvre and other museums (see Figure 5). A sculptor himself, he kept a mask he had made of the blinded Oedipus in his workshop, and used it for inspiration for his own (unmasked) expression in the play. One night Joséphin Péladan claimed he could detect at least a hundred statues in Mounet-Sully's performance in *Oedipe-Roi*.[61] Oedipus' growing anxiety in the pivotal scene with Jocasta was said to have been subtly conveyed as Mounet-Sully gazed absently into the distance and slightly raised his arm (no doubt in direct imitation of some Graeco-Roman sculpture).[62]

Mounet-Sully's female counterpart, Sarah Bernhardt – the leading lady at the Comédie Française until 1880, when she became actor–manager at the Théâtre de la Renaissance and later at the Théâtre-Sarah-Bernhardt – shared both his talent and his interest in the visual arts. For Bernhardt, as for Mounet-Sully, her work as a sculptress was parallel to and interdependent with her career in the theatre. When Francisque Sarcey commented upon her performance as Phèdre in 1893, he detected 'an artistic beauty that made one quiver with admiration, the look of a fine statue'.[63] What is notable here is that

5. H. Bellery-Desfontaines, engraving, of Mounet-Sully as Oedipe in the Comédie Française production of *Oedipe-Roi*

these two outstanding French actors from the end of the nineteenth century and the beginning of the twentieth were not only both sculptors; they were both also understood to 'self-sculpt' as they performed on the stage.[64] Their performances were intrinsically sculptural and had no need (we infer) of a Pygmalion to mould them – they were themselves, the creators/sculptors of their performances. In this sense, they represent the culmination and the end of a long tradition in European theatre history, in which the theatrical ideal was classical and essentially sculptural.[65]

The sculptural ideal in the modern theatre can be traced back, at least, to Winckelmann's privileging of sculpture in ancient art in his *Geschichte der Kunst des Altertums* (published 1764),[66] and it became common currency in the literary sphere through Schlegel's Vienna *Lectures*. If sculpture, according to Winckelmann, was the supreme ancient art form and the condition to which all other arts aspired to a greater or lesser extent, the most sculptural art form, according to Schlegel, was tragedy. In practical and popular terms, as we have seen, this formulation was readily translated into a 'sculptural' style of tragic acting, in which the tragedian assumed set 'attitudes' which were copiously learned from well-known (mostly Graeco-Roman) copies of statues on display in museums. Just as Quintillian had advised Roman orators to model their stance upon statuary, so now we find that late eighteenth- and nineteenth-century handbooks for actors (such as William Cooke's *The Elements of Drama Criticism* of 1775)[67] and indeed the playwrights themselves (notably Goethe) recommend the study of ancient statues in order to achieve (in Cooke's terms) that 'grace, and give that je ne sais quoi, so much admired in the whole department of action'.[68] The sculptural ideal involved a fixity of stance – an 'attitude', a marmoreal appearance (actresses often white-washed their arms to achieve this effect), a use of cotton and/or muslin (often dampened to enhance the folds).

In this sense, Mounet-Sully was one of the Winckelmann-esque statues that dominated the nineteenth-century European stage. He had been drawn to the theatre because it united all the arts – as a talented painter, sculptor, designer, pianist and singer, here was an art form which would engage and satisfy all his talents. He attended a course by the French archaeologist and curator of oriental antiquities and ancient vases at the Louvre, Léon Heuzey, who published two books on Greek costume (*Du Principe de la draperie antique* (Paris 1893) and *Le Péplos des femmes grecques étudié sur le modèle vivant* (Paris 1921)). What made Heuzey's classes especially notable was that each one ended with a practical session, when the students dressed live models with costumes.[69] According to Heuzey, Greek costume was 'natural' for the human form and the very formlessness of Greek dress constituted its appeal: it depended literally on the human form and its movements for its shape; and once shaped by the human body, the costume obeyed human *gestes*, the undulations of human passions, as well as the effect of light and shade.

In many ways the 'sculptural' performance was both a cause and a product of the nineteenth-century star system, for the sculptural style depended absolutely on stage pictorialism, even though theorists very often felt it was being defined against this (Schlegel, for example, deemed modern music and the picturesque to be in contradistinction to the sculptural). This style grew out of the proscenium arch theatre (which in turn became established once the introduction of limelight enabled the actor to retreat behind the proscenium and still be fully seen by the audience), with its increasingly archaeologically detailed sets. It was often noted that Mounet-Sully's statuesque Oedipus carried an otherwise indifferent production; and the Theban chorus very often receded, literally and metaphorically, into the background as he dominated the set.[70]

Exceptionally, Mounet-Sully appears to have had the verbal dexterity and the sheer physical presence to self-sculpt beyond the proscenium – in the newly excavated and reconstructed open-air Roman theatres in southern Europe.[71] In 1899 after the company had performed *Oedipe Roi* in the Theatre of Dionysus in Athens, under the aegis of the French Archaeological Society, Mounet-Sully's carriage was unhitched from its horses and borne aloft by a jubilant crowd through the streets of Athens: 'Long live Mounet-Sully! Long live

France!' chanted the ecstatic crowd. Similar cries greeted him in Romania. Nation and star actor had become inseparable in the minds of foreign audiences; and Oedipus was reincarnated as an honorary Frenchman, or, more importantly, through the power of Mounet-Sully's interpretation of Sophocles' tragic role, Oedipus had become Everyman.[72]

Even though the sculptural ideal in the theatre fell from fashion in the age of high Naturalism, it lived on largely uncensored through the performances of Mounet-Sully right up to his death in 1916. His final appearance in the theatre was as Oedipe in the Courtyard of the Sorbonne on 11 July 1915. After Oedipus had left the scene, one reviewer commented that he suddenly realised that there were two statues left on the set, which no one had previously noticed.[73] Mounet-Sully had so dominated the space that even the setting had receded into the background. This sculptured actor – as so very rarely had happened in the nineteenth century – had exceptionally managed to transcend, rather than be contained by, the theatrical space in which he performed.

NOTES

1. John Dennis, *The Impartial Critic* (London 1693), 190.
2. Hippolyte Jules Pilet de La Mesnardière, *La Poëtique* (Paris 1640), H.
3. J.D. Lyons, *Kingdom of Disorder: The Theory of Tragedy in Classical France* (West Lafayette, IN 1999), 145.
4. There was an earlier Italian vernacular version, *Edippo* by Anguillara (1565), but there is no evidence that this was performed. For discussion, see Salvatore Di Maria, 'Italian reception of Greek tragedy in culture', in Justina Gregory (ed.), *A Companion to Greek Tragedy* (Oxford 2005), 428–44.
5. David Kimbell, *Italian Opera* (Cambridge 1991), 36–9. The score for the four odes is extant and is reproduced in L. Schrade, *La Représentation d'Edipo Tiranno au theatro Olimpico (Vicenza 1585): Étude suivi d'une édition critique de la tragédie de Sophocle par Orsatto Giustiniani et de la musique des choeurs par Andrea Gabrieli* (Paris 1960).

6. A. Ingegneri, 'Del modo di Rappresentare le favole Sceniche', in Schrade (1960), 57, 59. Cf. Antonio Riccoboni, a professor from Padua, in his letter to the mayor, reprinted in R. D. Dawe (ed.), *Sophocles: The Classical Heritage* (New York and London, 1996), 10, who complains that the words were not sufficiently audible.

7. Riccoboni, in Dawe (1996), 2. For the civic dimension of Giustiniani's translation, see P. Vidal-Naquet, 'Oedipus at Vicenza and Paris', in J.-P. Vernant and P. Vidal-Naquet, *Myth and Tragedy in Ancient Greece*, 2 vols. (Cambridge, MA 1988), vol. I, 366–7.

8. J. T. Oosting, *Andrea Palladio's Teatro Olimpico* (Ann Arbor 1981), 141; and J. S. Ackerman, *Palladio* (Harmondsworth 1966), 178. Cf. Schrade (1960), who dates the decision to 1580.

9. Vitruvius, *I dieci libri dell'architettvra*, 1556 (tr. et commentati da monsignor Danielle Barbaro); Kimbell (1991), 36, for the influence of Orange.

10. Schrade (1960), 55.

11. See Filippo Pigafetta (1585) and Giacomo Dolfin (1585) for praise of the production, repr. in A. Gallo, *La Prima Rappresentazione al Teatro Olimpico con I progetti e le relazioni dei contemporanei* (Milan 1973), 53–8. Cf. Riccoboni, in Dawe (1996), 1–12, for his criticism of the overly lavish costumes of Oedipus and Jocasta, of the absence of choral dance, of the insubordinate chorus leader, of the dirge-like choral singing where the words were incomprehensible, and of the overly youthful Jocasta.

12. See Ackerman (1966), 180; and Di Maria, in Gregory (2005), 435.

13. See Michael Lurje, *Die Suche nach der Schuld: Sophokles' Oedipus Rex, Aristoteles' Poetik und das Tragödienverständnis der Neuzeit* (Leipzig 2004) for the early modern reception of Sophocles' tragedy generally.

14. C. Biet, *Oedipe en monarchie: Tragédie et théorie juridique à l'âge classique* (Paris 1994), 16–17. There was no new translation of Seneca until 1795.

15. For the French versions and Rapin and Brumoy see Biet (1994); for English Oedipuses at this time see Edith Hall and Fiona Macintosh *Greek Tragedy and the British Theatre* 1660–1914 (Oxford 2005), 215–42. P. L. Rudnytsky, *Freud and Oedipus* (New York 1987) erroneously dates the 'discovery' of Sophocles' tragedy to the German Romantic period, whereas both the earlier English and French proto-revolutionary Oedipuses show that this comes considerably earlier.

16. A. Joannidès, *La Comédie-Française de 1680 à 1920* (Paris 1921), s.v. Corneille and *Oedipe*.

17. For details see P. Hoffmann, 'L'Oedipe de Voltaire: Une Tragédie de la liberté', in J. Söring, O. Poltera and N. Duplain (eds.), *Le Théâtre antique et sa réception: Hommage à Walter Spoerri* (Frankfurt am Main 1994), 109, n. 1.

18. Voltaire, 'Troisième Lettre, contenant la critique de l'*Oedipe* de Sophocle', in *Oedipe Tragédie (avec Lettres écrites par l'auteur)* (Paris 1719), 103.

19. Biet (1994), 261. *Oedipe*'s initial run was from 18 November 1718 until 21 January 1719; it was then revived twice in March 1719 and twice in April 1719; and eighteen times in August 1720. This made *Oedipe* the most performed of all first plays by any author to date. See H.C. Lancaster, *French Tragedy in the Times of Louis XV and Voltaire 1715– 1774*, 2 vols. (New York 1977), vol. I, 53–4.

20. D. Jory. 'The Role of Greek tragedy in the search for legitimate authority under the *ancien régime*', in M.G. Badir and D.J. Langdon (eds.), *Eighteenth-Century French Theatre: Aspects and Contexts* (Edmonton, Alberta 1986), 12–13.

21. R.S. Ridgway, *La Propagande philosophique dans les tragédies de Voltaire*, Studies on Voltaire and the Eighteenth Century XV (Oxford 1961).

22. Voltaire, *Oedipe*, in *Théâtre du XVIIe Vol. I*, ed. J. Truchet (Paris 1972: Pléiade), Act II sc. IV, lines 531–2, 413. Subsequent references to the play appear in parentheses in the main text.

23. Biet (1994).

24. Voltaire, 'Sixième Lettre', in Voltaire (1719), 129.

25. M. Dominique, *Oedipe travesti: Parodie en vers de l'Oedipe de M. de Voltaire*, in M. Dominique, *Les Parodies du nouveau Théâtre Italien ou recueil des Parodies* Vol. I (Paris 1738), vol. I, 1–38.

26. 'Les dieux veulent du sang, et sont seuls écoutés'; 'Un prêtre, qu'il soit, quelque dieu qui l'inspire / Doit prier pour ses rois, et non pas les maudire'; 'Qu'eussé je été sans lui, rien que le fils du roi'. Voltaire (1972), 405, 423, 399. For comment see Lancaster (1977), vol. I, 53 ff.

27. Hall and Macintosh (2005), 215–42.

28. M. de La Tournelle produced four alone between 1729 and 1731, see Biet (1994), 17–18.

29. Pierre Brumoy, *Le Théâtre des Grecs*, 3 vols. (Paris 1730); published in English as Charlotte Lennox, *The Greek Theatre of Father Brumoy*, 3 vols. (London 1759), vol. I, cix. René Rapin, *Les Réflexions sur la poétique de ce temps et sur les ouvrages des poètes anciens et modernes* [Paris 1674], ed. E.T. Dubois (Geneva 1970), Chapter 20, 182.

30. Biet (1994), *passim*.

31. For Léonard's *Oedipe-Roi ou la fatalité* see Biet (1994), 314–15. For Marie Antoinette's promise to Sacchini see E.F. Jourdain, *Dramatic Theory and Practice in France 1690–1808* (New York 1921; repr. New York 1968), 190–1.

32. Biet (1994), 314–15.

33. John Lough, *Seventeenth-Century French Drama: The Background* (Oxford 1979), 73.

34. H.L. Nostrand, *Le Théâtre antique et à la antique en France de 1840 à 1900* (Paris 1934), 12.

35. Joannidès (1921), s.v. Voltaire's *Oedipe*.

36. 'La Grèce est sortie du tombeau', *L'Artiste*, 26 May 1844, 61–2. Cited in Nostrand (1934), 42. Sophocles' *Antigone* opened at the Hoftheater in the Neues Palais in Potsdam in 1841, having benefited from the combined efforts of leading classical scholars and theatre practitioners, and not least from the contribution of the composer Felix Mendelssohn, who provided the choral settings. See F. Macintosh, 'Tragedy in performance: nineteenth- and twentieth-century productions', in P.E. Easterling (ed.), *The Cambridge Companion to Greek Tragedy* (Cambridge 1997), 286–8.

37. See H. Patin, *Études tragiques grecs* (3rd edn, Paris 1865), vol. III, 29 n. Cited in Nostrand (1934), 47.

38. A.W. Schlegel, *Vorlesungen über dramatische Kunst und Litteratur*, 3 vols. (Heidelberg 1809–11); published in English as *A Course of Lectures on Dramatic Art and Literature*, trans. J. Black (London 1815).

39. Nostrand (1934), 200–14.

40. J. Lacroix, *Oeuvres*, vol. I, *Théâtre* (Paris 1874), 5: 'fidèlement, religieusement, et le transporter sur la scène française avec ses choeurs, vers pour vers, sans changements, sans nul sacrifice au goût moderne, simple et grandiose, dans toute son horreur tragique'.

41. 'Applaudissez, Athéniens! C'est du Sophocle!', cited by P. de Saint-Victor, *La Presse*, 26 September 1858; and A. Denis, *Revue et gazettes des théâtres*,

19 September 1858, repr. in J. Lacroix, *Oeuvres: Vol. III Opinions et jugements littéraires sur les pièces de théâtre* (Paris 1874), 293, 299.

42. J. de Premaray, *La Patrie*, 27 September 1858, in Lacroix, vol. III (1874), 300.

43. P. Boyer, *L'Artiste*, 12 December 1858, 228–33. See Nostrand (1934), 82. The cast list to Lacroix's text (Lacroix, vol. I (1874), 8) refers to a Chorus of Elders and a Chorus of Theban Women – as well as the two young Theban girls and a vast cast of extras, which includes priests, servants and 'people' (*peuple*).

44. '*Créon sort, accompagné d'une partie du peuple. On s'eloigne d'Oedipe, comme pour désapprover sa violence.*' Lacroix, vol. I (1874), 47: Act II sc. III.

45. 'Non, il fallait punir! – Aujourd'hui, sous mes lois / Est rangé ce pays, dont sa main fut gardienne'; 'Veux-tu désobéir à ma loi souveraine?' Lacroix, vol. I (1874), 22, 44.

46. Lacroix, vol. III (1874), 287: 'les agitations récentes de la société'.

47. 'Je ne sais rien de plus beau que ce Titan foudroyé ... Il pleure, et avec quelle abondance de larmes! avec quels accents de tendresse déchirante! Il n'y avait guère de femmes dans la salle; on aurait pu les compter. Mais j'en voyais quelqu'unes qui s'essuyaient les yeux'. F. Sarcey, *Opinion nationale*, 5 August 1861, in Lacroix, vol. III (1874), 306. The parts of Créon and Jocaste were taken by Jouanni and Mme Nathalie respectively. For full details see A. Penesco, *Mounet-Sully et la partition intérieure* (Lyon 2000), 17.

48. Lacroix, vol. I (1874), 6.

49. E. Thierry, *Le Pays*, 27 September 1858, in Lacroix, vol. III (1874), 296.

50. A. Escande, in *Union*, 12 August 1861, in Lacroix, vol. III (1874), 309.

51. J. Mounet-Sully, *Souvenirs d'un tragédien* (Paris 1914), 24–5.

52. Mounet-Sully (1914), 127: 'et chacun de ses cris est comme un secouement de chaînes invisibles'; 'Oedipe représente la révolte de l'instinct et de l'intelligence contre l'aveugle fatalité et la défaite terminale de l'homme.'

53. L. Vernay, 'Chez Mounet-Sully: À propos d'Oedipe Roi', *Revue D'art Dramatique* 11 (July–September 1888), 136–40: 'je n'ai vu qu'un homme, qu'un roi malheureux, j'ignore les secrets des dieux et je ne crois pas aux prédictions des oracles quand elles ne sont pas conformés à la justice. C'est le côté humain qui m'occupe toujours'.

54. Mounet-Sully (1914), 127: 'une responsabilité sacrée pèse sur moi'. He maintains also that he always has 'un respect religieux. J'entre en scène, chaque fois, comme un prêtre monte à l'autel'.

55. Armand Praviel, 'Le Théâtre en plein air', in *Le Correspondant* 204 (25 July 1910), 264–87. Cited in Nostrand (1934), 183.

56. See E. Noël and E. Stoullig, *Les Annales du théâtre et de la musique* (1881) (Paris 1882), 90.

57. Vernay (1888), 138: 'Je suis avec lui dans la complète intimité, je l'interroge, je discute'.

58. Ibid., 139.

59. Ernest Jones, *Sigmund Freud: Life and Work*, vol. I, *The Young Freud 1856–1900* (London 1953), 194, refers to the impact Mounet-Sully's performance had on Freud when he saw it in 1885. There is, however, considerable doubt that Freud actually saw the star perform in the role. There were no performances of *Oedipe Roi* in 1885 or 1886. Indeed there were no performances following the two in 1884 until 1888 (see Joannides (1921), s.v. *Oedipe*, but A. Soubies, *La Comédie Française depuis l'Époque Romantique 1825–1895* (Paris 1895) claims there were nineteen performances in 1887. See Richard H. Armstrong, 'Theory and Theatricality: Classical Drama and the Early Formation of Psychoanalysis', *Classical and Modern Literature* 26 (2006), 79–109, n. 11. See also Penesco (2000), 119.

60. Giannis Sideris, *To Archaio Theatro sti Nea Elliniki Skini* (Ancient Greek Theatre on the Modern Stage) (Athens 1976), 155–6. The conservative critic in question was G. Mistriotis, the professor of classics, whose dogged adherence to a fossilised concept of the 'classical' (especially in relation to the language question in Greece) led to a riot following a performance of the *Oresteia* in 1901. See P. Michelakis, 'Introduction', in F. Macintosh, P. Michelakis, E. Hall and O. Taplin (eds.), *Agamemnon in Performance 458 BC to AD 2004* (Oxford 2005), 16.

61. Penesco (2000), 110. See the painting by Louis Eduard Fournier – in the Musée Carnavalet, Paris, oil on canvas – of Mounet-Sully in his *loge*, in a typical sculptural *geste*, putting on make-up for the performance in 1893. For his mask see Vernay (1888), 139.

62. Francisque Sarcey detects a 'façon de trahir son inquiétude naissante par un mouvement du bras qui se lève et par un regard plongé dans

le vague.' Cited in a review of the press in *Revue d'Art Dramatique* XI (July–September 1888), 155.

63. Francisque Sarcey, *Quarante ans de théâtre*, 8 vols. (Paris 1900), vol. III, 8, cited in John Stokes, Michael R. Booth and Susan Basnett, *Bernhardt, Terry, Duse: The Actress in Her Time* (Cambridge 1988), 8.

64. Cf. J. Cocteau, *Portrait du Mounet-Sully* (Paris 1945): 'ce tragédien ne s'habillait pas, il se sculptait, il se drapait de telle sorte que la laine devenait du marbre et formait au tour de la personne des plus solonnels et définitifs' ('this tragedian doesn't dress himself, he self-sculpts, he drapes himself in such a way that the linen becomes marble-like and wraps itself around his person most solemnly and definitively').

65. See G. Marshall, *Actresses on the Victorian Stage: Feminine Performance and the Galatea Myth* (Cambridge 1998).

66. Johann Joachim Winckelmann, *Geschichte der Kunst des Alterthums*, 2 vols. (Dresden 1764).

67. William Cooke, *The Elements of Drama Criticism* (London 1775).

68. Ian Jenkins, *Archaeologists and Aesthetes in the Sculpture Galleries of the British Museum 1800–1939* (London 1995), 20, for the meaning of 'je ne sais quoi'.

69. Penesco (2000), 95. This was a widely held view at the time in England as well, where the Healthy and Artistic Dress Union was advocating dress reform, and especially the Greek style, in close association with the political emancipation of women.

70. E.g. L. McCarthy, *Myself and My Friends* (London 1933), 302: 'Nothing lived in it except Mounet-Sully, for whose acting no praise would be extravagant.'

71. He performed regularly in the Roman theatre at Orange from 1888.

72. Sideris (1976), 153; F. Lolière, *La Comédie Française: Histoire de la Maison de Molière de 1658 à 1907* (Paris 1907), 396.

73. Penesco (2000), 91.

CHAPTER 4

OEDIPUS AND THE DIONYSIAC

The classical/sculptural ideal, the supreme theatrical exemplar of which was the art of Mounet-Sully, was in reality a Romantic construct. Yet it remained largely unchallenged until the middle of the nineteenth century when German philosophers, notably Schopenhauer and later Nietzsche, together with the practice of Richard Wagner, made a theoretical and practical assault upon the privileged art form.

Schlegel's assertion in his Vienna lectures between 1808 and 1812 of the primacy of ancient sculpture over what he designated the modern privileging of a degenerate musical ideal was very soon challenged by Schopenhauer, who demoted the visual arts in general, and sculpture in particular, to the bottom of the aesthetic scale and concomittantly elevated music to the top. This negative antithesis between music and the visual arts was later in the century refined by Nietzsche towards a new synthesis located within Greek tragedy, in which the sculptural (now designated the Apolline, with its individuation, restraint and formal beauty) meets with and holds in check the life-enhancing/death-dealing Dionysiac music, with its collective, intoxicating, rapturous and murky depths.[1]

If the summation of the sculptural ideal in the theatre was found in Mounet-Sully's rendering of Lacroix's *Oedipe-Roi*, this chapter explores the way in which the *Oedipus Rex* of Max Reinhardt came to exemplify the newly configured Nietzschean relationship between the Apolline and the Dionysiac elements. Reinhardt's *Oedipus Rex*, in a version by Hugo von Hofmannsthal, was premièred in the Musikfesthalle in Munich on 25 September 1910 and went on to be performed throughout Europe until well into the 1930s (Figure 6). The French and the German/Austrian production were very often

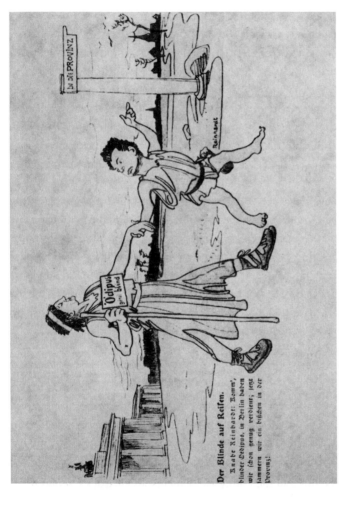

6. Young Reinhardt leading the blind Oedipus on a tour of the provinces in a cartoon postcard c.1910

held to be in contradistinction with one another – they overlapped for at least six years[2] – and each performance style had its adherents and its adversaries. Indeed there is a very real sense in which these two productions – one significantly named after its star performer, the other after its director – shaped twentieth-century scholarly responses to the play.

Sometime in early 1915, after several years of direct involvement in the triennial Cambridge University Greek play, John Sheppard concludes the Preface to his translation of *Oedipus Tyrannus* with the following comment: 'If you doubt whether in these days Greek tragedy still matters, you may learn the answer in Paris'.[3] Owing to the disruption of the Great War years, Sheppard's own translation of *Oedipus Tyrannus* did not in fact appear in print until 1920, some four years after the death of Mounet-Sully at the age of seventy-five. For Sheppard, Mounet-Sully's performance is proof that Greek tragedy still matters; and the formal beauty of the production demonstrates to him that 'Greek drama, not bolstered up by sensationalism, and not watered with sentimentality, has power to hold and move a modern audience'. The French production, in Sheppard's view, stood in stark contrast to the 'lavish, barbaric, turbulent' production of Reinhardt, which had opened at Covent Garden in London in January 1912.[4] According to Sheppard, Reinhardt's actors

> raged and fumed and ranted, rushing hither and thither with a violence of gesticulation which, in spite of all their effort, was eclipsed and rendered insignificant by the yet more violent rushes, screams and contortions of a quite gratuitous crowd.[5]

Sheppard was not alone in objecting to the crowd of about a hundred extras that was used in the London production (see Figure 7), some of whose members literally invaded the audience's space as they entered through the auditorium. The semi-naked torch bearers who preceded the crowd made occasional physical contact with audience members seated at the ends of rows. There was too much movement in the production for Sheppard, in marked contrast

7. Postcard of Mr Martin-Harvey as Oedipus in the London production of Reinhardt's *Oedipus Rex* at Covent Garden, January 1912

to the stillness that he and others praised in Mounet-Sully's performance. But what offended Sheppard, in particular, was that Reinhardt's
production was a kind of 'total theatre' assaulting the audience's senses
on every level; and instead of clarity – as had been the case with the
Mounet-Sully production – Reinhardt brought only obscurity,
summed up best, according to Sheppard, by the palace at the opening
of the play that was a 'black cavern of mystery'.[6] Hofmannsthal had
already provided the libretto for Strauss's *Elektra* (1909), which had
shocked and enthralled audiences by showing Greek myth as savage
and primitive.[7] And here in the production of *Oedipus Rex* audiences
were being offered further evidence of Nietszchean-inspired insights
into the ancient Greek world, with the collective Dionysiac experience
being held somewhat precariously in check by the Apolline action on
the raised platform.

It was not simply scholars who defined the Reinhardt production in
opposition to the French *Oedipe-Roi*. Lillah McCarthy, who took the
part of Jocasta in the London production of the German/Austrian
play, comments in her memoirs that the Comédie Française
production

> was cold, classical. Chorus: two women dressed in French classical style.
> No movement, the figures of the actors motionless, carved in marble.
> Nothing lived in it except Mounet-Sully, for whose superb acting no
> praise would be extravagant, but oh! for a Reinhardt to breathe into the
> other actors breath of life.[8]

Lillah herself received plaudits for her performance as Jocasta; and
whilst the startling performance of John Martin-Harvey in the title
role in London did earn him praise from many quarters, his earlier
experience as a star in melodrama seems to have denied him the
gravitas accorded to his French counterpart. Whilst the first part of
the play was generally deemed a success, the second half was said to
have resorted to melodrama. There was, for example, much criticism
of Oedipus' full-bodied assault upon the Shepherd, upon whom he
apparently leapt half way down the stalls and then proceeded to drag

8. Programme for the London production of *Oedipus Rex* at the Royal
Opera House, Covent Garden, January 1912

up the steps towards the palace.[9] Whilst Mounet-Sully had similarly
leapt upon the Shepherd, his movements and gestures were widely
acclaimed; in Martin-Harvey's case, by contrast, it was his voice alone
that attracted attention.[10] In the Nietzschean equation that the

Reinhardt production so vividly represented, the individual body was subsumed by the overwhelming Dionysiac collective.

However, it was not only the startlingly new performance style that made the Reinhardt *Oedipus* so significant in Britain. Its prominence was also guaranteed by the central role it played in an important moment in Britain's social and cultural history, when Sophocles' tragedy became embroiled with the Censor. In this sense, the Covent Garden production (Figure 8) – with a different cast, designer and eventually additional music – was in many ways of equal importance to the German/Austrian one that performed throughout Central and Eastern Europe.[11]

'PEOPLE'S THEATRE'

When the Russian theatre director Vsevolod Meyerhold writes about 'stylized theatre' in 1907, at a time when he was experimenting with alternatives to the theatrical naturalism of his master at the Moscow Art Theatre, Stanislavski, he says, 'The stylized theatre liberates the actor from all scenery, creating a three-dimensional art in which he can employ natural, sculptural plasticity.'[12] Mounet-Sully's outdoor performances, and especially that at the Sorbonne mentioned at the end of the previous chapter, may well stand as living testament to Meyerhold's 'natural, sculptural plasticity.'

However, finding new spaces generally led to a realisation that new patterns of movement needed to be sought. Indeed Meyerhold himself discovered in his own productions that if the performer and the set moved closer to the audience, the actors move as if in bas-relief.[13] And whereas in Mounet-Sully's classical/sculptural ideal, the body was merely a means of conveying the cerebral and the emotional qualities of the protagonist; now, for the Modernist directors, the sheer physical presence of all the actors (not just the protagonist) was to become a central part of the performance. In Reinhardt's case, he discovered that by moving his actors into new spaces – notably the arena space of the circus – he was able to energise the entire production by reconfiguring the relations between audience and performer. In Munich Reinhardt built the circus arena in direct imitation of the ancient Greek *orchestra*; he then went on to transfer the production to the genuine circus spaces of Vienna (the Zirkus Renz on 10 October 1910 and the following year in May at the Zirkus Busch) and Berlin (at the Zirkus Schumann, from 7 November 1910, where *Oedipus Rex* secured its iconic status with thirty performances). Thereafter Reinhardt always looked for an arena or circus space in which to stage his productions; and with the influence of Romain Rolland's *Le Théâtre du peuple* (Paris 1903), in particular, he developed his 'Theatre for the 5000', in which the theatre was to provide the site for political unity through a combination of high and popular culture in a festival atmostphere.[14]

Wagner had decried the 'awful solitude of one man carved out of stone' and advocated 'a countless multitude of real living people' in his music-theatre, but he had in reality no desire to include the ancient chorus in his highly hierarchical version of the *Gesamtkunstwerk*. At Bayreuth the chorus was dispensed with altogether and the modern orchestra acted as substitute, thereby making music the dominant element.[15] It was only once Reinhardt had experimented with a Greek chorus in *Oedipus Rex* and in his other Greek productions – *Elektra* (Kleines Theater, Berlin, 1903), *Medea* (Kleines Theater, Berlin, 1904), *Lysistrata* (Kammerspiele, Berlin, 1908), and the *Oresteia* (Ausstellungs Halle, Munich, 1912) – that the ancient chorus rediscovered its role on the modern stage. Reinhardt's work with vast crowds of extras, which developed alongside the experiments of the pioneers of what is now called 'modern dance' (notably Isadora Duncan) and the Ballets Russes, meant that the true limits of the theatrical sculptural metaphor were finally understood as the focal shift from the individual to the group became absolute. At first Reinhardt did not employ a singing chorus in his *Oedipus Rex* – the incidental music for trumpets and drums from behind the stage, by Reinhardt's young Swedish musical director, Einar Nilson, did not accompany the odes which were simply chanted. But when Martin-Harvey toured with the production it included musical settings for the odes by William H. Hudson, which had been written in the Dorian and Phrygian modes.[16] Finally, then, the Wagnerian *Gesamtkunstwerk* in which movement, speech and song figured equally was realised.

Reinhardt was renowned for his direction of crowd scenes, but in Munich and later in Berlin he put those skills to a severe test by directing a crowd of three hundred extras who represented the citizens of Thebes, together with a chorus of twenty-seven Theban elders (there were fewer in both the crowd and the chorus in London). Few who saw the production failed to be impressed by the sheer scale and grandeur of the formal patterns of movement. The play began with the trumpet clarion and the entrance of the half-naked torch bearers, who streamed through the darkened circular performance space. They were followed by the vast crowd, who engulfed the space in front of the palace steps and began chanting for Oedipus. A murky blue light broke through the darkness, partially revealing the chanting, groaning crowd; and after a strong yellow light had been cast over the altar and steps, the entrance of Alexander Moissi's Oedipus from the central doors, dressed in a brilliant white gown, was captured in spotlight. If the Mounet-Sully production had downplayed the Theban context in order to highlight the sufferings of Oedipus in his relations with the gods, here was a Nietzschean-inspired production in which individual (Apolline) suffering was to be seen against a background of the general (Dionysiac) suffering of the chorus/crowd.

But however major the monumental aspects of the production were, Reinhardt was also celebrated for his attention to naturalistic detail – he had trained at the Deutsches Theater under the so-called father of stage naturalism, Otto Brahm; and Hofmannsthal's version, no less than the version of Jules Lacroix, focused on the individual suffering of Oedipus. Hofmannsthal's text dates from 1905, and had been written as part two of a trilogy which began with *Ödipus und die Sphinx* and was to end with the events of *Oedipus at Colonus.* Indeed

Hofmannsthal's thinking about Oedipus at this time did not stop with the idea of a trilogy: he produced two further plays – *Ödipus-Monolog* and a fragment called *Die Königin Jokaste*. Although the third play in the trilogy never saw the light of day, the other plays all received some kind of performance between 1905 and 1906.[17]

The first play in the trilogy encompasses Oedipus' fatal encounter with Laius at the crossroads and culminates in the incestuous marriage and a strong note of foreboding. Hofmannsthal's Oedipus is a thoroughly Modernist, fragmented hero who needs to find himself through the extraordinary unfolding of the events of his life – his journey may be a forward one in terms of plot time, but it is in reality retrospective, analogous to an analysand on his journey of self-discovery in psychoanalysis.[18] But when Freud saw the Reinhardt production of Hofmannsthal's *Oedipus Rex* in 1910,[19] he might well have been puzzled. For even if the Apolline individual was central to the director's conception, and central to his text, there are many moments in the production when the Dionysiac collective breaks through the dykes. When the crowd surged through the darkened auditorium at the start of the play in London, it reminded *The Times* critic of 'some huge living monster'.[20] In this sense, paradoxically, the German/Austrian production turns out to be less Freudian than Mounet-Sully's interpretation, notwithstanding the Freudian qualities detectable in Hofmannsthal's text.

The startling light score in the opening scene, with the torchbearers and burning offerings upon the altar in the darkened auditorium, owed much to the pioneering work of Adolphe Appia. The lights were operated from on high in the theatre by technicians who were clearly visible to the audience. Especially effective was the black set against which the principal actors stood out in sharp relief; and many noted the ingenious use of the spotlight both to highlight and to isolate Oedipus at moments of great tension.

Reinhardt's three performance levels in Alfred Roller's design were recognised as being heavily indebted to Edward Gordon Craig.[21] The space in front of the palace, with its black marble facade and columns, was reserved for the principal actors; the palace steps, with the altar midway, acted as the gathering place for the chorus; and the circular space in front of, and on a level with, the audience was the preserve of the crowd. Reinhardt made especially good use of these contrasting levels to heighten the pitch and to amplify the emotional range in his production. We have already heard how Oedipus' indecorous descent into the lower space to drag the Theban Shepherd up to the palace gates caused considerable discomfort to many spectators. Even greater shock waves were felt when Reinhardt sought to alter the ending of Sophocles' text (and indeed Hofmannsthal's too) by having his Oedipus make an intrinsically Nietzschean, cathartic exit from Thebes, as he groped his way through the audience under the spot-light. This non-Sophoclean ending offended many (Oedipus, it was averred, should have exited through 'those great copper gates, which should have blotted him out like a symbol of blindness'[22]). But it was deemed by others to be so effective that many audience members averted their gaze as Oedipus passed them by, his bloody face picked out in the spotlight in the otherwise darkened auditorium. Reinhardt's 'people's theatre' had achieved its desired effect: the audience was being united in a theatrical experience in which affective participation was impossible to resist.

STAGING SOPHOCLES' OEDIPUS IN LONDON

From 1911 Reinhardt began looking for a London venue for his *Oedipus Rex*. Pioneers of staging Greek plays in England – notably Granville Barker, whose productions of Euripides' plays in Gilbert Murray's translations had been performed at the Court Theatre from 1907 – had seen the Berlin production and were determined to bring it to London. Barker had gone to Berlin in October 1910 and wrote enthusiastically to Murray about what he had seen.[23] In mid-February 1911, Reinhardt's emissary, Richard Ordynski, came to London saying that Reinhardt himself wanted to stage a London production using

Murray's translation. The theatrical impresario the Great Lafayette had promised, together with Martin-Harvey, to finance the London production;[24] and Lafayette was proposing to build a new theatre in the Aldwych, in which the entire floor space would be made available for the performers. Negotiations were also conducted on Murray's behalf by Frederic Whelen to produce the play at the Kingsway Theatre. But with Lafayette's untimely death in a fire at the Edinburgh Empire in May 1911, all these plans came to nought. Reinhardt then turned his attention towards the Albert Hall – its dimensions were comparable with those of the Zirkus Schumann – but secular theatrical performance was prohibited there and no exception would be made in this case.[25] By the end of July there were firm plans for a production of the *Oedipus* in January 1912 at Covent Garden, with Martin-Harvey in the leading role and Barker's wife, Lillah McCarthy, as Jocasta. Covent Garden was thus the compromise – and the impossibility of allocating the entire stalls' space to the players resulted in the removal of only the first few rows of seats and the consequent necessity of using the central and side aisles for the entries and exits of the performers.

London audiences were overwhelmed by what they saw; and although certain aspects of the production came in for criticism, Martin-Harvey continued to tour with the play for many years after the event, winning for himself the same distinction as his hero Mounet-Sully of being a truly great Oedipus. Amongst the criticisms levelled at the production was that audiences were being offered undiluted Reinhardt rather than pure Sophocles, and this particular barb led Gilbert Murray to make a spirited defence of Reinhardt and his production in a letter to *The Times*:

> After all Professor Reinhardt knows ten times as much about the theatre as I do. His production has proved itself: it stands on its own feet, something vital, magnificent, unforgettable. And who knows if the more Hellenic production I dream of would be any of these?[26]

In the programme note to the play, the production was hailed as 'the first performance of the play in England since the seventeenth century'.[27] This is a clear allusion to Dryden and Lee's *Oedipus* of 1678; and although it ignores all revivals of the Dryden and Lee version, an early eighteenth-century *Oedipus* by J. Savill Faucit (1821), and both the recent Cambridge production of 1887 and the Comédie Française tour to Drury Lane in 1893, the claim to be the 'first ... since the seventeenth century' was not without some foundation.[28] In many ways, the significance of the London production cannot be fully grasped without reference to its immediate prehistory.

In 1904 Sir Herbert Beerbohm Tree – inspired by Mounet-Sully – had sent his secretary at His Majesty's Theatre, Frederick Whelen, to ask the Lord Chamberlain's Examiner of Plays about the possibility of mounting a production of Sophocles' tragedy in London. Despite the recent precedents in Cambridge and at Drury Lane, the examiner said that a London production was out of the question on account of its incestuous subject matter.[29] Tree's informal inquiry led to a flurry of activity. First and most significantly, W. B. Yeats seized the opportunity to use the ban as a means of putting the Abbey Theatre in Dublin on the theatrical map of the English-speaking world when it opened at the end of the year. The Lord Chamberlain's Office had no jurisdiction in Dublin; and it was recognised by the founders of the Abbey that there could be no more effective beginning to a national theatre's career than to stage a play which would enable the theatre to go down in history as the champion of intellectual freedom: Ireland would liberate the classics from the English tyranny.

When Yeats announced the establishment of the Abbey Theatre in 1904, he added:

> *Oedipus the King* is forbidden in London. A censorship created in the eighteenth century by Walpole, because somebody has [*sic*] written against election bribery, has been distorted by a puritanism which is not the less an English invention for being a pretended hatred of vice and a real hatred of intellect. Nothing has suffered so many persecutions as the intellect, though it is never persecuted under its own name.[30]

Yeats's interpretation of the censor's 'real hatred of intellect' masquerading behind a 'pretended hatred of vice' is highly apposite because comical treatments of unorthodox sexual relations were routinely licensed by the Lord Chamberlain's Office.[31] And the banning of Sophocles' tragedy was confirmation for Yeats that England was the mean-spirited stifler of the intellect that Ireland would proudly defy.

Almost immediately, Yeats wrote to Murray asking him to write a translation of Sophocles' play for the newly founded Irish theatre. Murray was working on Euripides at the time and had been since the late 1890s; he found Sophocles conventional in comparison.[32] He wrote to Yeats, declining his invitation on the grounds that the *Oedipus Tyrannus* was 'English-French-German ... all construction and no spirit', with 'nothing Irish about it'.[33] However, Yeats's letter clearly opened up new areas of concern to Murray:

> I am really distressed that the Censor objected to it. It ought to be played not perhaps at His Majesty's by Tree, but by Irving at the Lyceum, with a lecture before ... and after. And a public dinner. With speeches. By Cabinet Ministers.[34]

The banning of such a significant play, according to Murray, should be taken to heart by the British establishment. And, indeed, some years later when he had completed his own translation of Sophocles' proscribed tragedy, Murray (then Regius Professor of Greek at Oxford) appropriately became the person to take the play to the heart of the establishment, when it was his translation that was used in Reinhardt's production at Covent Garden in 1912.[35]

Martin-Harvey had (like Sir Herbert Tree) been inspired by Mounet-Sully's performance as Oedipus; and he approached W. L. Courtney, drama critic of the *Daily Telegraph*, to produce a free version of the play.[36] As a former classical scholar with an intimate knowledge of the professional stage, Courtney was an ideal choice. But despite his impeccable credentials, Courtney's version was denied a licence by the Examiner of Plays, George Alexander Redford. So significant was the ban that the rejected play was submitted as evidence before the Joint Select Committee in 1909; and its presence guaranteed that a high profile was granted to Greek tragedy in general, and

Sophocles' play in particular, throughout the proceedings of the committee.

Before considering the findings of the Joint Select Committee in detail, it is important to provide some background as to how Sophocles' play found itself at the centre of controversy at this time. Although between 1895 and 1909, out of some eight thousand plays submitted for licence, only thirty were banned,[37] amongst the thirty was Sophocles' *Oedipus Tyrannus*, which was being widely read by schoolboys and had been performed (as we have heard) by under-graduates at Cambridge in 1887. When the Shelley Society mounted a production of Shelley's controversial play about incest, *The Cenci*, at the Grand Theatre, Islington, some seventy years after it was written, Sophocles' tragedy became linked with it. An editorial in the *Era* of, 22 May 1886 insists that just because Greek drama has become very voguish,

> we must beware of mistaking a passing craze for a national artistic development. It would not do (to take a parallel instance) to suppose that because *The Cenci* has been placed on the stage and listened to with attention, not to say avidity, by a mixed audience of old men, young men, and maidens, that our public taste in matters of morality had become sufficiently degraded to permit of the sin of incest forming a common and acceptable motif for a modern drama.[38]

Indeed there were others, as we will see, who deemed the 'public taste in matters of morality' to be so delicate that the inclusion of 'the sin of incest' in any drama was problematic.

When the Shelley Society thrust *The Cenci* into the limelight, they thus established a similarly high profile for Sophocles' tragedy on account of the shared treatment of incest. And from 1886 until 1910, when Sophocles' play was finally granted a licence after much public pressure (*The Cenci* had to wait until 1922 to receive a licence) the fates of these two plays were inextricably linked, featuring prom-inently in almost every important debate concerning theatrical censor-ship. Furthermore, it may be argued that it was the eventual prising apart of the two plays that led to the dilution of the case against censorship in 1910, when the increasingly splintered opposition was left without a cause célèbre around which to rally.

The linking of the plays was perhaps inevitable given that both plots involved incest and parricide. Although Shelley drew on Sophocles' *Electra* as well during his composition of *The Cenci*, in the Preface to the published edition of the play he refers to the Oedipus plays, although he himself refrains from pointing to the obvious thematic parallels.[39] And the members of the Shelley Society followed his example in their Preface (written by John Todhunter), similarly invoking the Sophoclean precedent without drawing explicit parallels between the two plays.[40] Furthermore, a glance at the evidence given to the Joint Select Committee in 1909 shows that not only had the twinning of the plays become habitual by this time, but that the two playwrights were now united in the cause against censorship as well.[41] When the playwright Henry Arthur Jones was unable to attend the Joint Select Committee to give evidence in person, he issued a vitriolic pamphlet in which Sophocles and Shelley become bywords for the absurdity of the licensing system. Jones writes: 'Thus the rule of Censorship is "Gag Shelley! Gag Sophocles! License Mr Smellfilth! License Mr Slangwheezy!"'[42]

It is extremely difficult to assemble the evidence for the case for censoring Sophocles' play, particularly since the evidence given by the Examiner of Plays to the Joint Select Committee in 1909 is terse, to say the least. Redford was asked why the version of the *Oedipus* by Courtney had been refused a licence. When asked by the Member of Parliament Robert Harcourt, who had introduced the Theatres and Music Halls Bill designed to abolish the censorship, if an alleged impropriety had led to the banning of Courtney's version whilst the *Oedipus* of Dryden and Lee was apparently exempt from such strictures, Redford replied: 'Mr Courtney's version was submitted and it was considered; Mr Dryden's version was not considered.'[43] Harcourt's line of enquiry here is an attempt to ascertain the extent to which precedent determined the fate of newly submitted plays. And it is clearly precedent in the case of *Oedipus Tyrannus* that is affecting its fortunes at the hands of the censor. For the analogy with *The Cenci*, and the refusal of a licence to Oscar Wilde's *Salomé* in 1893 – Wilde's play remained unlicensed until 1931 – meant that any play dealing with incest in any shape or form was deemed indecent and unfit for stage representation.[44]

Harcourt was determined to keep the Sophoclean scandal at the forefront of the committee's concerns. Even Sir Herbert Tree, who (like most actor–managers of the time) was against abolition per se, nonetheless admitted under Harcourt's assiduous questioning that the Lord Chamberlain's stance over the *Oedipus Tyrannus* was clearly mistaken.[45] When the half-million-word report on the committee's findings and recommendations appeared in November 1909, the frequency with which references to Sophocles' play occurred made it inevitable that a production would be mounted in London before too long.

By the middle of 1910, two leading theatre managers were planning to stage *Oedipus Tyrannus*.[46] Sir Herbert Tree, undeterred by Redford's previously negative response, was again hoping to mount a production at His Majesty's Theatre; and Herbert Trench, the new manager of the Theatre Royal in the Haymarket, had approached Murray for his almost completed translation of Sophocles' tragedy.[47] Together with his close friends and colleagues, Barker and Shaw, Murray was actively involved in the 1909 campaign, and this had undoubtedly led him to a temporary rejection of Euripides in favour of a translation of Sophocles' now notorious play.

It may seem incredible to us that Sophocles' tragedy was reduced at this time by the incumbents of the Lord Chamberlain's Office to a play about incest *tout court*. Dryden and Lee's play, with its parricidal and unashamedly incestuous Oedipus, had begun to fall from favour from the end of the eighteenth century. The ban on Sophocles' *Oedipus Tyrannus* in Edwardian England was really one of mistaken identity for it was the Restoration tragedy (bizarrely not banned) that was effectively on trial as the discussion focused unerringly upon the mother–son relationship, which Sophocles deliberately downplays.[48] So jealously did the Lord Chamberlain's Office guard their role as the custodians of public morality that they were in danger of confusing representation with imitation. For as Henry Arthur Jones wryly observed at the time:

> Now, of course, if any considerable body of Englishmen are arranging to marry their mothers, whether by accident or design, it must be stopped at once. But it is not a frequent occurrence in any class of English society. Throughout the course of my life I have not met more than six men who were anxious to do it.[49]

But anxieties concerning consanguineous sexual relations had become increasingly acute throughout the first few years of the century, culminating in the passing of the Punishment of Incest Act of 1908. Prior to 1908 – with the exception of the interregnum years, and in marked contrast to Scotland where incest had been a crime since 1567 – incest in England and Wales had been dealt with by the ecclesiastical courts, despite numerous attempts to make it a criminal offence.

The new legislation of 1908 undoubtedly lurks behind the ludicrously 'literalist' reading of Sophocles' tragedy proffered by the Examiner of Plays, which can be found in the copy of Murray's translation of *Oedipus Tyrannus* that was submitted to the Lord Chamberlain's Office in November 1910. On the first page, in the list of *dramatis personae*, Jocasta is described as '*Queen of Thebes; widow of Laius, the late king and now wife to Oedipus*'. '*Now wife to Oedipus*' is underlined in blue pencil – the only such underlining in the text – and the reason for this becomes clear from Redford's comment in his letter to Lord Spencer, the current Lord Chamberlain. Redford writes:

> I have read the Gilbert Murray version. In many respects it differs from Mr Courtney's treatment, but it follows the classic story throughout, and the character of Jocasta 'now wife of Oedipus', is represented and all the well known situations of the play are retained.[50]

Redford's comments are overwhelmingly naive – indeed by implying that a version of Oedipus without Jocasta would be permissible, he might as well be asking for a Hamlet without the ghost.

When Trench sent Murray's translation to the Lord Chamberlain's Office, Redford was all set to return it with the customary rejection based on precedent. He wrote to the Lord Chamberlain for his seal of approval, adding what we now realise was a highly significant caveat:

> Mr Trench and Dr Gilbert Murray are opponents of the office, and no doubt desire to make capital out of a prohibition of an ancient Greek classic so familiar to every school boy etc etc.[51]

The caveat was evidently heeded because the Lord Chamberlain's comptroller, Colonel Sir Douglas Dawson, acted swiftly, telling Redford to inform Trench that the play was under review, and Murray's translation was to be granted the dubious distinction of being the first play to be referred to the newly appointed Advisory Board.[52] When Dawson wrote to members of the Advisory Board to seek their advice concerning the Murray translation, he broadly adopted Redford's terms. Dawson wrote,

> Some years previously a translation of the same drama was made by Mr W.L. Courtney and was refused a licence for stage performance on the ground that it was impossible to put on the stage in England a play dealing with incest.
>
> There was a precedent for the action which the Lord Chamberlain took on this occasion in the refusal of successive Lord Chamberlains to license 'The Cenci'.[53]

All the members of the board felt that a ban would be hard to sustain, although the retired actor–manager Sir John Hare recommended that 'the greatest caution should be exercised and the matter very seriously and deliberately considered in all its bearings before a licence is granted'.[54] Professor Walter Raleigh from Oxford, however, injected some common sense into the debate when he pointed out – as neither side, for obvious political purposes, had done before – that 'any supposed analogies' with *The Cenci* should not 'be allowed to have weight' because the treatment of incest in both plays is of such a different order and degree.[55]

The recommendations of the Advisory Board were heeded and Murray's translation of Sophocles' play, entitled *Oedipus, King of Thebes*, was finally granted a licence on 29 November 1910. And perhaps by no means coincidentally, on the same day the Lord Chamberlain's Office issued a licence for Strauss's opera *Salomé*, which used Wilde's play (albeit in the German translation of Hedwig Lachmann) as the basis for the libretto, and the opera was performed a few days later at the Royal Opera House, Covent Garden, on 8 December.

Reviews of the Reinhardt *Oedipus Rex* remained curiously silent about the play's recent history at the hands of the British censor. Shortly after the opening at Covent Garden, Barker drew attention to this serious omission in a letter to *The Times*:

> Sir, – Public memory is short. In no review of the production of *Oedipus Rex* at Covent Garden has it been recalled that until a year ago this was a forbidden play. But neither has any critic even suggested that it is a thing unfit to be seen. This is a famous case against the Censorship. It is, as it were, brought to trial, and judgement goes by default. Why have the Lord Chamberlain's champions, eager to support him in principle, never a word to say in defence of any of his important acts? Here is a chance for them; and if they feel it is one to be missed, will they not in fairness offer a vicarious apology to the public and the theatre, who have been for several generations wantonly deprived of their property in this play? – Yours etc.[56]

Even though no theatre critic found Sophocles' play 'a thing unfit to be seen', there were some people who clearly did. When Martin-Harvey took the Reinhardt production on a tour around Britain in 1913, the manager of the New Theatre in Cardiff (no less a person than the brother of George Redford, former Examiner of Plays) refused to allow *Oedipus* to be performed in his theatre, and Martin-Harvey and his company had to find an alternative venue.[57]

Oedipus Tyrannus may have been finally freed but the British stage was to remain under the shadow of the censor for another fifty years. The new Examiner of Plays was even more stringent than his predecessor, and his high-handedness provoked a petition that was presented to King Edward on 11 June 1912 with the signatures of over sixty dramatists. In the petition, the recent success of Reinhardt's *Oedipus Rex* was held up as evidence of the absurdity of the system of censorship. The statement avows:

> That the Lord Chamberlain's Department by working on custom and not on ascertainable results has been grossly unjust to managers, authors and the public, and has cast discredit on the administration of the Department by its treatment of classical plays, and of plays in which scriptural characters appear, as may be instanced by the repeated refusals to many managers of a licence for Sophocles' great play *Oedipus Rex*, which now, at last permitted, has been produced with every indication of public approval.[58]

However strong a statement of protest the petition contained, a censored *Oedipus Tyrannus* had clearly been a far more effective weapon against the Lord Chamberlain's Office than a liberated one could ever be. Moreover, Barker's concerns, expressed to Murray in 1910 before the ban on *Oedipus* was lifted, were proving prophetic. Barker had written:

> My fear is that the Lord Chamberlain means to scotch opposition by making as many concessions as he can – we – the general body of opposers – are so rottenly divided on the question of principle – that it would be an easy job if he had the wit to set about it. Personally one will be glad to see the *Oedipus* through but – at once – everyone will bless the name of the committee and say that nothing more need be done.[59]

Redford may not have had sufficient 'wit' to scotch the opposition single-handedly; but by implying in his letter to the Lord Chamberlain that the Sophoclean tragedy was the opposition's trump card, he had unwittingly guaranteed his office's survival for some more years. For by withdrawing the *Oedipus Tyrannus* from the fray, the Lord Chamberlain had deftly wrongfooted the opposition; and the British stage had to wait until the 1960s for its freedom.

DIONYSIAC DECADENCE

Reinhardt's *Oedipus Rex* is thus central to European theatre history on aesthetic and political grounds. The Reinhardt example, as Sheppard himself partly acknowledges in his Preface of 1915 with which this chapter began, was to carry with it perils as well as potentialities. Not least his 'people's theatre', with its inclusive agenda in terms of class and physical spatial relations, was eventually re-formed and de-formed as it served as the model for the Nazi mass rallies in the 1930s.[60] But in Britain, in the first decade of the twentieth century, the perils of the 'people's theatre' were conceived less in terms of its political than its moral potential.

The Edwardian era ushered in a new Europeanisation in Britain, which led in many (essentially patriarchal) circles to a nostalgia for a 'healthier' time, when 'modern' problems (often of a sexual nature) did not exist. New frank discussion about gender roles and sexuality in general fuelled these anxieties, as had been the case in the last two decades of the nineteenth century.[61] The English retreat from what was increasingly considered to be Continental decadence was, perhaps, best illustrated during this period with reference to its institutionalised moral custodians, and its theatre censor, the Lord Chamberlain, was one of the most powerful.[62]

Whilst the new corporeality in Reinhardt's *Oedipus Rex* initially engendered amazement within the audience, it also eventually brought moral outrage and scandal. The dance experiments of both Isadora Duncan and Maud Allan at the beginning of the century were hailed as revivals of the 'totality' of ancient Greek dance, combining expressive qualities with a religious/spiritual and educative function. For many critics, W. B. Yeats's famous (and, somewhat later, Duncan-inspired) question 'How can we know the dancer from the dance?' was the hallmark of this 'modern/ancient' pattern of movement. Neither Duncan nor Allan were able to sustain their high status as 'serious' dancers in the post-Great War world, and this was in part on account of their own personal tragedies. But their eclipse from high cultural circles was also symptomatic of the Anglo-Saxon world's retreat from what was perceived as 'cosmopolitan' corporeality, which Reinhardt's theatre, and his *Oedipus Rex* in particular, had so demonstrably embodied.[63]

That the classical establishment in Britain and elsewhere in Europe in the first part of the century should have favoured the French over the German/Austrian production is hardly surprising given the ostracism afforded to Nietzsche and Nietzschean-inspired scholarship at this time.[64] Indeed, the hero-centred readings of Greek tragedy, which were to last for at least the first half of the twentieth century, are linked in important ways to Lacroix's version of *Oedipe Roi* as it was mediated through the powers of Mounet-Sully. Behind Sheppard's comments in the Introduction to his *Oedipus Tyrannus*, as with the Anglo-Saxon retreat from 'cosmopolitan' corporeality generally, there is more than a touch of anti-German feeling during the war years. In Britain, and in France too (as we will see in the next chapter), the Dionysiac collective was now deemed decadent and dangerous in aesthetic terms, many years before the German-speaking world was to translate the ideology of the collective into its most pernicious form in the political arena.

NOTES

1. For the nineteenth-century German philosophical background, see M. S. Silk and J. P. Stern, *Nietzsche on Tragedy* (Cambridge 1981).
2. Mounet-Sully died in 1916 and his brother, Paul, who had previously played Tiresias, took over the role of Oedipus. The film version with Mounet-Sully, however, continued to be available (see Chapter 5). Martin-Harvey performed Reinhardt's Oedipus until at least 1936. For

details of the European tours of the Reinhardt production see J.L. Styan, *Max Reinhardt* (Cambridge 1985); for Martin-Harvey tours throughout the English-speaking world see the Martin-Harvey Papers in the Theatre Museum, London.

3. J.T. Sheppard, *Sophocles' Oedipus Tyrannus* (Cambridge 1920), xi.
4. Ibid., x–xi, ix.
5. Ibid., ix.
6. Ibid., ix. Cf. the reviewer in *Theatre Journal* 14 (1911), 56–60, who noted the symbolic significance of the use of light and darkness in the production: 'Out of the darkness into which they [the chorus] disappear comes all the ill-fortune that besets Oedipus, bit by bit, until finally, overwhelmed by an accumulation of tragedies, blind, powerless and deserted, he is driven into the darkness himself, followed by the same mob, which does not even touch him now, for fear of pollution.'
7. S. Goldhill, *Who Needs Greek? Contests in the Cultural History of Hellenism* (Cambridge 2002).
8. Lillah McCarthy, *Myself and My Friends* (London 1933), 302.
9. For the melodramatic second half see *Cambridge Daily News*, 25 January 12; for comments on Martin-Harvey's lack of an 'imposing air' see *Punch*, 24 January 1912, 68–9; for his excess in grief, J.T. Grein in the *Sunday Times*, 21 January 1912; for criticism of the scene with the shepherd see *Observer*, 20 January 1912. The *Referee*, 21 January 1912, finds Martin-Harvey too ordinary and too wounded in comparison to Mounet-Sully's 'wounded lion'. Martin-Harvey Papers, Box 6, Theatre Museum, London.
10. See *New York Times*, 4 February 1912; and Herbert Farjeon in *The World*, 23 January 1912. Cf. *The Spectator*, where there is criticism of the inaudibility of the English actors with their 'old-fashioned English methods of declaiming verse'. Martin-Harvey Papers, Box 6.
11. The production opened in Munich (25 September 1910), and went to Vienna (10 October 1910), and Budapest before Berlin (7 October 1910). In 1911 it toured to Riga, St Petersburg, Stockholm, Prague, Budapest (again), Zurich and Leipzig, Berlin (again), Amsterdam and The Hague. In 1912, whilst the English company performed in Covent Garden and then around Britain and Ireland, the German company toured to St Petersburg (again), Moscow, Riga (again), Warsaw, Kiev,

Odessa and Stockholm (again). It was revived in 1916–17 at the Volksbühne, Berlin, with a different cast. Cf note 2 above.

12. Vsevolod Emilevich Meyerhold, 'The Stylised Theatre', in *Meyerhold on Theatre*, trans. and ed. E. Braun (London 1969), 58–64, 62.

13. See J.L. Styan, *Modern Drama in Theory and Practice*, vol. III, *Expressionism and Epic Theatre* (Cambridge, 1981), 78, for Meyerhold's productions of *Sister Beatrice* and *Hedda Gabler* in 1906.

14. Erika Fischer-Lichte, 'Invocation of the dead, festival of peoples' theater or sacrificial ritual? Some remarks on staging Greek classics', in Savas Patsalidis and Elizabeth Sakellaridou (ed.), *Displacing Classical Greek Theatre* (Thessaloniki 1999), 251–63. For an account of the Berlin production see also R.C. Beacham, 'Revivals: Europe', in J.M. Walton (ed.), *Living Greek Theatre: A Handbook of Classical Performances and Modern Productions* (New York and Wesport, CT 1987), 304–14.

15. Meyerhold citing Wagner in *Meyerhold on Theatre* (1969), 87–8. For Wagner and the chorus see M.S. Silk, 'Das Urprobleme der Tragödie': notions of the chorus in the nineteenth century', in Peter Riemer and Bernhard Zimmerman (eds.), *Der Chor im antiken und modernen Drama* (Stuttgart and Weimar 1999), 195–226.

16. The music was used from 1912 onwards on the English tour (see *Freeman's Journal, Dublin*, 20 May 1912; *Southport Visiter*, 22 October 1912 (Box 7, Martin-Harvey Papers)).

17. Walter Jens, *Hofmannsthal und die Griechen* (Tübingen 1955), 91 n. 31; cf. J.L. Styan, *Max Reinhardt* (Cambridge 1985), 131.

18. Jens (1955), 94–5.

19. W. McGuire, *The Freud/Jung Letters*, trans. R. Manheim and R.F.C. Hull (Princeton 1974), 422.

20. *The Times*, 16 January 1912.

21. For the lighting, see *Electric Times*, 25 January 1912; for the debt to Craig see *Observer*, 20 January 1912 (Box 6, Martin-Harvey Papers).

22. *Observer*, 20 January 1912 (Box 6, Martin-Harvey Papers).

23. C.B. Purdom, *Harley Granville Barker: Man of the Theatre, Dramatist and Scholar* (London 1955), 114–15.

24. *Court Journal*, 8 February 1912; *Western Scotsman*, 27 January 1912 (Box 6, Martin-Harvey Papers).

25. Styan (1985), 80.

26. *The Times*, 23 January 1912.

27. The note is written by F. B. O'Neill.

28. For revivals of Dryden and Lee see Chapter 1 above; for Faucit's Oedipus see Edith Hall and Fiona Macintosh, *Greek Tragedy and the British Theatre 1660–1914* (Oxford 2005), 240–2.

29. *Censorship and Licensing (Joint Select Committee) Verbatim Report of the Proceedings and Full Text of the Recommendations* (London 1909), 68.

30. W. B. Yeats, 'Samhain: 1904', in W. B. Yeats, *Explorations* (London 1962), 131–2.

31. On censorship generally at this time see F. Fowell and F. Palmer, *Censorship in England* (London 1913); and the letter from Barker to Murray dated August 1910 in Purdom (1955), 113: 'You know I suppose that the Little Theatre opens with the Lysistrata – blessed by Redford.'

32. Yeats to Murray, 24 January 1905, in the Bodleian Library, reprinted in D. R. Clark and J. B. McGuire, *W. B. Yeats: The Writing of Sophocles' King Oedipus* (Philadelphia 1989), 8–9; for Murray's attitude to Sophocles, see P. E. Easterling, 'Gilbert Murray's reading of Euripides', *Colby Quarterly* 23 (1997), 113–27, 119.

33. Murray to Yeats, 27 January 1905, in R. J. Finneran, G. Mill Harper and W. M. Murphy (eds.), *Letters to W. B. Yeats*, 2 vols. (London 1977), vol. I, 145–6.

34. Ibid., 145.

35. For details of the Abbey attempt to mount the play see Fiona Macintosh, 'An Oedipus for our times? Yeats's version of Sophocles' *Oedipus Tyrannos*', in Martin Revermann and Peter Wilson (eds.), *Performance, Reception, Iconography: Studies in Honour of Oliver Taplin* (Oxford 2008), 524–47.

36. J. Martin-Harvey, *The Autobiography of Sir John Martin-Harvey* (London 1933), 391–403.

37. Richard Findlater, *Banned: A Review of Theatrical Censorship in Britain* (London 1967), 79.

38. *The Era*, 22 May 1886. For the taste for 'Greek' plays in London at this time see Hall and Macintosh (2005), 462–87.

39. Although Shelley does not refer explicitly to their thematic parallels, he was fully aware that such parallels would not be missed. Thomas Love Peacock, who had vainly submitted the play to Covent Garden at

Shelley's request, doubted that *The Cenci* would have been granted a licence anyway because other treatments of incest (including Dryden and Lee's *Oedipus*) had been banned from the stage in recent times. See G.E. Woodberry, Introduction, in *The Cenci by Percy Bysshe Shelley*, ed. G.E. Woodberry (Boston and London 1909), xxxiii–xxxv.

40. See A. Forman and H.B. Forman's Introduction to the Shelley Society edition of the play (Percy Bysshe Shelley, *The Cenci: A Tragedy in Five Acts … with an Introduction by A. Forman and H.B. Forman and a Prologue by J. Todhunter* (London 1886). Todhunter was a veritable polymath: as well as being a doctor of medicine, he was a well-known playwright and also the author of a study of Shelley in 1880.

41. See *Censorship and Licensing* (1909), *passim*.

42. Henry Arthur Jones's pamphlet, written in the form of a letter to Herbert Samuel, chairman of the Joint Select Committee, is reprinted in *Censorship and Licensing* (1909).

43. *Censorship and Licensing* (1909), 68.

44. There were other plays involving incestuous relationships that were also banned at this time; e.g. M.G. d'Annunzio's *La Città Morta* – which Eleonora Duse had tried to stage in London – was denied a licence in 1903.

45. *Censorship and Licensing* (1909), 74.

46. See the Barker–Murray correspondence in Purdom (1955), 99–102.

47. See Murray to Barker, 6 August 1910, in Purdom (1955), 112.

48. See note 39 above.

49. Cited by Fowell and Palmer (1913), 275, n. 1.

50. *Censorship and Licensing* (1909), 68.

51. Letter from Redford to Lord Spencer, 11 November 1910. Lord Chamberlain's Plays' Correspondence File: *Oedipus Rex* 1910/814 (British Library).

52. Letter from Dawson to Redford, 11 November 1910; and from Dawson to Sir Edward Carson, 11 November 1910. Lord Chamberlain's Plays' Correspondence File: *Oedipus Rex* 1910/814 (British Library). The other members of the board were Sir Squire Bancroft, Sir John Hare, Professor Walter Raleigh and S.O. Buckmaster.

53. Letter from Douglas Dawson to Sir Edward Carson, 11 November 1910. Lord Chamberlain's Plays' Correspondence File: *Oedipus Rex* 1910/814 (British Library).

54. Sir John Hare, in Lord Chamberlain's Plays' Correspondence File: *Oedipus Rex* 1910/814 (British Library).

55. Professor Walter Raleigh, 22 November 1910. Lord Chamberlain's Plays' Correspondence File: *Oedipus Rex* 1910/814 (British Library).

56. *The Times*, 18 January 1912.

57. Martin-Harvey (1933), 490.

58. The petition is quoted in full in Fowell and Palmer (1913), 374–6.

59. Purdom (1955), 116.

60. Erika Fischer-Lichte, 'Between text and cultural performance: staging Greek tragedies in Germany', *Theatre Survey* 40 (1999), 1–30.

61. Samuel Hynes, *The Edwardian Turn of Mind* (London 1968), 132–71.

62. Ibid., 212–53.

63. For a discussion of Duncan and Allan and 'cosmopolitan' corporeality at this time see Hall and Macintosh (2005), 542–54.

64. Silk and Stern (1981).

CHAPTER 5

EVERYMAN AND EVERYWHERE

In 1945 Jean Cocteau recalled Mounet-Sully's appearance as Oedipus at the opening of a production of *Oedipe-Roi* many years previously:

> Suddenly an arm emerged from behind a column. This arm brought with it a profile, similar to a Greek shepherd's crook, to Minerva's helmet, to the horse at an angle on the pediment of the Acropolis. This profile sat on top of an astonishing breastplate, on a chest full of melodious roaring.[1]

What is striking here is Cocteau's vivid, almost surreal, childhood memory of an event that had taken place at least thirty years previously (Mounet-Sully's last performance was in 1915 at the Sorbonne). For Cocteau, it is a memory of a bas-relief that only belatedly emerges as a three-dimensional shape as it comes out fully from behind the column. We saw in Chapter 3 how Mounet-Sully represented in many ways the pinnacle of the sculptural style in the theatre. Cocteau's memory here provides us with a clue to the durability of his acting style: as a consummate performer, he is able to adumbrate and even usher in the performance style of the succeeding generation, where the frontal (sculptural) style very often gives way to a profile style of performance which is more reminiscent of the frieze or bas-relief (see, for example, the profile of Oedipus on the cover). And it is notable that Mounet-Sully is almost always presented in profile in photographs or engravings – except in the final scene, where the mask-like quality of his facial expression is being highlighted.[2]

It may well have been this profile (rather than frontal) style that enabled Mounet-Sully's performances to translate so well into the recently inaugurated open-air theatres of southern Europe. Alternatives to the proscenium arch stage, as we have seen with Reinhardt's 'people's theatre', led to new patterns of movement. Once the Wagnerian concept of the *Gesamtkunstwerk* was adopted and applied beyond the operatic realm, the shortcomings of the sculptural ideal were finally overcome. Now the ideal of the fixity of the statuesque, individual performer was replaced by a new interest in the kinetic movement of the group. The performer is no longer the statue; in Meyerhold's designation, the performer is now hieroglyph:

> *Only via the sports arena can we approach the theatrical arena.*
> Every movement is a hieroglyph with its own peculiar meaning. The theatre should employ only those movements which are immediately decipherable; everything else is superfluous ...[3]

In these new outdoor performance spaces where the circle (as opposed to the picture frame) provided the dominant focus, the archaeological metaphor had to change: vase-painting or the architectural frieze, not sculpture, provides the reference point for the Modernist performer/director/choreographer.

Furthermore, it was no doubt Mounet-Sully's ability both to self-sculpt and to perform in profile that led to his ready and successful involvement with the twentieth century's most popular and truly pioneering art form, cinema. Cocteau's memory of Mounet-Sully in the theatre underpins what was for him a lifelong fascination with the figure of Oedipus; and many others, notably the playwright Saint-Georges de Bouhélier and the composer George Enescu, publicly acknowledge their debt to Mounet-Sully's theatrical performances. What is regularly overlooked, however, is the extent to which Mounet-Sully's translation of Oedipus to the screen had an equally significant legacy.

This chapter explores the legacy of Mounet-Sully in the productions and versions of Sophocles' tragedy in France during the inter-war period and immediately after the Second World War. What is truly remarkable is the longevity of his impact, which lasted nearly sixty years across the stages of Europe, thirty of which were posthumous. Freud may well have theorised the concept of Oedipus as Everyman, but it was Mounet-Sully who pioneered and popularised the interpretation in both his theatrical and cinematic performances. But it was the numerous adaptations and versions, which relate and respond to Mounet-Sully's performances in the inter-war period in France in particular, which perpetuated the concept and made the Everyman appear to be everywhere.

MOUNET-SULLY AND THE CINEMA

Cinema developed at a time when ancient vase-painting grew in status; and the links made between early cinema and Attic black- and red-figure vase-painting were both regular and productive, with important lessons being learnt from both about kinesis and stasis.[4] Whilst it might seem surprising that an actor renowned for his extraordinarily powerful voice should have turned to silent film in the last phase of his life, Mounet-Sully's dependence upon *gestes* and profile style would have made that transition a particularly appropriate and easy one. His silent film of *Oedipe Roi* of 1912, in which he performed and which he directed, was released not just in France but in America (in January 1913) and Austria (in March 1913).[5] It was unusually long (it lasted just over one hour and is therefore longer than any other extant silent film of an ancient play of the period), but it is its structure which is most striking and which clearly left an important legacy in readings of Sophocles' tragedy.

The film itself has not survived but its structure can be inferred from the publicity surrounding it and from stills in the French Bibliothèque du Film: the first act involves Oedipus' encounter with the Sphinx, in which Oedipus (we infer from comments from the German Censor), unlike his Greek counterpart, kills the Sphinx and then decapitates her and brings the head to Thebes; only the last two acts involve the Sophoclean play. Although Hofmannsthal's *Ödipus und die Sphinx* directed by Max Reinhardt in 1906 – inspired by

Joséphan Péladan's version of the same episode – had already treated this part of the legend in the theatre (see Chapter 4 above), what is important about Mounet-Sully's film is that it is clearly not a record of a stage performance, but an attempt to retell the Oedipus story in filmic terms. Mounet-Sully's versatility at this moment of great technological and performative change enabled him to adapt and his style to endure.

This extraordinary development in the reception of Sophocles' tragedy had, as we will discover, an important legacy. It encouraged the viewer of the film to 'read' the myth differently. *Oedipus Tyrannus*, the neo-Aristotelian paradigm, admired in France since at the very least Dacier's commentary on the *Poetics* of 1692 as the pinnacle of tragic form, had for obvious reasons never previously been so radically recast. But now, with the very different demands of the new genre, Sophocles' retroactive plot can be refigured as *Bildungsroman*. Oedipus' life as evolutionary, causal plot was, of course, central to Freud's reading of the myth which dictated a return to the 'roots' of Oedipus' trauma. But for Freud – as with the Sophoclean plot and equally with the analyst's method – that journey was always a retracing of steps rather than a linear development, unfolding in time. For Otto Rank, however, Freud's surrogate son, the encounter with the Sphinx was central to the myth because it was here that the primary trauma of birth was articulated.[6] Furthermore, with the developments in anthropology, in which myths began to be read both across time and across cultures, the Oedipus myth was finally liberated from the Sophoclean straitjacket in a way that it had not been since the English Renaissance, when Alexander Neville had retold Oedipus' story as a medieval morality tale (see Chapter 2).

It is this new evolutionary structure which lies behind many of the versions of Sophocles' tragedy that appeared in France over the next two decades – Bouhélier's *Oedipe, roi de Thèbes* (1919, dir. Firmin Gémier, Cirque d'Hiver), Cocteau's adaptation, *La Machine infernale* (1934, dir. Louis Jouvet, Comédie des Champs-Élysées), and Enescu's *Edipe* (dating from the early 1920s but not premièred until

1936). André Gide's *Oedipe* (1932, dir. Georges Pitoëff, Théâtre des Arts) may not trace the earlier episodes of Oedipus' life in sequential order but it does broaden the Sophoclean streamlined plot to include the brothers/sons Polynices and Eteocles, and the sisters/daughters Antigone and Ismene. However, it is the Stravinsky/Cocteau *Oedipus Rex* (1928, Ballets Russes, Théâtre Sarah-Bernhardt) that is the exception that proves the rule, with its close (albeit truncated) similarity to Sophocles' tragedy.

OEDIPUS *POUR NOS JOURS*

What is striking about the first of these inter-war French Oedipuses, Bouhélier's *Oedipe, roi de Thèbes*, is that it is another radical recasting of Oedipus for popular consumption; and, more particularly, it is strongly reminiscent of a medieval mystery play, with its octosyllabic verse form, familiar style and paratactic structure. Although Bouhélier himself had been inspired by Mounet-Sully's performances as Oedipus, he deliberately set out to resist what he deemed the restrictive, neoclassicising and Romantic alexandrines of Lacroix's text. He also strongly rejected the other, more recent, German-inspired 'scientific'/authenticating trend in the appropriation of ancient tragedy, which he felt had reduced the artist to slavish archaeologist and which had been most closely associated with the pre-war adaptations of ancients plays staged at the Odéon and in the open-air theatres of southern France. What the Modernists resisted was the concern with external detail – the dependence upon the archaeological findings of over half a century and the desire to incorporate in art the findings of the all-encompassing German classical scholarship, *Altertumswissenschaft*. Instead, Bouhélier sought to remake the material for his contemporaries, just as the ancient tragedians had done; and like them, to write for an inclusive audience, in class terms.[7]

As early as 1901 Bouhélier had written that 'the theatre will shortly become a place for the celebration of the sacred rites in which the people may participate';[8] and his collaboration in 1919 with the actor–manager Firmin Gémier made that aspiration a serious one. Gémier planned a genuine 'people's theatre' at the Cirque d'Hiver (he went on to become the first director of the Théâtre National Populaire); and the audience was to be very far from the *haut bourgeois* spectators at the Comédie Française. During one performance of *Oedipe, roi de Thèbes*, Bouhélier was delighted when a team of firemen, lured into the circus ring by the excitement generated by the performance, wandered onto the set.[9]

Gémier took his cue in many ways from Reinhardt in his desire for a 'people's theatre', in his choice of venue, as well as in his decision to put Oedipus onstage together with a huge crowd of extras. The monumental Craig-inspired set also looks back in many ways to Reinhardt's *Oedipus Rex* (see Chapter 4 and Figure 9). But Gémier went even further than Reinhardt in trying to re-create the performance conditions of the Festival of Dionysus in Athens. In addition to the play, with its cast of two hundred (including javelin and discus throwers and high jumpers), he sought to re-create in the interval an Olympic Games (five years before Paris hosted the games in 1924) and to make theatre truly 'popular'. Audiences loved it, but critics were less enthusiastic – this was a *Gesamtkunstwerk* that was too ambitiously inclusive.[10]

Bouhélier's recasting of Sophocles is radical indeed: three acts and thirteen tableaux which take us from Corinth to Thebes, from the interior of the Theban palace to a road outside the city walls. If we look for a forebear, the best place to start would probably be Dryden and Lee's Shakespearean/Sophoclean/Senecan *Oedipus*. Bouhélier's earlier scenes of domesticity between Jocasta, her nurse and the children recall Dryden and Lee's intimate scenes between husband and wife; and the political agitation of the Theban people is not unlike the scenes of the baying mob in the English Restoration *Oedipus* (see further Chapter 2 above). Bouhélier's play moves effortlessly between a tragedy of state and a domestic tragedy – even the appearance of Oedipus after the blinding occurs in Jocasta's room, when following

9. E. Bertin, engraving, set of Saint-Georges de Bouhélier's *Oedipe, roi de Thèbes* at Cirque d'Hiver, directed by Firmin Gémier (1921)

the Nurse's scream, a blood-smeared Oedipus terrifies his own children as he claws the walls and literally (re)pollutes his wife/mother when he touches her in desperation.[11]

If we detect Shakespeare as influence in these early scenes, Seneca's imprint emerges in the final scene, when Bouhélier's blinded Oedipus (played by Gémier himself) wends his way into exile, as ritual scapegoat, with Antigone at his side. In this final scene, as in Seneca, Jocasta comes centre stage: following Oedipus and Antigone's exit, she begins her own slow descent down the monumental staircase towards the plaintive crowd below. Down in the circus ring, she begins a highly plangent, ritualised dance of agony in their midst, strikingly reminiscent of the 'hysteric' case study of Elektra in the 1909 Hofmannsthal/ Strauss opera (p. 228).

The production made great use of the contrasting performance levels and especially the staircase that joined them: Tiresias is thrown down the steps by a demotic, intemperate Oedipus ('Creon paid you, didn't he! It's him who advised me to call you! What justice! I don't know what restrains me from smashing your face in! Dog, that you are' *[He throws him to the bottom of the steps.]*[12] p. 85). And when Oedipus discovers the truth about himself, he falls down the huge staircase. A long silence ensues, before Oedipus sits up and, to the accompaniment of a Bach fugue, holds his forehead in his hands. When Oedipus finally rises to his feet, newly steeled for his superhuman action to come, he remounts the vast sweep of steps to re-enter the palace.

Gémier then once more directs the audience's attention to the circus ring below as the Chorus begin a *danse tragique* to the offstage cries of Jocasta. This choral dance served as a prelude to Jocasta's own climactic dance which was to follow. Both Gémier and Bouhélier conceived of the Chorus, down below in the circus ring, as analogous to bas-reliefs on the temple pediments,[13] and this scene demonstrated their centrality to the performance absolutely as they enact in emotional counterpoint the offstage tragic dénouement.

Bouhélier's amplificatory choral dance, however, does not (as in Greek tragedy) temporarily arrest the fast, almost unstoppable, flow of the linear plot that unfolds towards the end of the play. Here in this prolix version, the plot moves hectically sideways after the *danse tragique*, to wrap up the other loose strands in its multivalent plot: first, to a street scene in which Creon is urged by Arsakes to take power, before he himself urges Hymon to forget Antigone. It is only after this circuitous path that Bouhélier's plot moves back on track to the anticipated intimate scene in which the blinded and bloodied Oedipus stumbles in upon his family in Jocasta's room.

EVERYMAN OR ARCHETYPE?

If the parallels with Shakespeare and Dryden and Lee make Bouhélier's text sound old-fashioned, the final dance of Jocasta, as we have seen, was very *au courant* with its psychologically probing significance. Enescu's opera, similarly inspired by Mounet-Sully's performance, was begun in 1909 and largely written in the early 1920s, but not produced until 1936, when it received a monumental production at the Paris Opéra with 350 players including singers, chorus and dancers.[14] The libretto, by the poet Edmund Fleg, charted the fortunes of Oedipus from birth until his end at Colonus. Freud's imprint is felt in Oedipus' anxieties about incestuous dreams; and anthropological readings of Oedipus as scapegoat in Act II, following his self-blinding and departure from Thebes together with Antigone, soon give way to Christianised readings of a redeemed Oedipus by the end of Act III.[15] The riddle is changed by Fleg into a question concerning who has power over destiny, but since the answer 'man' remains unchanged, Enescu's *Oedipe* ultimately becomes a vind-ication of its protagonist's human-centred response. The opera's Wagnerian epic sweep and its use of leitmotifs may well draw atten-tion to the period of its genesis, but critics at its première did not seem to find it outmoded. And as with Bouhélier's text, Enescu/Fleg's diachronic presentation of a noble, suffering and fate-beset hero met with popular acclaim: here again was an Oedipus, in Enescu's words, in whom 'people ... [could] find ... something common to themselves'.[16]

Stravinsky's opera-oratorio *Oedipus Rex*, by contrast, met with no such critical acclaim at its première in 1927. Even if the repressed Freudian subtext creeps in with the echoes of Bizet's *Carmen* in Jocasta's arias, Stravinsky produced an Oedipus out of his time – distant rather than empathetic – and in a form that was streamlined rather than prolix. Bouhélier's text deliberately eschewed the restrictive alexandrines of neoclassical tragedy, whereas the desire for order, reason and clarity embodied by the neoclassical ideal is clearly reflected in Stravinsky's work. Though hardly 'French', and indeed thus representative of the very cultural diversity that provided the source of the vibrancy of 1920s Paris, Stravinsky's opera-oratorio nonetheless can be seen in its use of Latin to be very close to the post-war French, Catholic conservative classicising traditions.[17]

Stravinsky had admired Cocteau's highly compressed *Antigone* when he saw it in 1923 at the Théâtre d'Atelier, and he asked Cocteau to produce a similarly condensed *Oedipus*. Stravinsky promptly pared down Cocteau's text even further and arranged for it to be translated into Latin by the priest Jean Daniélou. For Stravinsky, the language had to be lapidary and elevated; and following Stravinsky's recent conversion to Orthodox Christianity, the music drew on plainsong and the Easter Orthodox liturgy, making Oedipus into a quasi-priestly figure as well as a kind of ritual scapegoat (as he had been at the end of Bouhélier's version and the end of Enescu's third act). Despite the numerous allusions to baroque and Romantic composers for all the characters, Oedipus, in Stravinsky's conception, is less Everyman than archetype – not at all like the flesh and blood Oedipuses which are generally characteristic of the inter-war period.

The 1927 première at the Théâtre Sarah-Bernhardt in Paris was only a concert performance because Stravinsky (perhaps deliberately) continued to write the score up until the last minute.[18] The libretto shows that Cocteau had planned to use masks for all the characters except

Tiresias, the Shepherd and the Messenger; and movement for all the other singers was to be limited to arms and heads. The masked Chorus in the original designs are half-obscured by an ascending staircase upon which they are grouped in three tiers, and Oedipus and the main characters were to give the impression of 'living statues'.[19] Now we can see this hieratic and pared-down piece as characteristic of the period; and with the visual symmetry in Cocteau's set, we can detect parallels with the cinema of the period. The 1961 Eisenstein-inspired designs by Farrah for the British première chose to highlight these affinities.[20] In some ways this static, highly charged, high Modernist paring down was an intensification of many of the strengths of the late nineteenth-century Comédie Française house style, but in its use of masks it was removed from both the star system that produced Mounet-Sully and the subsequent 'demotic' versions by Gide and Cocteau himself.

In many ways, Cocteau got his own back on Stravinsky's editorial sleight of hand on his libretto when his *La Machine infernale* appeared at the Comédie des Champs-Élysées in 1934. Here paratactic form replaced the hypotactic structure favoured by Stravinsky, with the Sphinx scene of Act II being presented as if in flashback (the narratorial voice explains that this episode in fact occurred simultaneously with the opening scene on the battlements).

This modern-dress, *boulevardien* vernacular version refuses to allow its audience to forget about the ancient myth's connections with the world outside the theatre: Jocasta is despised by the people because of her foreign (do we infer 'German'?) accent and her weakness for Tiresias (her analyst?), to whom she confides her dreams. The shadowy figure of Créon, who only appears in the final act, is chief of police; and in this class-obssessed, enervating city (first beset by the Sphinx, later by the plague), there is always a discontented mob fomenting trouble in the background. As the Soldier explains, it is only dead kings who communicate with the people of Thebes in Cocteau's world.[21]

In place of aesthetic order, then, Cocteau now substitutes mechanisms of political control. Furthermore, in the first production, the 'machine' of the title, in which the paradigmatic Oedipus is entrapped by the gods, was replicated on the stage in Christian Bérard's designs, where a four-by-four-metre platform served as the performance space, giving the illusion that the characters were being manipulated by a greater, all-seeing force.[22] As with the Narrator in Cocteau's libretto, the voice who provides a summary at the start of each act further serves to distance the audience from the characters, whose fate they appear to be watching from afar.

For Cocteau, as he openly admitted, the character of Oedipus dominated his *oeuvre* – even when he was not the subject at hand; and this was because Cocteau's own life narrative could only be written with reference to Oedipus' own, and especially the Freudian Oedipus. Even if Sophocles' protagonist did not suffer from the Oedipus complex, Cocteau (who had lost his father young and who had an overly close mother) felt that he himself did, and his own creative work became the space in which he sought to unearth his childhood emotions.

The voice, in the first production the recorded voice of Cocteau himself, explains to the audience before the characters appear how the parricide and the incest have occurred. The first (explicitly and parodically) Hamlet-like act of *La Machine infernale* introduces the Freudian mother–son motif, which then reaches its crescendo in the third act, in Jocasta's suitably vibrant red bedroom, 'red like a small butcher's shop' ('rouge comme une petite boucherie').[23] The large bed covered in white furs, with an animal skin at its foot, dominates the set, but the inclusion of the incongruous cradle transports the scene far away from the tacky venality of the low-budget pornographic film into the world of psychoanalytical theory absolutely, especially when Oedipus rests his head upon his own cradle. For the actress Marthe Régnier, who played Jocasta, this was a daring scene, upon which her reputation would either stand or fall. When Oedipus rests his head upon his own cradle, Jocasta is finally able to act out her maternal incestuous desires. The critics were divided (Colette was ecstatic), but today it all feels horribly dated.[24] A revival at the Lyric,

Hammersmith, in 1986 met with howls of derision when the set of Act II opened to reveal a vulva-like entrance to the bedchamber.

The centrality of the episode with the Sphinx to Cocteau's version is, as we have heard, in keeping with developing psychoanalytical theory. Cocteau's Oedipus may have been at the top of his year in his studies in Corinth, but he is no cerebral hero and no swashbuckling adventurer of the kind played by Mounet-Sully in his silent film. He is arrogant, deeply ambitious, selfish and unfeeling (even in his dealings with his wife/mother), but he is more a teenager with promise than a complete wastrel. Cocteau's Sphinx gives Oedipus the solution to the riddle because of his seductive powers, but later on this Oedipus pretends to Jocasta that he has killed the Sphinx with a knife.

Even if Oedipus fails to play the hero of mythical and theatrical tradition, he is nonetheless acutely aware of his failing, and especially of his position in mythical tradition. After the Sphinx has died for him, he agonises about how best to carry his quarry into town; he decides against carrying her body, arms outstretched, in front because it reminds him of an unconvincing tragic actor from Corinth, who took the part of a king grieving over his dead son: 'That pose was pompous and didn't move anyone' ('La pose était pompeuse et n'émouvait personne'; p. 91). Finally, Cocteau's Oedipus decides that Heracles with his lion is his best model and he slings the corpse over his shoulder.

It is undoubtedly this diachronic account of the life of a charismatic and doom-laden hero that attracted Cocteau to Sophocles' play. In 1937 he directed his uncut version of *Oedipe-Roi* at the Théâtre Antoine, with the exquisite costume designs of Coco Chanel. Oedipus' white swaddling bands wonderfully set off the body of Jean Marais (Cocteau's lover at the time), making this Oedipus the Lothario again – although this time it was Oedipus as gay icon par excellence. When Stravinsky's opera-oratorio received its famous production (available on record) at the Théâtre des Champs-Élysées in 1952, with Cocteau as Speaker, it also included a number of *tableaux vivants* designed by Cocteau himself (taken from his last film, *Le Testament d'Orphée*). These *apparitions* punctuated the libretto and visually injected the events from *La Machine infernale* into Stravinsky's honed-down text (notably the plague, the Sphinx, the bedroom scene, the daughters). If *La Machine infernale* was Cocteau's revenge on Stravinsky, this expanded production of Stravinsky's opera/oratorio in 1952 showed that Cocteau had temporarily, at least, conquered the imperious Russian. In 1963, however, it was Stravinsky who had the last word when he denounced both the tableaux and the Speaker.[25]

When Gide had seen Cocteau's *Antigone* in 1924 he had been appalled at what he felt was its snapshot view of its subject. When he wrote his *Oedipe* towards the end of his life, he succeeded in writing a contemporary version without sacrificing the Sophoclean form. The three-act structure of Gide's play bears much resemblance to Sophocles' tragedy in its retrospective unravelling of Oedipus' past; its only gesture towards the contemporary wide-angled versions is its inclusion of Oedipus' brother/sons, Polynices and Eteocles, its magnification of the roles of Ismene and Antigone and the epigraphs to each act which are drawn from *Antigone*, *Phoenician Women* and *Oedipus at Colonus* respectively.

The Oedipuses of this period are not simply aesthetically untrammelled, as we have seen; and what Gide's play shares with Cocteau's and what makes it so very different from the Mounet-Sully model is its self-reflexive and occasionally burlesque tone, which encourages a kind of aesthetic distance. His Oedipus introduces himself as a *personne* at the start of the play – a person (not a king) and also a character in a play. For Gide, as for Cocteau, there is a strong sense that his Oedipus is appearing at the end of a long tradition. If Mounet-Sully's Oedipus was noble and cerebral, and Cocteau's Oedipus beautiful and sentient, the Gidean Oedipus is man of action, self-made and increasingly a man on a trajectory towards intellectual discovery; and as is the case at the end of Cocteau's version, Gide's Oedipus is man at war with authority, especially divine authority.

For the sixty-year-old Gide especially, and for the radicals of his own and Cocteau's generations, Classics provided an alternative to Christian authority. In Gide's case that meant repressed and repressive Protestantism. The inclusiveness of Hellenism, and especially its tolerance of sexual diversity, enabled Gide to negotiate his own sexual development.[26] The Gidean hero is free of conventional belief and proud of his bastard state; and for Oedipus, unlike Creon, there is nothing particularly shocking about the incestuous desires his sons have for their sisters, nor for the filial/conjugal love he feels at one and the same time for Jocasta.[27] Ancient Greece is liberating for France trapped in a world dominated by Christian (essentially Catholic) orthodoxy. At the end of Gide's *Oedipe*, Oedipus blinds himself in a defiant gesture of free will against the merciless and treacherous divine authority, whose structures of power on earth (typified by Tiresias) are based on fear. Even the pious Antigone at the end of his play renounces the Church and finds God in her heart and in the company of her atheist father.

It is the very modernity of the myth that makes it important for both Gide and Cocteau; and it is the clash that it affords between conformity and independence of spirit, between the ancient and modern, that makes it urgent. The original production gestured rather more towards 'German' archaeological accuracy in Georges Pitoëff's production at the Théâtre des Arts in February 1932: simple as the set was, it was very Greek in conception. Pitoëff's Russian accent in the part of Oedipus was deemed problematic; and he failed miserably, to the chagrin of some critics, to wear his *peplos* authentically, in marked contrast (it was noted) to Mounet-Sully. The main problem, however, was the mismatch between the authentically Greek set and costumes and the topicality of the language and the jokes. For this reason, Gide much preferred the set for the Darmstadt production later in June 1932, where the Notre Dame de Paris was projected behind the neoclassical building in the foreground.[28] The modern had to be conjoined with the ancient to make this *Oedipe* speak to contemporary audiences.

The occasionally flagrant burlesque tone in both Cocteau and Gide's versions is not only born out of deep familiarity with the classics; it is also due to the fact that both playwrights are still publicly settling scores with a conservative and predominantly Catholic cultural elite, whose Classics had none of the liberationary qualities that made it so potent a force for the radicals. For Jacqueline de Romilly the dominant tone of these twentieth-century French versions is irreverence.[29] This 'irreverent' tone is profoundly radical in a way that is hard for us to appreciate and easy for us to overlook. By dethroning Oedipus and the star of the Comédie Française, by putting him in line with the ordinary man, Gide and Cocteau invite us to see Oedipus as the figure who showed his audiences how to resist the authority structures that oiled the Infernal Machine, which ultimately led France to Vichy.

OEDIPUS IN POST-WAR PARIS
AND ENGLAND

In the immediate post-Second World War period, there were two star-studded productions of Sophocles' tragedy that have gone down in the annals of theatre history. The first was Michel Saint-Denis's Old Vic production, at the New Theatre in London in October 1945, starring Laurence Olivier and Sybil Thorndike as Oedipus and Jocasta respectively. The second, directed by the French film star Pierre Blanchar, opened at the Théâtre des Champs-Élysées in December 1947; and Blanchar took the lead together with the well-known actress of stage and screen Valentine Tessier, who played Jocasta. Star actors notwithstanding, there were other stellar contributions to these two productions: in both cases there were striking set designs by highly distinguished artists – the war artist John Piper in London, and no lesser luminary than Pablo Picasso in Paris. Picasso had already designed the set for Cocteau's controversial version of *Antigone* in 1922; his fascination with the ancient world had continued and in

10. Laurence Olivier as Oedipus in the Old Vic production of *Oedipus* in 1945

1947 he had just finished illustrating Ovid's *Metamorphoses* and Aristophanes' *Lysistrata.*[30]

Piper's monumental statues of the gods were decidedly more Celtic than Greek (see Figure 10), but they were deliberately sited alongside neoclassical buildings.[31] There was a similarly disjunctive feel to Picasso's set: this time an upside-down stylised Chinese boat with an all-seeing, emblematic eye looking down from above framed a classically inspired inner performance space, in which steps led up to a separate level with three neoclassical doors (Figure 11). In both cases the multiply suggestive sets came about in part because there was not always a clear correspondence between the design intention and the directors' aims: in London, the designer responded perhaps more intuitively to the W. B. Yeats translation which was used for the

11. Pablo Picasso's set for Pierre Blanchar's production of *Oedipe-Roi* at Théâtre des Champs-Élysées, Paris (1947)

production; or, at least, he took his cue from Yeats much more than the director had done. Indeed the choice of translation was not Saint-Denis's own, but had been made by Tyrone Guthrie, who had originally conceived of the production and had intended himself to act as director (see further Chapter 6 below).

There were tensions from the outset between Blanchar and Picasso because the director wanted less stylisation than the artist desired and a set that was 'authentically' Greek in atmosphere. Picasso had designed masks for the protagonists and the chorus leader, but in the event these were replaced by face paint, beards and wigs. For some critics, the set was merely a poor shadow of the 'real' Picasso; for others (notably those from the communist press), Picasso delivered a triumph of subtlety. The real problem, however, was that the set arrived only after the rehearsal process was well under way, and inevitably some critics detected a distinct lack of coherence in the production as a whole.[32]

Whilst the music by Anthony Hopkins appears to have been the least remarkable feature of the Old Vic production, Arthur Honneger's choral settings in Paris for percussion and ondes Martenot (the electronic instrument recently invented by Maurice Martenot) were considered notable enough to merit (an albeit non-commercial) recording in advance of the production.[33] The Chorus played a significant role in both productions – in London there were fifteen chorus members, including Nicholas Hannen as the Leader; in Paris, Jan Doat was the Leader of a chorus of eight members. But the chanting and unison delivery were deemed, as is so often the case, the least successful aspect of both productions.[34]

The production photos show uncanny similarities between the costumes for the London and Paris choruses: each member wore silver, black and red gowns. The similarities are perhaps not so surprising after all because, in many ways, the quintessentially 'British/Irish' *Oedipus* was also French in inspiration. The costumes at the New Theatre were designed by Michel Saint-Denis's cousin, Marie-Hélène Dasté, daughter of Jacques Copeau and wife of the actor Jean Dasté. In Paris they were the work of François Ganeau, who had cut his teeth and made his mark as stage designer during the five years he spent as prisoner of war in Germany; but it was (the Copeau-trained) Louis Jouvet who chose to promote Ganeau and introduced him to Blanchar.[35]

Sophocles' tragedy clearly spoke to the audiences of Europe in the immediate post-war period because it showed an exemplary hero embattled and yet ennobled by his suffering at the hands of a seemingly arbitrary fate. As Michel Saint-Denis commented some years later: 'I put on *Oedipus Rex* just after the war because the tragedy of the hero caught in the snare of Fate seemed to me to correspond to the tragedy of our time.'[36] However, there was a shared feeling behind both these productions that the post-war audiences needed some equivalent to the ancient satyr play in order to counter the bleakness of the Sophoclean ending. Most unusually, these *Oedipus* pieces – instead of presenting a consolatory diachronic version which concluded with the events of *Oedipus at Colonus* – were followed on the same evening by comic afterpieces: in London the comedy was Sheridan's *The Critic* (see Figure 12); in Paris it was Mérimée's *Le Ciel*

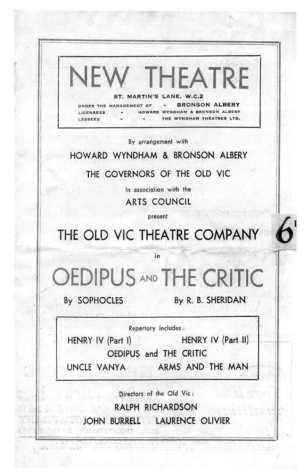

NEW THEATRE

ST. MARTIN'S LANE, W.C.2
UNDER THE MANAGEMENT OF - BRONSON ALBERY
LICENSEES - HOWARD WYNDHAM & BRONSON ALBERY
LESSEES - - THE WYNDHAM THEATRES LTD.

By arrangement with

HOWARD WYNDHAM & BRONSON ALBERY

THE GOVERNORS OF THE OLD VIC

In association with the
ARTS COUNCIL

present

THE OLD VIC THEATRE COMPANY 6'

in

OEDIPUS AND THE CRITIC

By SOPHOCLES   By R. B. SHERIDAN

Repertory includes :
HENRY IV (Part I)   HENRY IV (Part II)
OEDIPUS and THE CRITIC
UNCLE VANYA   ARMS AND THE MAN

Directors of the Old Vic :
RALPH RICHARDSON
JOHN BURRELL   LAURENCE OLIVIER

12. Programme for the 1945 Old Vic production of *Oedipus* and *The Critic* at the New Theatre, London

et L'Enfer. Both the London and the Parisian audiences were thus subjected to a complete gear change as they went on to watch a light-hearted but subversive coda to Sophocles' tragedy, which provided an interesting retrospective commentary on the themes and the form of the ancient tragedy.

These two productions, separated by just a couple of years, may be said both to have continued and to have marked the end of the essentially Freudian Mounet-Sully line in the performance history of Sophocles' tragedy. Olivier had regularly consulted Ernest Jones on matters of psychology in relation to Hamlet and Othello.[37] Now it seemed his Oedipus was being subjected to Freudian insights as well. In the Yeats translation (where the Chorus is marginalised), Olivier gave a consummate performance as the lonely hero pushed beyond the bounds of normal human endurance.

When Olivier's Oedipus discovered the truth about himself, he emitted his (now famous) cry, in direct imitation, we are told, of the wailing of ermine entrapped by the barbarous practices of huntsmen. In the suggestively open translation of W. B. Yeats, Sophocles' *eeiou* is rendered 'O! O!', instead of the more usual exclamatory spelling of 'oh!' with the 'h'.[38] The magnificent potentiality of the Yeatsian 'O! O!' was precisely what Olivier appreciated: by omitting the 'h', Yeats is implying pure sound: an open, hollow, primal scream rather than a desperate *cri de coeur* of any potentially self-pitying kind. Olivier comments, 'After going though all the vowel sounds, I hit upon 'Er'. This felt more agonised and the originality of it made the audience a ready partner in this feeling.'[39] For the critic Kenneth Tynan, Olivier's Oedipus cried 'a new born baby's wail'; and according to the reviewer of the *New Statesman and Nation*, '…we hear rung from him two groans, half-animal and as expressive of astounded pain as a woman's cry the moment when her child is born. And in a sense it is a rebirth for Oedipus'.[40]

Indeed, in many ways, Olivier was offering audiences Freud's Oedipus, now in 1945 being crudely wrenched anew from his mother's womb. That it was this moment from the production in particular that entered the annals of British theatre history is perhaps not surprising. For Olivier's 'wail' in many ways looks forward to important developments in theatre and in psychoanalytical theory in the post-war world: it not only anticipates the Beckettian scream, it also recalls the newly ascendant Kleinian psychoanalytical theory, in which the first and crucial trauma occurs on departure from the birth canal (see further Chapter 6 below).

Blanchar's Oedipus was regularly compared to Mounet-Sully's.[41] His choice of André Obey's adaptation of the translation by Paul Mazon may well have been dictated by a desire to free Sophocles' text from the neoclassical accretions of the Lacroix version, but it was nonetheless the human-centred reading proffered by Mounet-Sully which Blanchar sought to replicate in his production. Picasso's early sketches for the set had been a deliberate attempt to resist the psychological reading of the tragedy; and with Blanchar's rejection of Picasso's masks, he demonstrated his determination to keep the human dimension in view.

These two productions are not just notable because of their immediate post-war context, nor indeed because of their uncanny similarities. Their importance is also on account of their wide impact: we have already heard how Olivier's scream has entered into theatre history, but so too has the virtuosity (and sheer nerve) demanded by a double bill, which necessitated a speedy change from a bloodied Oedipus to a bewigged Mr Puff on the same night. George Steiner has recalled the impact this made on him as a young boy:

> As blinded blood-dripping Oedipus, with both eyes streaming with blood, with hands filled with blood, at the end he cascaded down the stage (it was one of his great physical, athletic *coups de théâtre*), down a long flight of steps, rolling over and over, the blood pouring onto the steps. The house lights were kept down, and there was no applause: only a total numbness at the immensity of the performance at that moment. The house lights blaze up, the curtain rises – on Olivier in the dandy's costume of Sheridan's Mr Puff. And the house exploded, stood and roared in a kind of numb relief and strangeness, but also resentment. It's

as near as I've come to some silly, primitive guess as to what might have been the *Stimmung* of the audience as it leaves the theatre of Dionysus in Athens after a satyr-play mocking, contravening, deconstructing the tragic play before it.[42]

Steiner is remembering a performance by Olivier in New York, after the London production had transferred to the Century Theatre in April 1946 for six weeks, with a new Jocasta (now Eva Burrill) and a chorus of twelve rather than fifteen. The Old Vic Company had already toured to Paris, Hamburg and the British military post at the remains of the concentration camp in Belsen before arriving in New York 'on a victory tour for a battered but triumphant Western culture'.[43] In addition to the *Oedipus Rex/The Critic* double bill, the repertoire consisted of *Henry IV Parts I* and *II* and Chekhov's *Uncle Vanya*. But it was undoubtedly the virtuoso double bill that captured the audience's, as the young George Steiner's, hearts and imaginations. As the *New York Times* critic commented (and to the chagrin of Orson Welles, whose *Around the World in Eighty Days* had recently opened at the Mercury Theatre a few blocks away): 'The spring seems to be given over to Laurence Olivier.'[44]

Olivier himself notes that it was the 1945–6 season that 'made our names' and that in New York the 'reception was as happy as a marriage-bell'.[45] Olivier's performance lived on in the American popular imagination for the next decade and surfaced again, somewhat surprisingly, in Vincente Minelli's 1953 film *The Band Wagon*.[46] The Michel Saint-Denis/Olivier production is clearly the model behind the Broadway production of *Oedipus Rex* featured in Minelli's film, where the suave Jack Buchanan plays Oedipus in a declamatory, portentous style. Although the Buchanan character is supposedly based on José Ferrer, who at one time had four productions running simultaneously on Broadway, the indefatigable and multitasking Buchanan (attempting to turn the Faust legend into a modern musical) is also a clear allusion to Olivier, who moved seemingly effortlessly not just from Astrov to Hotspur in one season, but from Oedipus to Puff in one night.

Minelli had even written to Yeats's widow to get permission to use her husband's translation for the five-minute scene from *Oedipus Rex*; but when he received no reply, he hired Norman Cowin to adapt a few scenes and the actor Louis Calhern to coach Buchanan in the part. The shooting of the five-minute scene took many days and, according to the pianist Oscar Levant, who appears in the movie, 'Recreating the fragments of the tragedy *Oedipus Rex* is no stylistic exercise, but displays Minelli's recognition of its psychoanalytic centrality and of its meanings for his own work, and, more generally the musical.'[47] In case audiences missed that centrality, the film's biggest number, 'That's Entertainment', included the following lines:

> The plot can be hot, simply teeming with sex;
> A gay divorcee who is after her ex.
> It could be *Oedipus Rex*,
> Where a chap kills his father
> And causes her a lot of bother.

Blanchar's Parisian *Oedipus* was similarly fêted and well-travelled: it previewed in November and December of 1947 in Lyons at the Théâtre des Célestins and in Brussels at the Théâtre Royal des Galeries before opening in Paris at the Champs-Élysées on 19 December. It too reached a wide public, not only extending its Paris run into the second half of January, but also touring to Verviers, Antwerp and Ghent in Belgium before its second Paris run.[48] In the opinion of some, the true star of this show was the Picasso set;[49] and indeed Picasso's 'eye' loomed long and large in the public imaginary and enjoyed a recent resurgence of interest in exhibitions at the Picasso Museums in both Antibes and Paris between 1999 and 2001.[50] In many ways this all-seeing eye – which alluded to the Greek word for theatre, *theatron*, the 'viewing place' – encapsulated the thematic heart of Sophocles' tragedy: it was the Sun (all-seeing Apollo, who masterminds the plot) as well as the cyclopean eye of Oedipus himself, myopic and vulnerable to assault from without. It also evoked knowledge – partial, distorted and ultimately forbidden knowledge, as the lights made the eye change to a bloody red with Oedipus' discovery of the truth about himself. Picasso's set for the 1947 *Oedipe-Roi* led to a new wave of commissions for theatrical designs. Yet it is, perhaps, not until the twenty-first century that we can fully appreciate Picasso's prescience here: as we will see in the final chapter, this Oedipal eye in many ways anticipated the predominant views of Oedipus over the next few decades both as 'all-seeing' philosopher and, more controversially, as the 'panoptic' and repressive establishment figure of the post-war period.

NOTES

1. Jean Cocteau, *Portrait de Mounet-Sully* (Paris 1945), 5: 'soudain, un bras sortait d'une colonne, ce bras entraînait un profil pareil à la houlette du berger grec, pareil au Casque têtu de Minerve, pareil au cheval de l'angle du fronton de l'Acropole. Ce profil se dressait sur l'étonnante cuirasse d'une poitrine pleine de rugissements mélodieux'.

2. See, e.g., the painting by Louis Édouard Fournier (1893) – in the Musée Carnavalet, Paris, oil on canvas – of Mounet-Sully in his *loge*, in typical profile *geste*. The lithograph on the cover shows the blinded Oedipus in profile.

3. 'The actor of the future and biomechanics', a report of Meyerhold's lecture in the Little Hall of the Moscow Conservatoire, 12 June 1922, in *Teatralnaya Moskva* 45 (1922), 9–10, repr. in Edward Braun (ed.), *Meyerhold on Theatre* (London 1969), 200, original emphasis. Significantly, when the publicity appeared for the Eva Palmer-Sikelianou production of *Prometheus Bound* in the ancient theatre at Delphi in 1927, the performers were photographed in poses strikingly reminiscent of the letters of the Greek alphabet.

4. F. Naerebout, '"In search of a dead rat": the reception of ancient Greek dance in late nineteenth-century Europe and America', in F. Macintosh (ed.), *The Ancient Dancer in the Modern World* (Oxford 2010).

5. I am indebted to Pantelis Michelakis for having shown me chapters from his forthcoming monograph on Greek tragedy and film for Oxford University Press; and his findings are reproduced here and in the next paragraph. Although no clip from the silent film survives, Michelakis has tracked down a very short film of Mounet-Sully in a stage performance of *Oedipe Roi*.

6. See Otto Rank, *The Trauma of Birth* (London 1924), for an analysis of the relationship between the Greek verb *sphingo* meaning literally 'I strangle', and the Sphinx.

7. Paul Blanchart, *Firmin Gémier* (Paris 1929), 52–3. On pre-war Classics generally, and especially the Parnassiens, see Fernand Desonay, *Le Rêve hellénique chez les poètes Parnassiens* (Paris 1928).

8. Saint-Georges de Bouhélier (1901), Preface to *La Tragédie du nouveau Christ* (Paris 1901), cited in Dorothy Knowles, *French Drama of the Inter-war Years 1918–39* (London 1967), 302.

9. Blanchart (1929), 123, note 1.

10. Ibid., 124.

11. Saint-Georges de Bouhélier, *Oedipe Roi de Thèbes – pièce en 3 parties et 13 tableaux* (Paris 1919). All subsequent references to this edition appear in brackets in the text following the citation.

12. 'Créon t'a payé? / C'est lui qui m'avait conseillé / De t'apeller. Sainte justice! / Je ne sais ce qui me retient / De te casser la tête! Chien / Que tu es! *[Il le jette à bas des marches].*'

13. Blanchart (1929), 127.

14. Noel Malcolm, *George Enescu: His Life and Music* (London 1990), 156.

15. Michael Ewans, *Opera from the Greek: Studies in the Poetics of Appropriation* (Aldershot 2007), 106–14.

16. Boris Kotlyarov, *Enescu: His Life and Times* (Neptune City, NJ 1984), 107–9 cited in Ewans (2007), 114. For the reception of the première see Malcolm (1990), 158–9.

17. See Martha Manna, *Mobilization of the Intellect: French Scholars and Writers during the Great War* (Cambridge, MA 1996) for an excellent account of the Catholic conservative traditions during the First World War and in the 1920s.

18. Stephen Walsh, *Stravinsky* (London 2002), 25.

19. Cocteau cited in David Nice, 'The person of fate and the fate of the person: Stravinsky's *Oedipus Rex*', in *ENO Opera Guide: The Oedipus*

Rex and The Rake's Progress (London 1991), 7–16, 10, for an excellent account of the designs. For an account of the staging see Stravinsky, 'From a *Greek Trilogy* (1968)', repr. in the same volume, 32–3.

20. The British première took place at Sadler's Wells in 1961, directed by Michel Saint-Denis, with designs by Abd'Elkadder Farrah, and conducted by Colin Davis.

21. Jean Cocteau, *La Machine infernale: Pièce en 4 actes* (Paris 2006), 63.

22. Gérard Lieber, 'Introduction' to Cocteau (2006), 12.

23. Cocteau (2006), 97. Subsquent references to the text appear in brackets following the citation.

24. See Lieber in Cocteau (2006), 18–20 for the play's contemporary reception.

25. André Boucourechliev, 'Rituel et monolithe', programme note for Chatelet Théâtre Musical de Paris, 26–31.

26. See Helen Watson Williams, *André Gide and the Greek Myth: A Critical Study* (Oxford 1967), 13–16.

27. André Gide, *Théâtre: Saul, Le Roi Candaule, Oedipe, Perséphone, Le Treizième Arbre* (Paris 1942), 263.

28. Knowles (1967), 217.

29. Jacqueline de Romilly, 'Les Mythes antiques dans la littérature contemporaine', *Bulletin de l'Association Guillaume Budé* (1960), 171.

30. Dominique Dupuis-Labbé, 'Une Rencontre insolite', in *Picasso et le théâtre: Les Décors d'Oedipe-Roi* (Musée Picasso, Antibes and Musée national Picasso, Paris 2001), 54–5, 54. This volume was published to accompany the exhibition *Oedipe-Roi*: Picasso et le théâtre at the Musée national Picasso, Paris, April to June 2001.

31. See *The Times*, 19 October 1945, 6. Piper's set introduced a 'suggestion of Galway into Thebes'. Cf. Harcourt Williams (who took over the role of Tiresias from Ralph Richardson), *Old Vic Saga* (London 1949), 193, who describes Piper's set as 'surrealistic with a very real house portico in the middle of it'.

32. Marie-Noëlle Delorme, 'L'Histoire des dessins d'*Oedipe-Roi*' in Picasso et le théâtre (2001), 8–47, 13, 42, 46–7.

33. Williams (1949), 193, alone seems to comment 'on the very exciting music of Anthony Hopkins'. There is no mention of it in *The Times*, 19 October 1945, 6; the *Spectator*, 26 October 1945, 283; or the *New*

Statesman and Nation, 22 October 1945, 279. For details of the (lost) recording made on 25 June 1947 of Honneger's settings by Ginette Martenot and Pierre Boulez and the extant recording from INA (broadcast 26 December 1948) see Delorme (2001), 41.

34. E.g. *Spectator*, 26 October 1945, 383; and François de Roux, *L'Époque*, 20 December 1947.

35. Marie-Noëlle Delorme, 'François Ganeau', in *Picasso et le théâtre* (2001), 48–53, 48.

36. Interview with Michel Saint-Denis in *Le Théâtre dans le Monde* 4 no. 4 (1957), 281–3, 281.

37. James Forsyth, *Tyrone Guthrie: The Authorised Biography* (London 1976), 165.

38. Cf. E.F. Watling's translation for Penguin Classics, 'Oh God'. For the scream, see Laurence Olivier, *Confessions of an Actor* (London 1982), 154. For the Yeats translation generally see Fiona Macintosh, 'An Oedipus for our times? Yeats's version of Sophocles' *Oedipus Tyrannos*', in Martin Reverman and Peter Wilson (eds.), *Performance, Reception, Iconography: Studies in Honour of Oliver Taplin* (Oxford 2008), 524–47.

39. Olivier (1982), 154.

40. Kenneth Tynan cited in Dominic Shellard, *British Theatre since the War* (New Haven and London, 1999), 3–5, 5; Desmond MacCarthy, 'Sophoclean discovery', *New Statesman and Nation*, 22 October 1945, 279.

41. François de Roux, *L'Époque*, 20 December 1947.

42. George Steiner, 'Tragedy, pure and simple', in M.S. Silk (ed.), *Tragedy and the Tragic* (Oxford 1996), 534–46, 545, n. 2.

43. Claudia Roth Pierpont, 'The player kings: how the rivalry of Orson Welles and Laurence Olivier made Shakespeare modern', *New Yorker*, 19 November 2007, 70. Steiner (1996) erroneously dates the American tour to 1942. For further details of the New York run see Karelisa Hartigan, *Greek Tragedy on the American Stage* (Westport, CT 1995), 40–1.

44. Cited in Roth Pierpont (2007), 70.

45. Olivier (1982), 157.

46. I am indebted to Kathleen Riley for first drawing this to my attention, and for the subsequent discussion.

47. Oscar Levant, *Memoirs of an Amnesiac* (New York 1965), 201, cited in Bruce Babington, 'Jumping on the band wagon again: Oedipus backstage in the father and mother of all musicals', in Bill Marshall and Robynn Stilwell (eds.), *Musicals: Hollywood and Beyond* (Chicago 2000), 31–9.
48. Delorme, 'L'Histoire des dessins' (2001), 42–4.
49. See *Ce Soir*, 21 December 1947; and Blanchar in a radio interview with Jacques Espargnao, *Radio revue*, 21 December 1947.
50. For details of the exhibitions, see note 32 above.

CHAPTER 6

OEDIPUS DETHRONED

Whilst Oedipus was everywhere during the first part of the twentieth century, by the last third of the century it was hard to find an Oedipus anywhere on the stage that has endured in the public memory.[1] It is not so much that Sophocles' tragedy has been shunned altogether – indeed most prominent theatre directors today have tried their hand at *Oedipus Tyrannus* (notably Yukio Ninagawa, Tadashi Suzuki and Peter Hall) – but that none of their *Oedipus* productions could be ranked amongst their best works. The figure of Oedipus, it seems, has somehow eluded them. Success has come more readily from small-scale companies – as with the British touring company Northern Broadsides, whose *Oedipus* in the Yorkshire dialect of Blake Morrison's craggy text proved that a consistently demotic translation set in a non-cosmopolitan context could bring Sophocles' tragedy alive to contemporary audiences. Morrison's bluff, often bombastic, Oedipus was completely dethroned to emerge as an insecure grandee from a small town in the heart of the dales. Percussive speech rhythms and the clashing of stones together in choral accompaniment injected a new pulse and resonance into the tired bourgeois familial tragedy that Freud had theorised a century earlier.[2]

Institutional changes within the theatre – and especially the demise of the star system from the 1950s onwards – have played some role in determining this sharp turn in the performance history of Sophocles' tragedy. When Arthur Miller proclaimed the nobility of the 'ordinary man' in his landmark essay 'Tragedy and the common man' in the *New York Times* on 27 February 1949, theatrical stars were being toppled from thrones throughout the theatres of the Western world. Oedipus as king, as hero, in what was increasingly being deemed the post-tragic world of post-war Europe, began to feel anachronistic, alien even.[3]

In some ways this radical change in the performance repertoire of ancient plays came about because the ubiquitous Oedipus of the first half of the twentieth century had enjoyed an overexposure, which led inevitably to a cloying of taste. Although Freudian psychology was both prominent and entrenched within theatrical discourse by the 1950s and 1960s, it became evident by the 1970s within society at large that Freud's theories were no longer immune from close critical scrutiny. In clinical practice, it was the Kleinian psychoanalytical model, in which the mother replaces the father as the focus for exploration, which began to eclipse Freudian orthodoxy.[4]

About this time French academic discourse, in a move strikingly evocative of, if not directly inspired by, eighteenth-century Jesuitical readings, began to refigure Oedipus with reference to the ambiguities in the designation *tyrannos*. The Freudian familial romantic drama became once again Sophocles' political tragedy.[5] These critiques were coincident with the countermoves in psychoanalytical theory in which the figure of Oedipus began to come under sharp attack. If the eighteenth-century Oedipuses were insouciant tyrants, by the end of the play they were very frequently at odds with the tyrannical side of their own nature.[6] Now in post-modern Paris, and in Foucault's terms in particular, Oedipus is a tyrant through and through: if Picasso's omniscient eye from the 1947 Paris production was emblematic of Oedipus' status as Enlightenment subject, this 'eye' was now designated as one aspect of the repressive panoptic society that Western liberal democracies have become.

In these new readings, Mounet-Sully's victim of an unjust world has himself become the prime cause of social injustice. Foucault's critique gains even greater force and prominence in *L'Anti-Oedipe* of Deleuze and Guattari (Foucault wrote the Introduction to the English translation), where Oedipus is a symbol of restraint and repression – racist, capitalist, patriarchal and imperialist.[7] The Anti-Oedipus/'antihero' of Deleuze and Guattari turns out to be another mythical construct, a joyous (misunderstood Laingian) schizophrenic, who has much in common with Nietzsche's Dionysiac boundary-breaking chorus.

The Nietzschean terminology is not merely fortuitous here. Much of French psychoanalytical theory is (consciously or not) indebted to Nietzsche: Julia Kristeva is but one such example in her distinction between (Apolline) symbolic male phallic discourse and the (Dionysiac) semiotic, pre-Oedipal feminine/maternal world of the prelingual.[8] In many ways, Oedipus has suffered in the late twentieth century because he is just too Apolline for the post-1960s world: too much associated with the light, with knowledge, with the *polis* rather than the Furies. Indeed, when Luce Irigaray proclaimed in her first manifesto *Speculum of the Other Woman* that matricide and not parricide was the founding act of Western civilisation (referring, inter alia, to the primacy of Aeschylus' *Oresteia* over Sophocles' *Oedipus Tyrannus*), she was summarily dismissed by Jacques Lacan from her teaching post at Vincennes.[9]

This chapter examines the various ways in which Oedipus has been dethroned and displaced within his own play in the theatre in the last few decades. It opens with a discussion of Tyrone Guthrie's *Oedipus Rex* in Stratford, Ontario, which began life in 1954. The importance of Guthrie's production cannot be overstated: in many ways, it is pivotal in marking the culmination of a glorious period in the performance history of Sophocles' tragedy. It also marks a watershed because when it was filmed in April 1956 the producer, Leonid Kipnis (aka Lola), like Aristotle before him, once more liberated Sophocles' text: in Aristotle's case, from fifth-century Athens (see further above, Chapter 1); in Kipnis's case, from an exclusively Western heritage. Now captured on film, *Oedipus Rex* becomes truly international in both its appeal and its reach.

From the 1960s onwards, however, Oedipus' place in the repertoire has been neither dominant nor secure. The distinguished German playwright/theatre director Heiner Mueller presciently noted in 1975, 'In the century of *Orestes* and *Electra*, which is upon us, *Oedipus* will be a comedy'.[10] We have already detected a burlesque tone in the interwar versions of Cocteau and Gide; but there has been a long-standing parodic Oedipal tradition – which includes Heinrich von Kleist's *The Broken Jug* (1808) and J.M. Synge's *Playboy of the Western World* (1907) – in which comic antiheroes either unwittingly enact the Oedipus pattern in bawdy and bathetic key (as in the German play) or pretend to an act of parricide in order to enhance their own otherwise insignificant stature (as in the Irish version). Mueller's claim that the Oedipus of today demands recasting in the comic mould may well be borne out by numerous recent versions, where the comic has dominated over the tragic element as in Giuseppe Manfridi's iconoclastic *Cuckoos* or in the recently devised piece by the innovative Irish company Pan Pan, *Oedipus Loves You.*[11] In Manfridi's hilariously shocking version, Oedipus is literally locked for the first part of his play in anal intercourse with his mother under a parachute. Is this where Sophocles' play has ended up? It is as if the tragic Oedipal tradition is too heavy a burden to bear; and to reduce its weight or, very often, to recharge its potency, it is first necessary to strip it of its (especially Freudian) accretions through comic deflation.

If Oedipus has enjoyed a position, it is very often in radically new guises, as if the outsider hinted at in the title – the *tyrannos* – were now his strength, not a source of vulnerability. The most successful of the stage versions thoroughly cleanse the spectators' Freudian perceptual filters: either by radically re-siting the play in a non-Western, non-metropolitan context, where bourgeois, familial crises are irrelevant – as with Ola Rotimi's *The Gods Are Not to Blame*;[12] or by challenging Freud's reading of the play head-on – so the anti-Freudian rewriting of Steven Berkoff, *Greek.* One final way in which the problematic Freudian accretions are overlaid (rather than obliterated) is in the feminist rewritings, such as those by Martha Graham and Hélène Cixous, in which Kleinian psychoanalytical theory provides the frame. Oedipus has become marginalised in all these plays: he is colonial subject rather the representative of Western Enlightenment; no longer the star of London's West End, he hails instead, and with pride, from London's East End; or this new Oedipus is so thoroughly dislocated within his own drama that it is Jocasta who now comes centre stage, to tell her story.

GUTHRIE'S *OEDIPUS REX*

In many ways the last major twentieth-century *Oedipus Tyrannus*, Tyrone Guthrie's production in Stratford, Ontario, which premièred in 1954, was conceived in marked opposition to the Olivier production, and to the fading star system itself. Had Guthrie not resigned from the management of the Old Vic over Olivier's decision to mount Sophocles' tragedy in a double bill together with Sheridan's *The Critic* (an unabashed sop, one might infer, to the ego of the formidable star), Guthrie would have directed Olivier in the Oedipus role. That Guthrie is in some senses engaged in the process of downgrading the star in his own production in Stratford, Ontario is perhaps nowhere better evidenced than in the designs by Tanya Moiseiwitsch, which included vast expressionist masks for all the principal actors, and notably for the star performers who took the lead (see Figure 13), James Mason in 1954, and from 1955 onwards Douglas Campbell.

However, Guthrie's associations with Sophocles' tragedy pre-date the Old Vic production by at least twenty years. In 1923–4, Guthrie had taken the part of Tiresias as an undergraduate at Oxford; and soon after graduation, as assistant producer for James B. Fagins's Company at the Oxford Playhouse, he found himself again working on Sophocles' tragedy, this time in Gilbert Murray's translation. His long-standing association with Sophocles' tragedy, however, was not confined to the theatre: his regular pen name as an undergraduate had been Oedipus Biggs; and his overly close relationship with his mother made him acutely aware (as was Jean Cocteau) of his own resemblance to the protagonist of Freud's bourgeois familial drama.[13] It was during preparations for his production of *Hamlet* in 1937 that Guthrie and Olivier began their close friendship with Freud's biographer, Ernest Jones. Many years later in Stratford, Ontario, Guthrie could not resist the irony of having to suffer a swollen foot during the rehearsals for the première of *Oedipus Rex*, which meant that he was forced to conduct rehearsals from a cane chair.[14]

13. Douglas Campbell in the Stratford (Ontario) Festival's production of
Oedipus Rex, directed by Tyrone Guthrie, 1955

In some ways this overly close and uncanny relationship between
Guthrie and his tragic subject was to yield powerful consequences: it
was as if the very personal nature of those feelings meant that they had
to be aestheticised and transported onto another plane absolutely. No
doubt this was one of the reasons why he found Olivier's Oedipus
uncomfortably naturalistic when he saw it in 1945 (although he was
not alone in feeling this – even Olivier's leading lady in London, Sybil
Thorndike, noted that the 'realism' of the performance did not result
in the 'symbolic heights of tragedy'). On seeing Olivier in the final
scene with realistic blood pouring down his face, Guthrie was determined to direct the scene himself and to do it differently.[15]

Guthrie had two opportunities to work out his ideas about
Sophocles' play before his landmark production in 1954. The year
after the première of Olivier's stellar performance, Guthrie was invited

to Tel Aviv by the Habimah Theatre Company, where he staged *Oedipus Rex* in Hebrew, and in 1947 he received an invitation from the Swedish Theatre in Helsinki to direct the play in Swedish. The experience of working with Sophocles' play in languages not his own convinced him of the universality of its message, and provided him with further (non-personal) reasons for his pursuit of a thoroughly non-naturalistic production in Stratford, Ontario.[16]

Guthrie had himself suggested the Yeats text to Olivier, for whom (as we have heard) it served as a perfect vehicle for a Freudian reading of Sophocles' tragedy, with its marginalised Chorus and unerring focus upon an isolated Modernist hero. For Guthrie, however, the potential in Yeats's translation was altogether different: in both the prose sections and in the verse, Yeats regularly uses repetition and echo, which gives a sense of formal patterning that is on occasions almost incantatory in effect. Guthrie recognised that Yeats's translation could become, under his own direction, an archetypally ritualistic drama. As Guthrie and Moiseiwitsch so readily relished and exploited, Yeats's version is set in neither Thebes nor Dublin; we are nowhere in particular, and this enabled them to transport Oedipus into a mythopoeic sphere absolutely. But alongside this sense of being everywhere and nowhere in particular is the kind of detail that Guthrie and Moiseiwitsch imply in their description of a text that 'treads barefoot over steep sharp rocks'.[17]

For Guthrie, Yeats's text had the perfect combination of openness and specificity that enabled him to realise onstage the main tenets of the Cambridge ritualists, who had maintained that tragedy grew out of the ritual of the Year-Daimon. He writes:

> The theater is the direct descendant of fertility rites, war dances and all the corporate ritual expressions of which our primitive ancestors, often wiser than we, sought to relate themselves to God, or the gods, the great abstract forces which cannot be apprehended by reason, but in whose existence reason compels us to have faith.[18]

Guthrie refers in particular to 'the sacred drama of *Oedipus Rex*' in which the actor 'impersonates a symbol of sacrifice'.[19] His Oedipus wore *kothornoi* (Roman tragic boots) four and a half inches high, a gold robe and a half-mask in gold, bedecked with an enormous crown from which spikey rays protruded; with spectre in hand, this literally larger-than-life, hieratic performer was more god than human, more Apollo than Oedipus.

According to Guthrie and Moiseiwitsch, 'the audience must be prepared to enter into a world of symbols exactly analogous to the experience of dreaming.'[20] In the tent that served as the theatre at Stratford in 1954 – there was no permanent theatre building until 1956 and in the tent the spectators in the back row were only thirteen rows away from the stage – the proximity of the audience to the actors readily effected the requisite entry into a symbolic world. In the 1956 film version of the production, this accession is effected through a metatheatrical prologue, in which a narrator – played by Douglas Campbell, who will take the part of Oedipus – explains how the spectators are about to witness a re-enactment of the sacrifice of a king, just as the priest re-enacts in symbolic mode Christ's Last Supper during the Eucharist. Campbell then picks up his mask and invites the spectators to imagine the studio lights as the sun and the camera as 'eyes'; and it is as if he conjures before their eyes a smoke-enshrouded set (wafting up from four gigantic bowls of burning incense placed on the edges of the stage), from which the moaning crowd of suppliants eventually emerges, first vaguely discernible as swaying branches and finally as primeval creatures from another time and place.

The heat of the Canadian summer, especially from inside a tent, enforced an unwelcome break in the action. A ten-minute intermission was therefore reluctantly included, just after the arrival of the Corinthian Messenger, mak▓▓▓▓▓tal playing time ninety minutes. However, Guthrie made a r▓*the*▓▓e of what could have been a disastrous hiatus in the action: with a brilliant flashback sequence at the start of the second half, any interruption to the tragic rhythm was overcome. The second half opened with a replay of the emergence of Jocasta from the palace on her way to leave offerings at Apollo's altar; and then the arrival of the Messenger was similarly played again. The spectators were thus imaginatively taken back in time and in their memories to the emotional moment they were forced to leave behind when the house lights came up for the ten-minute interval.

In Guthrie's stridently anti-realistic production, the masked Oedipus does nót change his mask in the final scene but merely wears a gauze veil over it; and when the daughters come, they wrap themselves round him in a ritual dance, 'symbolically washing in his blood, [in] a purification ritual'.[21] Yeats's blinded Oedipus has only just emerged from the palace, proudly announcing to the chorus that it 'was my own hand alone, wretched that I am, that quenched these eyes'.[22] With Yeats's inspired choice of the verb 'quench' – with its multiple connotations of extinguishing something on fire and of cooling with liquid and thus soothing and satisfying – we see how Guthrie's image of Oedipus' daughters bathing in their father's blood is suggested on the lexical level as well. For Yeats, as for Guthrie (and for all those for whom tragedy is a ritual enactment of the Year Daemon), death in tragedy is really no death at all: it is a sacrifice of the individual which brings about renewal for all.

Guthrie's Oedipus, in marked contrast to Olivier's piercing scream, gives out a low moan (interestingly also finding sufficient freedom in Yeats's 'O, O!' to emit 'Ai – eee') before withdrawing in the fading light. The final scene is played out in half-light as the audience participate and share in Oedipus' new, deeper insight into reality. Departing from both the Sophocles and Yeats texts, Creon orders Oedipus to 'Go!'. There is no room here for mere pity: the Chorus retreat into the shadows, leaving Oedipus to fumble his way down the steps towards the camera, heavily obscured, almost blotted out as if in silhouette, by the half-light, before disappearing out of sight entirely. This is a far cry from Yeats's 1928 published text, where Oedipus (as with Sophocles) is sent back into the palace, followed by Creon and the children. Guthrie is offering the audience not only a greater magnification of the Yeatsian isolated Modernist hero; he has also translated Sophocles'/Yeats's tragic character into the (Senecan) ritual scapegoat absolutely.

OEDIPUS IN AFRICA

The film of Guthrie's production guaranteed that Greek tragedy was no longer the exclusive preserve of the Western world; and indeed from the 1960s onwards, Greek tragedy became increasingly cosmopolitan.[23] Ola Rotimi's version of Sophocles' tragedy, *The Gods Are Not to Blame*, is generally considered to be one of Nigeria's most important plays. Written in 1966, and premièred by the Ori Olokun Players in 1968 at the first annual Ife Festival of Arts (Rotimi was one of the festival's founders), *The Gods Are Not to Blame* went on to be performed across Nigeria and Ghana during the next couple of years, before winning the Oxford University (Nigeria) prize for literature in English. More recently it has enjoyed a high profile beyond Africa as well, enjoying productions in Britain in 1989 and 2004.[24]

Rotimi, like Soyinka and numerous West African writers, readily reworked Greek tragedy as a spirited riposte to the long shadow cast by imperial rule. For these writers the Greek material intermeshes seamlessly with Yoruba religious ritual; and much has been written about the affinities between the Yoruba and Greek pantheons, and more particularly about the ties between Ogun, the Yoruba god of iron whose powers include creativity, war and liberation, and the Greek god of contradictions, Dionysus.[25] Dionysus' followers carry the *thyrsus*, Ogun's carry the willowy pole bedecked with palm fronds; Dionysiac rites culminate in the rending of a live quarry (*sparagmos*), similarly the rites of Ogun culminate in the tearing apart of a live dog.

It is Ogun who presides over the action in *The Gods Are Not to Blame*, taking on many of the prophetic powers of Apollo and the destructive ones of Ares. His shrine remains downstage throughout

14. Femi Robinson as King Odewale in the première of Ola Rotimi's *The Gods Are Not to Blame*, performed by Ife University's Ori Olokun Players, Nigeria (December 1968)

the play, coming into dominant focus in the scene in which Rotimi's Oedipus, Odewale, ironically curses himself as he pledges vengeance on the dead King Adetusa's murderer (Figure 14):

> *[Odewale pulls out the matchet from the shrine, raises it and swears.]*
> ODEWALE   Before Ogun the God of Iron, I stand on oath. Witness
> now all you present that before the feast of Ogun, which

> starts at sunrise, I, Odewale, the son of Ogundele, shall
> search and fully lay open before your very eyes the murderer
> of King Adetusa. And having seized that murderer, I swear
> by this sacred arm of Ogun, that I shall straightway bring
> him to the agony of slow death …[26]

However, it is not simply in terms of religious ritual that the Greek plays
are easily assimilated into a Yoruba context. The form of Greek tragedy –
its combination of speech, song and dance – makes it especially congenial
in an African theatrical context, where traditional masked performances
of singing and dancing continue to enrich contemporary drama. Rotimi
himself insisted on founding his theatre in a traditional Yoruba courtyard, where the spectators sat around three sides of the performance
space. Staging an African/Greek play in this theatre made perfect sense;
much more, indeed, than in any Western-inherited, proscenium space
that had recently been erected at the University of Ife.[27]

Rotimi's play opens with a mimed prologue of the events surrounding the exposure of the baby, and the action is accompanied by choral
singing, drumming and (what Rotimi calls) 'symbolic sound-effects'.
Indeed it is the playwright's ability to create a kind of 'total theatre' –
with spoken and sung words together with highly orchestrated movement played out on an arena stage – that makes his drama much closer
to the tragedies performed in the fifth-century Athenian theatre than
most Western equivalents.

Although Rotimi had finished his play by 1966, the première took
place in 1968 at the height of the Biafran war – Nigeria's civil war that
lasted from 1967 to early 1970, during which there was an unsuc-
cessful attempt to split the federation that colonial rule had left behind
into separate states. It was inevitable therefore that the first audiences
of Rotimi's play should have interpreted the action in the light of their
immediate circumstances. As Rotimi comments, 'The root cause of
that war was tribal distrust which is what I've worked into the play as
the basic flaw of the hero, Odewale.'[28] When we examine Rotimi's
version, in which the question of tribal identity is dominant and the

Freudian familial interpersonal transgressions are refreshingly absent, we are reminded again just how much importance Sophocles also attaches to biological origins in Oedipus' quest for his own identity. In *Oedipus Tyrannus*, the emphasis is clearly placed on the blood relationships between the characters, rather than on the incest or the parricide. This distinction is not often made by commentators, but that it is an important one is borne out by Sophocles' very different handling of the myth in *Oedipus at Colonus*, where Oedipus' past is discussed exclusively in terms of guilt and pollution.[29]

In Rotimi's play, the parricide is unwittingly committed over a dispute about land; and that dispute is fuelled by tribal hostilities. The episode is hauntingly re-enacted onstage during a flashback scene in which Odewale relives the events that followed his departure from Ijekun (Corinth):

OLD MAN	*[stops laughing]*. You from the bush tribe, come to these parts and boldly call me 'THIEF'?
ODEWALE	Where am I from?
OLD MAN	*[calling his men]*. Gbonka ... Olojo – come, come, come quickly – come and listen to this man's tongue. *[Two men run over with their hoes.]*
ODEWALE'S VOICE	That is the end. I can bear insults to myself, brother, but to call my tribe bush, and then summon riff-raff to mock my mother tongue! I will die first. *(Act III sc. I, p. 46)*

Although Odewale goes on to invoke the spirit of the god Ogun as he commits the act of parricide, the gods of the title, like Sophocles' own gods, are generally absent from Rotimi's play. It is their very detachment from the action that makes them clearly analogous to the neocolonial 'gods' on the international stage, who have precipitated the events of the civil war by imposing arbitrary state boundaries, yet now preside in a state of seeming neutrality. In the 2005 London production, the masks around the walls of the theatre provided another lugubrious presence.

However, at the end of the play, when Odewale has learned the truth about his biological origins and the enormity of his unwitting crimes, he insists:

> No, no! Do not blame the Gods. Let no one blame the powers. My people, learn from my fall. The powers would have failed if I did not let them use me. They knew my weakness; the weakness of a man easily moved to the defence of his tribe against others ...   *(Act III sc. IV, p. 71)*

In Yoruba culture, fate is not fixed; tribal divisions stem from human frailties, not eternal verities, and to resist those weaknesses is the first step in bolstering oneself against the imperial gods, who proceed by exploiting vulnerability.

Like Oedipus before him, Odewale construes the accusations made by the priest Baba Fakunle (Tiresias) as part of a general conspiracy against him on account of his alien status. Later in the play, and with even greater reason than his Sophoclean counterpart, Odewale's fears for his own safety are compounded when he reflects upon the recent fate of the hereditary king: if the legitimate member of the royal house can be murdered, what horrors must lie in wait for him, the outsider?

Odewale discovers that he is not a member of the Ijekun tribe, with whom he had identified so strongly that he had been driven to murder in its defence; he is a Kutuje after all. Rotimi is clearly saying not only that tribal allegiances are damaging in an African context, but also that they may be entirely illusory; and that there exist between individuals in Africa far deeper ties that its citizens ignore at their peril.

If Sophocles' tragedy could be said, at the very least, to be reflecting contemporary debate about Pericles' citizenship law and biologically determined identities, Rotimi's play unequivocally condemns the over-emphasis upon tribal origins that prevents an appreciation of true like-nesses. In Odewale's case, his tribal allegiance prevents him from recognising his true, pan-Nigerian, pan-African identity. Oedipus' question, 'Who am I?', thus becomes a truly pressing metaphor for black consciousness in the postcolonial world, where the struggle to forge an identity in the wake of the colonial past is a particularly arduous one.

OEDIPUS IN THE EAST END

One of the very few Oedipuses in Britain to have found a distinctive voice in the post-Freudian world has been Steven Berkoff's Eddy in *Greek*. Berkoff's highly controversial and often deeply shocking re-engagement with the myth premièred at the Half Moon Theatre in London on 11 February 1980, and went on to inspire a major post-modern opera by Mark-Anthony Turnage in 1992. In many ways Berkoff's version gestures towards and may well be situated within the Oedipal parodic tradition, and could readily be invoked in support of Heiner Mueller's claim about the comic Oedipus becoming the norm. But what makes Berkoff's radical reworking both representative and striking is not so much its generic mutation, as its defiant refutation of both Sophocles and Freud. Shamelessly and in many ways obsessively Freudian, this latter-day Oedipus flagrantly becomes in the final analysis both anti-Sophocles and anti-Freud, as Eddy celebrates his complex in what is essentially an anti-Cartesian, mind–body unity. In this sense, and perhaps not surprisingly, the post-Freudian Oedipus turns out, in its assault on the ideology of authority, to be no less Oedipal than its forebears.

Berkoff trained in the essentially cerebral English performance tradition, but he also received training in mime from the school of Jacques Lecoq. Berkoff was in many ways uniquely well placed in his generation of actors to achieve this desired unity of mind and body. As a faithful adherent of the theories of the French director Antonin Artaud (Berkoff claimed that whilst the English had merely flirted with Artaud before their flings with Brecht and subsequently Grotowski, he alone had remained faithful to him[30]), Berkoff subscribes to the Artaudian notion that theatre should provide a site for the revelation of a pre-rational heightened reality. And like Jean-Louis Barrault (Artaud's disciple of the 1960s), Berkoff aims for a psycho-physiological unity: what Berkoff cynics might term his visceral, 'in-yer-groin' drama.

That Artaud and Barrault are aiming to convey, in the theatre, what in psychoanalytical terms would be called the realms of the unconscious as well as the conscious mind (the id as well as the ego) is abundantly clear. And so when Berkoff uses Freudian terminology in his critiques of the contemporary theatre, it is therefore not merely fortuitous: he bemoans the absence of British directors imaginative enough to enter 'the interior of man's soul' (his subjects, equally Freudian, are always male and semi-autobiographical), and elsewhere in his autobiography we learn that theatre should be 'closer to Freud than to the political columns of the *Daily Rant*'.[31]

For Berkoff, however, there is a deeply political dimension behind his espousal of Barrault's ideal of 'total theatre'. If there had been a clear hierarchy in the hero/choral divide in the Oedipus productions of Mounet-Sully and Laurence Olivier, the ensemble performance is seen by Berkoff as the aesthetic correlative to the classless society. Berkoff, the young working-class Jewish actor from the East End, found the pecking order of the 1950s Royal Court and the RSC totally alienating; and when he set up his London Theatre Group in 1968, it was in large measure to counter the essentially class-based hierarchy that pervaded the star system in London theatrical circles. And when he chooses to write a play inspired by the Greek model, it becomes clear that the chorus for him (in marked contrast to those star-dominated forerunners) is integral to the action: Berkoff's Oedipus and his chorus are one, as the chorus serves to amplify the emotional strains of the protagonist.[32]

Berkoff's choice of Sophocles' *Oedipus Tyrannus* for updating can also be traced to the interests of his forebears. The key chapter in Artaud's *Theatre and Its Double* (1938) is entitled 'Theatre and the plague', in which he argues that the theatre should seek to (re-)present the plague from which the audience will emerge either dead or purged. And not only was the plague a recurrent trope in Artaud's own theoretical and practical works, he was also drawn time and again to plays with incestuous relationships (notably Ford's *'Tis Pity She's a Whore*, Shelley's *The Cenci* and his own play *The Spurt of Blood*), in which the ideology of patriarchal authority is challenged. When Artaud's principle English disciple, Peter Brook, staged an ancient play in 1968, he not surprisingly chose the *Oedipus* (albeit Seneca's, in Ted Hughes's version). And as a deep admirer of Brook as well as of Artaud, Berkoff's own choice of the Oedipus legend begins to seem inevitable; in *Greek* we find verbal echoes of Hughes's text, which are testimony to that genealogy.

In Berkoff's case, as was the case with Guthrie, there is no attempt to disguise the autobiographical reasons that inform his choice of Oedipus as chosen subject. Berkoff's formation of an ensemble company had been informed by psychological as much as political needs. His various accounts of the company's experiences on tour and in rehearsal reveal that for Berkoff the actors had become his surrogate family[33] – the family he never had – because although his mother was caring and involved, he remained unable to make contact with his cantankerous and distant father. So now writing his version of Sophocles' play, he confesses he is able to use it 'as a mask for [his] own feelings and ambitions'.[34]

Berkoff explains that it was important for him not to take the part of Eddy in *Greek* (unusually for Berkoff, he did not appear in the play until the 1992 revival at the Wyndham's Theatre, when he was too old for the part of Eddy and so appeared as the father); instead he wanted the necessary distance to be able to 'analyse' the material that was far too close to his own life experiences (as the material is, he says in the Author's Note to the printed edition of his play, for many other young men, who in turn identify with his protagonist). Towards the end of Berkoff's autobiography, Oedipus is held up as the representative protagonist:

> What did Oedipus tell us except the torments inside the mind of man? Torments of the soul. Show me a tormented man … You tell me where I can see this on stage and I will run, since I too am a spectator at the feast.[35]

For Berkoff, as for Artaud and Barrault, the star has been replaced with the archetype of Jungian psychology. This is another version of Oedipus/Eddy as Everyman; and as Eddy becomes narrator and participant in his own drama, very often veering between past, present and future in the course of one speech, the multiple levels of reality within the play mirror (as Freud saw in the Sophoclean tragedy) the process of unravelling that constitutes the psychoanalytical method in practice.

Berkoff's vision is in many ways pure Freud in its delight in laying bare Eddy's consciousness. The moment of recognition in Berkoff's play comes during Eddy's stepfather's account of how the young toddler was discovered. The pivotal moment in the play similarly draws on the nautical imagery used in Sophocles' tragedy. However, it also recalls both Klein's archetypal birth trauma and the birth mimes in the work of Barrault (in *As I Lay Dying*), Grotowski, the Living Theatre and Richard Schechner (in *Dionysus in 69*).

In a quasi-messenger speech, Dad tells how London's Tower Bridge opened up 'to allow the steamers' funnels through like some big lazy East End tart from Cable Street opening her thighs' (see Figure 15).[36] And the bridge's opening reveals carefree East Enders on deck enjoying a Sunday outing down the river moments before their Southend steamer gets blasted to smithereens by an unexploded bomb, scattering limbs and torsos to the wind. From the debris and confusion, a toddler is miraculously pulled to safety:

> when all had gone and dawn arose we saw what seemed a little doll clinging to a piece of wood but on closer butchering revealed a little bugger of about two he were, struggling like the fuck and gripping in his paw a greasy old big bear, which no doubt helped to keep him up. We threw the bear back in the slick, and lifted the toddler out all dripping wet and covered in oil looking like a darkie so, no one about we took him home and washed him … (p. 136)

Eddy's arrival in his surrogate family is, like Oedipus' in Sophocles, really a rebirth into another world; but Eddy's new world is a terrifyingly solipsistic one. That sex and language are intimately interconnected in Berkoff's Freudian-informed world is underlined by the images of masturbation that recur in this first disjunctive part of the play. At this stage in his life, Eddy can only glimpse the Artaudian heightened reality (here albeit couched in highly sexist fantasies of

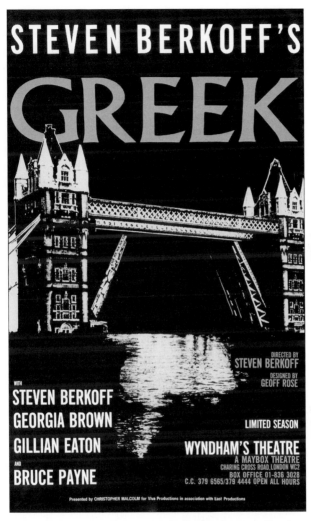

15. Poster from the revival of Steven Berkoff's *Greek* at Wyndham's
Theatre, London (1988)

priapic conquest), before he is rudely awakened into 'the seething
heaving heap of world in which I was just a little dot' (p. 113).

Eddy's arrival at the mythological crossroads – here Skidrow (aka
Heathrow) Airport – involves a crisis of identity that is underlined by

Berkoff in a deftly enacted choral improvisation. The Family as chorus provides an accompaniment of airport sounds and noises to a syntactical muddle, in which we hear a clear allusion to that other Oedipal play, which depends on linguistic confusions, Synge's *Playboy of the Western World*:

> All this confused me / who needs to go / do I, do you, do he / I decided to stay and see my own sweet land / amend the woes of my own fair state / why split and scarper like ships leaving a sinking rat / *I saw myself as king of the western world* / but since I needed some refreshment for my trials ahead, I ventured into this little café / everywhere I looked … I witnessed this evidence … of the British plague.   *(pp. 113–14; added emphasis)*

As the German Romantic poet Friedrich Hölderlin said of Sophoclean death scenes in general,[37] the words here in Berkoff's play are truly deadly in the scene of Eddy's (Ted Hughes-meets-Batman) onomatopoeic parricide:

[*They mime fight*]

EDDY	Hit hurt crunch pain stab jab
MANAGER	Smash hate rip tear asunder render
EDDY	Numb jagged glass gouge out
MANAGER	Chair breakhead split fist splatter splosh crash
EDDY	Explode scream fury strength overpower overcome
MANAGER	Cunt shit filth remorse weakling blood soaked
EDDY	Haemorrhage, rupture and sell. Split and cracklock jawsprung and neckbreak
MANAGER	Cave-in rib splinter oh the agony the shrewd icepick
EDDY	Testicles torn out eyes gouged and pulled strings snapped socket nail scrapped
MANAGER	Bite swallow suck pull
EDDY	More smash and more power
MANAGER	Weaker and weaker
EDDY	Stronger and stronger

MANAGER	Weak
EDDY	Power
MANAGER	Dying
EDDY	Victor
MANAGER	That's it
EDDY	Tada.
WAITRESS	You killed him / I never realized words can kill.

(pp. 116–17)

Eddy's subsequent sexual union with the waitress/mother brings with it a new, liberated and elevated diction, and eventually new economic benefits without any gross exploitation of others, as their greasy café thrives under its new fecund management. However, ten years on in Act II, Eddy is forced (like Cocteau's Oedipe) to encounter the other face of womankind in the form of the Sphinx (revealingly played by the same actress who plays his wife/mother). The Sphinx is the Kleinian anti/stepmother – accusatory, not loving – and here in Berkoff she is also a kind of eco-warrior Gaia, whose lot is to preside over the anti-generative state (where sex peepshows provide light relief and abortion clinics terminate would-be geniuses), which has come about because of the pollution and oppression at the heart of Eddy/Everyman (p. 123).

If Eddy, like Sophocles' Oedipus, is both the instrument of hope and the source of destruction, he differs from his forebears in his act of defiance in the final moments of the play. According to Berkoff, Eddy possesses a 'non-fatalistic disposition';[38] and in a chillingly bold act of defiance, his protagonist interrogates both Sophocles and Seneca, as well as Freud, in his refusal to give up his ideal wife, even if she is his mother. The casting of Linda Marlowe as wife/mum in the 1980 production was no doubt deliberate: as one critic commented, she at least made incest 'understandable'.[39]

Like Cocteau and Gide's Oedipuses before him, Eddy is fully aware of the tradition of which he is a part as he vacillates between following convention and following instinct:

> Oedipus how could you have done it, never to see your wife's golden face again, never again to cast your eyes on her and hers on your eyes ...

> What a foul thing I have done, I am the rotten plague, tear them out,
> scoop them out like ice-cream, just push the thumb behind the orb and
> push, pull them out and stretch them to the end of the strings and then
> snap! Darkness falls. Bollocks to all that …(p. 138)

This Oedipus prefers incestuous union with his mother to violence
and destruction: 'it's love I feel it's love, what matter what form it
takes' (p. 139), Eddy utters, thereby not only illustrating the complex,
but ultimately denying the need for its very existence.

This daringly optimistic and celebratory ending gestures in many
ways towards the Yiddish theatre enjoyed by Berkoff's grandparents in
London's East End of the late nineteenth century. But if the carnival-
esque ending of *Greek* recalls Yiddish theatrical traditions, its moral
bearings lie elsewhere. Eddy's radical moral relativism is, of course,
very far removed from the Sophoclean model, in which the erotic
implications of the mother–son union are scrupulously avoided. It is
far, too, from the world of Freud's Vienna, where such feelings could
only be repressed and never fully expressed. Eddy's final speech takes
us instead towards that chillingly amoral universe of Jacobean tragedy,
and more specifically to Giovanni's (antipatriarchal) advocacy of
brother–sister incest in Berkoff's favourite tragedy, *'Tis Pity She's a
Whore* (itself a distant relative of Euripides' lost tragedy of brother–
sister incest, *Aeolus*).[40] Berkoff, as many have acknowledged, heralds
the amoral universe of 'in-yer-face' drama of the late 1990s, which
uses sex and violence to plumb and probe the emotional depths of
both dramatic subject and audience alike. Plays such as Sarah Kane's
Phaedra's Love (drawing as it does on both Euripides' *Hippolytus* and
Seneca's *Phaedra*) pay more than a passing nod to Berkoff, as they
celebrate a world in which the taboo of incest no longer pertains. By
the end of *Greek*, Berkoff has succeeded in some senses in dragging his
spectators through the Artaudian plague and forcing them to emerge
either purged or dead, according to their levels of tolerance.

Berkoff's version joins the other post-1960s versions of Sophocles'
tragedy in showing the *tyrannos*-outsider and his eponymous play now

re-sited on the margins of modern Western society. From this new peripheral perspective, Aristotle's paradigmatic tragedy has assumed a different kind of importance in the repertoire: Oedipus is still crucial, it seems, but in strikingly non-canonical ways. Moreover, in a world in which the traditional definitions of 'parenting' are constantly under review, in which traditional rites of passage and the gaps between generations are blurring, where the practice of IVF may well bring with it a decrease in the status of biological parents, we can readily envisage more than one way in which both Rotimi and Berkoff's refutation of both Sophocles and Freud might be deemed pathbreaking.

EXIT OEDIPUS; ENTER JOCASTA CENTRE STAGE

In the same year as the première of the Blanchar/Picasso *Oedipe-Roi*, a select audience at Cambridge High School in Cambridge, Massachusetts witnessed another milestone in the performance history of Sophocles' *Oedipus Tyrannus* with Martha Graham's pioneering ballet, *Night Journey* (1947). Most accounts of Oedipus in the twentieth century move from Paris of the 1920s and 1930s to the general reception of the 1960s and beyond, with Pasolini's film (*Edipo Re*, 1967), and (maybe) Rotimi's version. But Graham's earlier ballet is a very important point in the reception history of Sophocles' play, and serves as a salutory reminder both to historians of theatre and to those students of classical reception of the necessity of including dance within their sphere of study.[41]

Graham's Greek-inspired ballets in general are predicated upon the complex relationship between myth, literature and psychoanalytical theory, and are thus central to any serious discussion of mid-twentieth-century reception of the plays. Furthermore, Graham's 'mythic' cues come directly from the giants of literary Modernism, Joyce and Eliot; and like them, her intuitions are often strikingly prescient. The première of *Night Journey* took place on 3 May 1947, just one year after *Cave of the Heart*, Graham's version of Euripides'

Medea, her first dance drama based on an ancient Greek tragedy. Initially entitled *Serpent's Heart*, Graham's refiguring of Euripides' play focuses on a Medea, who dominates the stage in a seering performance of reptilian and then raging revenge.[42] That Graham's feminist sympathies should have attracted her to the spurned wife and child-killing mother was hardly surprising in the aftermath of the Second World War, when settling scores was high on the public agenda and Medea seemed to catch the mood on both sides of the Atlantic. Furthermore, no more surprising was the fact that working with *Medea* led Graham the following year to Sophocles' paradigmatic ancient Greek tragedy; what was surprising, however, was how Graham chose to refashion it.[43]

In some ways it was inevitable that dance should become the most powerful medium with which to explore the inner life; and Graham's own interest in psychoanalysis was essentially Jungian in her desire to tap into and express through movement the contents of the collective unconscious. But she was also heavily influenced by the political and gender-based critiques of Freudian psychology proffered by Erich Fromm, and these in particular inform her reading of *Oedipus Tyrannus*.

In *Night Journey*, Martha Graham radically refigures the Sophoclean text in order to allow the mother figure, Jocasta, to come centre stage. And Graham's un-Sophoclean insistence upon the erotic nature of the incestuous encounter between mother and son, and the dance drama's concern with the act of incest to the exclusion of the parricide, owe a clear debt to Fromm's theories of love and freedom. Her inclusion of a female chorus and the centrality of the traditionally bisexual Tiresias to the structure of the dance drama bring a decidedly feminist reading to the ancient text. Indeed, all Graham's departures from Sophocles' tragedy are especially significant in hindsight because we can now see them as emblematic of a general shift in attitudes that becomes commonplace in many late twentieth-century reworkings of the Sophoclean tragedy.

Night Journey opens with Jocasta entering the stage, rope in hand ready to hang herself. As Tiresias slowly arrives, he strides rhythmically across the stage, beating his staff as if tolling the bell of doom. The blind priest goes to remove the rope from Jocasta's hands; but it is not to prevent her suicide, it is merely to postpone it. For here, in Martha Graham's dance drama, based on Sophocles' *Oedipus Tyrannus*, Jocasta has become protagonist; and she is forced (Noh-like) to relive the horrors of her life as she stands on the threshold of death.

Graham's work owes as much to Yeats's Plays for Dancers as it does to psychoanalytic theory; and like Yeats's Noh-inspired plays, it hovers between the realms of life and death, reality and other layers of consciousness. The 'night' of this particular journey refers equally to the dream world and to familial descent into lugubrious chaos. As Graham's Jocasta falls upon the schematic bed by the renowned Japanese designer Isamu Noguchi, more rack-like than canopy, her dream world begins to unfold before our eyes.

In Jocasta's dream world, we dream back with her to the arrival of a victorious Oedipus, ceremoniously welcomed by an all-female Chorus carrying stylised laurel branches; and we watch him tread upon the raised stepping stones that lead him to the royal bed and to his prize. Lifting the queen upon his shoulders, covering her head with his cloak before placing an imperious foot upon her thigh, he is alternately tender child and dominant warrior in courtship. Slowly the victory dance gives way to an erotic and highly charged physical union that brings with it painful forebodings for Jocasta. She nurses Oedipus, then mounts his lap in a beautiful sequence of caress and enfurlment as they both become entwined in the (now umbilical) rope and the bed beneath. But when the Chorus returns, to the staccato strings of the orchestra and the dissonant piano accompaniment in William Schuman's score, the lovers' passion is reduced to (rather than con-summated with) a series of restricted jerks.

Tiresias re-enters, his familiar pounding staff now evoking Oedipus' legendary lameness; and when the tip of the staff touches the 'umbilical' cord, husband/son and wife/mother collapse to the ground. The truth has been signalled: Oedipus discards the rope, reeling from the bed and recoiling upon the Chorus in horror. Only once more, momentarily, does passion return before moral rectitude prevails to curb the errant son. Now that the skein of Jocasta's memory has broken in this familial drama of intergenerational chaos, future precedes the present as the husband/son appears to blind himself prematurely before taking flight from the incestuous bed. Alone now, Jocasta rises from the bed, removes her royal cloak, grabs the rope of kinship and of memory, wraps it round her neck and falls. Tiresias returns, his staff tapping in Noh-like invocation of the spirits of the dead; and as he walks, he walks on past the corpse which remains centre stage, presaging as he does the exile of Oedipus to come.

Graham's *Night Journey* was the first of numerous feminist reworkings of Sophocles' tragedy for the stage. One of the most striking of these is André Boucourechliev's opera, *Le Nom d'Oedipe*, with a libretto by Hélène Cixous (originally entitled *Le Chant du corps interdit*),[44] which was premièred at the Festival d'Avignon in May 1978 under the direction of Claude Régy. Even though the opera only received three performances at Avignon, it has attracted considerable attention owing to the high profile of the librettist.[45]

Just as psychoanalytical theory from Rank and Klein onwards has emphasised, it is the mother–child relationship which is primary in *Le Nom d'Oedipe*, just as it was in Martha Graham's *Night Journey*; and Jocasta's perspective predominates in both these representative rewritings of the Oedipus myth. But the treatment of incest in the opera is different: in marked contrast to Graham's version, and very much along the lines of Berkoff's *Greek*, there is no sense of horror at the taboo of incest in *Le Nom d'Oedipe: Chant du corps interdit*, despite the 'forbidden body' referred to in the subtitle. Boucourechliev had conceived his composition as a post-Freudian, Kleinian piece in its celebration of the pre-Oedipal state in which incest can be enjoyed without taint. This is a very allusive piece – with echoes of Mahler, Debussy and, perhaps inevitably, Stravinksy; but it also (like Debussy) uses Balinese gamelan to extend beyond the immediate Western operatic tradition.

It was only after he had written his opera that Boucourechliev turned to Cixous, on whose sympathy for his treatment of the material he knew he could depend and whose own version was already written. Cixous made it very clear that by asking for a version of '*Oedipus*', Boucourechliev had very much made a 'man's' request. For her, the myth of Oedipus was not her subject; instead her concern was with the incestuous structures in which every man and woman is caught once passion enters their relationship. By speaking of 'incest', we are already commiting an act of repression – a repression of those natural incestuous feelings that underpin every successful heterosexual relationship.[46] Forty years after Graham, Cixous's libretto articulates Graham's earlier intuitions in order to participate in a widely contested intellectual debate concerning France's late twentieth-century identity. Oedipus is celebrated in the opera for his assimilation into a Dionysiac, pre-Oedipal unity; and as he struggles with an Apolline-imposed identity, we see him finally, albeit tragically because belatedly, reject his 'name' and with it the baggage that comes with being branded France's post-war bête noire.

In *Le Nom d'Oedipe*, Oedipus' story is told by Jocasta in the last few days of her life, as she relives her own experiences both with him and in her childhood. Her song is really one long lament for the loss of the forbidden body that she enjoyed in the pre-Oedipal state she shared with her son; but it is also a celebration of that earlier union between them. It is not incest that is taboo here; instead it is the Cartesian mind/body divide that is derided by Boucourechliev and Cixous.

The bipartite title encapsulates the two worlds within the opera and their contrapuntal relationship; and the adoption of two Oedipuses and two Jocastas makes the psychological splitting a visual one as well. One Oedipus was played in a calm baritone by Claude Meloni in a red cape. This Oedipus cut a dignified public figure, strikingly reminiscent of the Oedipus of the first half of Sophocles' tragedy, who finds out he has unwittingly committed regicide. The other Oedipus was played by the fiery actor Michel Lonsdale in a crushed linen suit: this was the Oedipus of the contemporary world, the one who discovers he is a parricide. But it was the two Jocastas who dominated the stage: one literally sang the 'song of the forbidden body' referred to in the subtitle, the blonde-haired soprano Sigune von Osten, who was dressed in a wedding dress. The other, the dark-haired actress Catherine Sellers, wearing a mauve cocktail dress, articulated that song in highly wrought, heightened verse. Even Tiresias was played by two actors here.

Even though the orchestra of fifteen musicians, conducted by Claude Prin, were placed centre stage, there was no sense in which the music drowned the word: indeed there were many long stretches when the intensely lyrical libretto of Cixous was unaccompanied. Some critics wondered whether Boucourechliev had been overwhelmed by the power of the libretto; others suggested that this was a deliberate attempt to unite the spoken and sung voice. For some, the volcanic rocks of the set dominated; for others this was a perfect fusion between opera and theatre.[47] But the plurality of voices in the opera – spoken/sung, male/female, choric/individual, public/private – were part of its meaning as they served to mirror the shifting relationships between the protagonists. Just as Oedipus and Jocasta's unity is past rather than present, so the increasingly solipsistic worlds of mother–son, wife–husband, can only be conveyed through 'splitting' – psychological 'splitting' and the physical disjunction of selves. Everyone is in search of the Other here – even the subject.

It is not self-discovery that determines the breakdown of the mother–son relationship, but Oedipus' discovery of his public self: Thebes, 'La Ville', which becomes his 'lover', who woos him away, and provides him with his name in a thoroughly quotidian world. In the Kleinian, pre-Oedipal timeless state that life with Jocasta represented, sentient experience collapses the boundaries between self and other, *je/lui, toi/moi*. It is a world of the body, blood, the sea (*mer/mère* are played upon), song, without gender (*l'enfant*) and without linear time; where present, future and past are collapsed: 'Tu étais là, tu serais là, l'avenir / est arrivé' ('You were there, you will be there, the future has arrived').[48]

The intrusion of La Ville and the Plague lure Oedipus away: first metaphorically as he sits onstage refusing Jocasta his life-sustaining gaze; and later literally when his departure from the stage leads to her physical collapse and her sense that she has changed body. Now lying on her deathbed, hearing only silence, she vainly tries to re-hear the song of peace they made together; as she proclaims that '[l]a danse est morte' (p. 73), she has nothing to do except turn to the wall herself and die. The androgynous Tiresias, father and mother here, sings Jocasta back in time into her childhood sleep of death; and as he does so, she imaginatively re-enters the world of pre-Oedipal peace at a genderless, giant breast.

Oedipus arrives too late to enjoy any union with Jocasta in life; but now in a beautiful sequence of free indirect style, his voice, her voice and a mediating narratorial third person merge in the linguistic equivalent of the Dionysiac eternal unity: 'Je suis là / Ma bien aimée mon enfant / Il est revenu pour toi! / Oedipe est là. Je t'avais dis' ('I am here, my [female] lover, my child. He has come back for you. Oedipus is here. I had told you') (p. 81). The Cixous/Boucourechliev baritone Oedipus is very far from Sophocles' cerebral tragic figure, whose blinding is the one independent act possible in a world circumscribed by oracles; here his flesh and body combine with Jocasta's own once he feels her again, himself now encompassed by 'ma nuit', 'mer'.

CONCLUSION

In uncanny resemblance to his experiences within Sophocles' play, the vagaries of Oedipus' *Nachleben* have very often entailed punishments that far outstrip the crimes that he committed without intent. As regicide, he has endured comparisons with Judas, Cromwell and Charles II; and as perpetrator of incest, he has suffered ostracism in the form of censorship. More recently, after some decades of unparalleled prominence on the stage, the Oedipus of Sophocles' *Oedipus Tyrannus* has experienced a new form of ostracism: the ignominy of being linked with imperialism and the repressive and oppressive powers of the bourgeois state by his anti-Freudian adversaries in France.

There may be considerable consolation to be had in the fact that parricide has been relegated to secondary consideration in the postmodern Western psyche. The focus is no longer unerringly upon sons who enter into perpetual conflict with their patriarchal forebears. That Oedipus has succeeded on occasion in escaping the imprint of Freud is no bad thing; and with Jonathan Kent's stunningly beautiful and occasionally deeply moving production of *Oedipus* at the Royal National Theatre in London, it may well be that Sophocles' tragedy is beginning to escape from the metaphorical impasse in which Manfridi's Oedipus was shown to be so emphatically stuck.

NOTES

1. Whilst the stage productions have been ephemeral, there are two notable exceptions. First, Yeats's *Oedipus the King*, which premièred in 1926 at the Abbey, has endured way beyond the normal shelf-life of any translation for the stage. Used by Olivier and Michel St Denis in 1945, it still remains the text of choice for many small companies who are unable to afford a new commission. See Fiona Macintosh, 'An Oedipus for our times? Yeats's version of Sophocles' *Oedipus Tyrannos*' in Martin Revermann and Peter Wilson (eds.), *Performance, Reception, Iconography: Studies in Honour of Oliver Taplin* (Oxford 2008), 524–47. Second, Pasolini's film version *Edipo Re* (1967) has become a classic of the cinema; and it set a sentient (rather than cerebral) Oedipus within the arid landscape of North Africa. Neither of these will be discussed in this chapter, which focuses on productions which began in the theare.

2. Northern Broadsides' *Oedipus*, directed by Barrie Rutter, premièred at the Viaduct Theatre, Dean Clough, Halifax, on 6 September 2001 before embarking on a tour of England.

3. The *locus classicus* of the 'post-tragic' position is George Steiner, *The Death of Tragedy* (London 1961).

4. For an account of the Kleinian acendancy, see Nancy Chodorow, *The Reproduction of Mothering: Psychoanalysis and the Sociology of Gender* (Berkeley and Los Angeles 1978).

5. For the post-war period see Miriam Leonard, *Athens in Paris: Ancient Greece and the Political in Post-war French Thought* (Oxford 2005).

6. See, e.g., Marie-Joseph Chénier's *Oedipe-Roi* (1818). For discussion, see Chapter 3 above.

7. Gilles Deleuze and Félix Guattari, *Anti-Oedipus: Capitalism and Schizophrenia*, trans. R. Hurley, M. Seem, and H.R. Lane (Minneapolis 1983).

8. M. Ellmann (ed.), *Psychoanalytic Literary Criticism* (London and New York 1994), (1994), 25.

9. See Ibid., 23.

10. Heiner Mueller, *Projection 1975*, cited by C. Innes, *Avant Garde Theatre 1892–1992* (London and New York 1993), 201.

11. Peter Hall's production of Manfridi's *Cuckoos* (in a version by Colin Teevan) was produced at the Gate Theatre, March 2000; Pan Pan's *Oedipus Loves You* (by Simon Doyle and Gavin Quinn) premièred at Smock Alley Theatre, Dublin, in 2006 and toured to the Riverside Studios, London, in 2008.

12. Other African versions include Yaya Konate's *Oedipe noir ou le drame de la jeunesse*, performed in Upper Volta in 1971, and J. Leloup's *Gueido* (1984) and, less directly, Gilbert Kiyindou's *La Colombe de Kibouende* (performed Upper Volta 1981), which alludes to Oedipus. See Jacques Scherer, *Dramaturgies d'Oedipe* (Paris 1987), 176–9. Witness too the Deep South African-American version by Rita Dove, *Darker Face of the Earth* (1994); and compare Lee Breuer's *Gospel at Colonus* (1983). For comment on why the Oedipus myth still has resonances in a postcolonial context see Barbara Goff and Michael Simpson, *Crossroads in the Black Aegean: Oedipus, Antigone, and Drama of the African Diaspora* (Oxford 2007). See further Marvin Carlson (ed.), *The Arab Oedipus: Four Plays from Egypt and Syria* (New York 2005), for plays by Tawfig Al-Hakin, Ali Ahmad Bakathir, Ali Salim and Walid Ikhlasi; and for general comment see Ahmed Etman, 'Translation at the intersection of traditions: the Arab reception of the Classics', in Lorna Hardwick and Chris Stray (eds.), *Classical Receptions* (Oxford 2007), 141–52.

13. James Forsyth, *Tyrone Guthrie: The Authorised Biography* (London 1976), 41.
14. Ibid., 250.
15. Elizabeth Sprigge, *Sybil Thorndike Casson* (London 1971), 258; Forsyth (1976), 194–5. Thorndike also much admired the Guthrie production, which she saw at the Edinburgh Festival in 1956. At the time of his death, Guthrie was working on yet another even more ritualistic production of the play in Sydney. Influenced by his reading of Immanuel Velikovsky's study *Oedipus and Akhnaton* (London 1966), this Oedipus was to be messianic figure. Forsyth (1976), 312.
16. Tyrone Guthrie, *A Life in the Theatre* (London 1960), 233–46.
17. Tyrone Guthrie and Tanya Moiseiwitsch, 'The Production of *King Oedipus*', in Robertson Davies, Tyrone Guthrie, Boyd Neel and Tanya Moiseiwitsch, *Thrice the Brinded Cat Hath Mew'd: A Record of the Stratford Shakespearean Festival in Canada 1955* (Toronto 1955), 111–78, 120.
18. Guthrie (1960), 314.
19. Ibid., 313. Cf. Francis Fergusson, *The Idea of a Theater* (Princeton 1949).
20. Guthrie and Moiseiwitsch (1955), 154.
21. Robertson Davies, 'King Oedipus', in Davies, Guthrie, Neel and Moiseiwitsch (1955), 35.
22. W.B. Yeats, *Collected Plays* (2nd edn, London 1952), 513.
23. Edith Hall, Fiona Macintosh and Amanda Wrigley (eds.), *Dionysus since 69: Greek tragedy at the Dawn of the Third Millennium* (Oxford 2004).
24. The Talawa Theatre Company production in 1989, dir. Yvonne Brewster, was performed at London's Riverside Studios and in Liverpool; the Tiata Fahodzi Company production in 2005, dir. Femi Elufowoju, was at the Arcola Theatre in London.
25. See especially the essays in W. Soyinka, *Myth, Literature and the African World* (Cambridge 1976).
26. Ola Rotimi, *The Gods Are Not to Blame* (Oxford 1971), Act I sc. II, 24. All subsequent page references appear in brackets in the text following the citation.
27. C. Dunton, *Make Men Talk: Nigerian Drama in English Since 1970* (London 1992).
28. Rotimi quoted in Ibid., 149 n. 16.

29. There is an excellent article by D. Konstan, 'Oedipus and his parents: the biological family from Sophocles to Dryden', *Scholia* 3 (1994), 3–23, which develops this argument.

30. Berkoff cited by Ned Chaillet in *The Times*, 16 February 1980.

31. Steven Berkoff, *Free Association: An Autobiography* (London and Boston 1996), 5.

32. Ibid., 341.

33. Ibid., 283.

34. Ibid., 2. Berkoff also wrote a version of Sophocles' *Oedipus Tyrannus*, entitled *Oedipus*, which was premièred in 2008 by Blackeyed Theatre in the Wilde Theatre at South Hill Park, Bracknell, Berkshire (dir. Bart Lee). The text appears in Volume 3 of Berkoff's *Collected Plays* (London 2000), although the striking similarities with *Greek* suggest that the genesis of the text may well have pre-dated *Greek*.

35. Berkoff (1996), 390.

36. Steven Berkoff, *The Collected Plays, Volume 1* (London and Boston 1994), 135. All subsequent references to the play appear in brackets after the quotation.

37. Friedrich Hölderlin, 'Anmerkungen zur Antigone', in *Sämtliche Werke und Briefe*, 2 vols. (Darmstadt 1970), Vol. II, 370–458, 456.

38. 'Author's note', in Berkoff (1994), 97–8, 98.

39. Michael Billington, *Guardian*, 15 February 1980.

40. I am indebted to Edith Hall for pointing out that Ford's source is Ovid's *Heroides*, Letter of Canace to her brother, which in turn was based on the lost *Aeolus* by Euripides.

41. E.g. Jacques Scherer, *Dramaturgies d'Oedipe* (Paris 1987); Charles Segal, *Oedipus Tyrannus: Tragic Heroism and the Limits of Knowledge* (2nd edn, Oxford 2001). There is a 1961 recording of *Night Journey*, produced by Nathan Kroll, and available on DVD, *Martha Graham in Performance* (Kultur, USA, 2002), with Martha Graham as Jocasta, Paul Taylor as Tiresias, Bertram Ross as Oedipus.

42. *Serpent's Heart* (with music by Samuel Barber) premièred at McMillan Theatre, Columbia University (New York City), before being revised and retitled *Cave of the Heart* for performance at Ziegfeld Theater, 27 February 1947. It was then frequently revived under different titles (*Medea's Meditation* and *Dance of Vengeance*).

43. Cf. Jean Anouilh's *Medée* of the same year (although not performed until 1953); and Robinson Jeffers's *Medea*, which opened the following year in New York and remained in the repertoire for many years with Judith Anderson in the title role. For the interconnections in the performance histories of Medea and Oedipus Tyrannus, see Fiona Macintosh, 'Parricide versus filicide: Oedipus and Medea on the modern stage', in Sarah Annes Brown and Catherine Silverstone (eds.), *Tragedy in Transition* (Oxford 2007), 192–211.

44. Cixous finished the *Chant du corps interdit* in 1976, from which the libretto for the opera is taken. See Mathilde la Badonnie, 'Le Nom d'Oedipe à Avignon', in *Le Monde*, 28 July 1978, 16. The libretto is now published, with the old title as subtitle, as Hélène Cixous, *Le Nom d'Oedipe: Chant du corps interdit* (Paris 1978). For other recent feminist treatments of Sophocles' *Oedipus Tyrannus* see Helene Foley, 'Bad women: gender politics in late twentieth-century performance and revision of Greek tragedy', in Hall, Macintosh and Wrigley (eds) (2004), 77–112.

45. The front page of *Le Monde*, 30 May 1978, has a report by Jacques Longchampt of a dialogue between the composer and the librettist, which took place on 27 May before a concert première of the opera broadcast on Radio-France. See too Maurice Fleuret, 'Oedipe en Avignon', *Le Nouvel Observateur*, 12–18 August 1978, 54: 'Il y a bien longtemps qu'un musicien créateur n'avait eu librettiste de cette qualité' ('It's a long time since a composer has had a librettist of such calibre'). Even Matthieu Galey, in *L'Express* 1413 (7–13 August 1978), 17, who is otherwise hostile to the production, notes that the libretto merits serious attention.

46. Jacques Longchampt, 'L'Oedipe de Cixous et Boucourechliev: Cette Plainte de toutes les femmes', *Le Monde*, 30 May 1978, 1. See too *Revue des sciences humaines* 76, 205 (January–March 1987), 131–44 for an interview with Boucourechliev.

47. See *L'Express* 1413 (7–13 August 1978), 17 for a criticism of the set; *Le Nouvel Observateur*, 12–18 August 1978, 54 for assessment as successful combination of music and theatre.

48. Cixous (1978), 62. All subsequent references appear in brackets in the text after the citation.

SELECT BIBLIOGRAPHY

Chapter 1 Oedipus in Athens

Dawe, R.D. (2006), *Sophocles, Oedipus Rex*, rev. edn, Cambridge.

Easterling, P.E. (ed.) (1997), *The Cambridge Companion to Greek Tragedy*, Cambridge.

Edmunds, Lowell (2006), *Oedipus*, London and New York.

Gregory, Justina (ed.) (2005), *A Companion to Greek Tragedy*, Oxford.

Knox, Bernard (1964), *The Heroic Temper*, Berkeley and Los Angeles, CA and London.

— (1998), *Oedipus at Thebes: Sophocles' Tragic Hero and His Time*, new edn, New Haven and London.

Segal, Charles (2001), *Oedipus Tyrannus: Tragic Heroism and the Limits of Knowledge*, 2nd edn, Oxford.

Chapter 2 The Roman Oedipus and his successors

Biet, Christian (1994), *Oedipe en monarchie: Tragédie et théorie juridique à l'âge classique*, Paris.

Boyle, A.J. (1997), *Tragic Seneca: An Essay in the Theatrical Tradition*, London and New York.

Fitch, John G. (ed.) (2008), *Oxford Readings in Seneca*, Oxford.

Hall, Edith and Fiona Macintosh (2005), *Greek Tragedy and the British Theatre 1660–1914*, Oxford.

McCabe, R.A. (1993), *Incest, Drama and Nature's Law 1550–1700*, Cambridge.

Palmer, H.R. (1911), *List of English Editions and Translations of Greek and Latin Classics Printed before 1641*, London.

Smith, Bruce. R. (1988), *Ancient Scripts and Modern Experience on the English Stage 1500–1700*, Princeton.

Chapter 3 Oedipus and the 'people'

Dawe, R.D. (ed.) (1996), *Sophocles: The Classical Heritage*, New York and London.

Mounet-Sully, Jean (1914), *Souvenirs d'un tragédien*, Paris.

Mueller, Martin (1980), *Children of Oedipus and Other Essays on the Imitation of Greek Tragedy 1550–1800*, Toronto.

Nostrand, H.L. (1934), *Le Théâtre antique et à l'antique en France de 1840 à 1900*, Paris.

Penesco, Anne (2000), *Mounet-Sully et la partition intérieure*, Lyon.

Schrade, Leo (1960), *La Représentation d'Edipo Tiranno au theatro Olimpico (Vicenza 1585): Étude suivi d'une édition critique de la tragédie de Sophocle par Orsatto Giustiniani et de la musique des choeurs par Andrea Gabrieli*, Paris.

Chapter 4 Oedipus and the Dionysiac

Beacham, R.C. (1987), 'Revivals: Europe', in J.M. Walton (ed.), *Living Greek Theatre: A Handbook of Classical Performances and Modern Productions*, New York and Westport, CT, 304–14.

Fowell, F. and F. Palmer (1913), *Censorship in England*, London.

Hynes, Samuel (1968), *The Edwardian Turn of Mind*, London.

McCarthy, Lillah (1933), *Myself and My Friends*, London.

Purdom, C.B. (1955), *Harley Granville Barker: Man of the Theatre, Dramatist and Scholar*, London.

Silk, M.S. and J.P. Stern (1981), *Nietzsche on Tragedy*, Cambridge.

Styan, J.L. (1985), *Max Reinhardt*, Cambridge.

Chapter 5 Everyman and everywhere

Blanchart, Paul (1929), *Firmin Gémier*, Paris.

Cocteau, Jean (1945), *Portrait de Mounet-Sully*, Paris.

Ewans, Michael (2007), *Opera from the Greek: Studies in the Poetics of Appropriation*, Aldershot.

Forsyth, James (1976), *Tyrone Guthrie: The Authorised Biography*, London.

Malcolm, Noel (1990), *George Enescu: His Life and Music*, London.

Picasso et le théâtre: Les Décors d'Oedipe-Roi (2001) (Musée Picasso, Antibes, and Musée National Picasso), Paris.

Rudnytsky, P.L. (1987), *Freud and Oedipus*, New York.

Walsh, Stephen (2002), *Stravinsky*, London.

Chapter 6 Oedipus dethroned

Deleuze, Gilles and Félix Guattari (1983) *Anti-Oedipus: Capitalism and Schizophrenia*, trans. R. Hurley, M. Seem and H.R. Lane, Minneapolis.

Foley, Helene (2004), 'Bad women: gender politics in late twentieth-century performance and revision of Greek tragedy' in Edith Hall, Fiona Macintosh and Amanda Wrigley, *Dionysus since 69: Greek Tragedy at the Dawn of the Millennium*, Oxford, 77–112.

Guthrie, Tyrone (1960), *A Life in the Theatre*, London.

Hall, Edith, Fiona Macintosh and Amanda Wrigley (eds.) (2004), *Dionysus since 69: Greek Tragedy at the Dawn of the Millennium*, Oxford.

Leonard, Miriam (2005), *Athens in Paris: Ancient Greece and the Political in Post-war French Thought*, Oxford.

Macintosh, Fiona (2007), 'Parricide versus filicide: Oedipus and Medea on the modern stage', in Sarah Annes Brown and Catherine Silverstone (eds.), *Tragedy in Transition*, Oxford, 192–211.

— (2008), 'An Oedipus for our times? Yeats's version of Sophocles' *Oedipus Tyrannos*', in Martin Reverman and Peter Wilson (eds.) *Performance, Reception, Iconography: Studies in Honour of Oliver Taplin*, Oxford, 524–47.

Scherer, Jacques (1987), *Dramaturgies d'Oedipe*, Paris.

INDEX

196